Dear Rea

We're thril

families ar appearance! With this special Famous Families fifty-book collection, we are proud to offer you the chance to relive the drama, the glamour, the suspense and the romance of four of Harlequin's most beloved families—the Fortunes, the Bravos, the McCabes and the Cavanaughs.

Our third family, the McCabes, welcomes you to Laramie, Texas. A small ranching town of brick buildings, awnings and shady streets, Laramie is the kind of place where everyone knows each other. The little town is currently abuzz with wedding plans—and no McCabe is safe from the matchmaking! The path to the altar may not be smooth for the McCabes, but their humor-filled journeys will no doubt bring a smile to your face.

And in August, you'll be captivated by our final family, the Cavanaughs. Generations of Cavanaughs have protected the citizens of Aurora, California. But can they protect themselves from falling in love? You won't want to miss any of these stories from *USA TODAY* bestselling author Marie Ferrarella!

Happy reading,

The Editors

CATHY GILLEN THACKER

is married and a mother of three. She and her husband spent eighteen years in Texas and now reside in North Carolina. Her mysteries, romance comedies and heartwarming family stories have made numerous appearances on bestseller lists, but her best reward, she says, is knowing that one of her books made someone's day a little brighter. A popular Harlequin Books author for many years, she loves telling passionate stories with happy endings, and thinks nothing beats a good romance and a hot cup of tea! You can visit Cathy's website, www.cathygillenthacker.com, for more information on her upcoming and previously published books, recipes and a list of her favorite things.

FAMOUS FAMILIES

the McCABES

CATHY GILLEN THACKER

Santa's Texas Lullaby

HARLEQUIN®
entertain, enrich, inspire™

This book is dedicated to Madeline Ruth Thacker.
Your sunny personality is matched only by your smile.
Welcome to the family, darling girl.

Recycling programs for this product may not exist in your area.

ISBN-13: 978-0-373-36514-2

SANTA'S TEXAS LULLABY

This edition published by arrangement with Harlequin Books S.A.

For questions and comments about the quality of this book please contact us at Customer_eCare@Harlequin.ca.

www.Harlequin.com

Printed in U.S.A.

FAMOUS FAMILIES

The Fortunes

Cowboy at Midnight by Ann Major
A Baby Changes Everything by Marie Ferrarella
In the Arms of the Law by Peggy Moreland
Lone Star Rancher by Laurie Paige
The Good Doctor by Karen Rose Smith
The Debutante by Elizabeth Bevarly
Keeping Her Safe by Myrna Mackenzie
The Law of Attraction by Kristi Gold
Once a Rebel by Sheri WhiteFeather
Military Man by Marie Ferrarella
Fortune's Legacy by Maureen Child
The Reckoning by Christie Ridgway

The Bravos by Christine Rimmer

The Nine-Month Marriage
Marriage by Necessity
Practically Married
Married by Accident
The Millionaire She Married
The M.D. She Had to Marry
The Marriage Agreement
The Bravo Billionaire
The Marriage Conspiracy
His Executive Sweetheart
Mercury Rising
Scrooge and the Single Girl

The McCabes by Cathy Gillen Thacker

Dr. Cowboy
Wildcat Cowboy
A Cowboy's Woman
A Cowboy Kind of Daddy
A Night Worth Remembering
The Seven-Year Proposal
The Dad Next Door
The Last Virgin in Texas
Texas Vows: A McCabe Family Saga
The Ultimate Texas Bachelor
Santa's Texas Lullaby
A Texas Wedding Vow
Blame It on Texas
A Laramie, Texas Christmas
From Texas, With Love

The Cavanaughs by Marie Ferrarella

Racing Against Time
Crime and Passion
Internal Affair
Dangerous Games
The Strong Silent Type
Cavanaugh's Woman
In Broad Daylight
Alone in the Dark
Dangerous Disguise
The Woman Who Wasn't There
Cavanaugh Watch
Cavanaugh Heat

Chapter 1

Amanda Witherspoon had heard Riley McCabe was returning to Laramie, Texas to join the Laramie Community Hospital staff, but she hadn't actually seen the handsome family physician until Friday afternoon when he stormed into the staff lounge in the pediatrics wing.

Nearly fourteen years had passed, but his impact on her was the same. Just one look into his mesmerizing amber eyes made her pulse race, and her emotions skyrocket. He had been six foot when he left for college, now he was even taller. Back then he had worn his sun-streaked light brown hair any which way. Now the thick wavy strands were cut in a sophisticated urban fashion, parted neatly on the left and brushed casually to the side. His lanky body filled out his button-down shirt, V-necked Fair Isle sweater and jeans in an exceedingly appealing way. He looked solid and fit, mouthwateringly sexy, and every inch the kind of grown man who knew exactly who he was and what he wanted out of life. The kind not to be messed with. The sound of holiday music playing on the hospital sound system and the Christmas tree in the corner only added to the fantasy-come-true quality of the situation.

Had Amanda not known better, she would have thought Riley McCabe's return to her life would have been the Christmas present to beat all Christmas presents, meant to liven up her increasingly dull and dissatisfying life. But wildly exciting things like that never happened to Amanda.

"Notice I'm not laughing," Riley McCabe growled as he stormed close enough for her to inhale the fragrance of soap and brisk, wintry cologne clinging to his skin.

"Notice," Amanda returned dryly, wondering what the famously mischievous prankster was up to now, "neither am I."

Riley marched toward her, attractive jaw thrust out pugnaciously, thick straight brows raised in mute admonition. "I would have figured we were beyond all this."

Amanda had hoped that would be the case, too. After all, she was a registered nurse, he a doctor. But given the fact that the Riley McCabe she recalled had been as full of mischief as the Texas sky was big, that had been a dangerous supposition to make. "All what?" she repeated around the sudden dryness of her throat. As he neared her, all the air left her lungs in one big whoosh.

"The practical jokes! But you just couldn't resist, could you?"

Amanda put down the sandwich she had yet to take a bite of and took a long sip of her diet soda. "I have no idea what you're talking about," she said coolly. Unless this was the beginning of yet another ploy to get her attention?

"Don't you?" he challenged, causing another shimmer of awareness to sift through her.

Deciding that sitting while he stood over her gave him too much of a physical advantage, she pushed back her chair and rose slowly to her feet. She was keenly aware that he now had a good six inches on her, every one of them as bold and masculine as the set of his lips. "I didn't think you were due to start working here until January 2," she remarked, a great deal more casually than she felt.

He stood in front of her, arms crossed against his chest, legs braced apart, every inch of him taut and ready for action. "I'm not."

"So?" She ignored the intensity in the long-lashed amber eyes that threatened to throw her off balance. "How could I possibly play a prank on you if I didn't think you were going to be here?"

"Because," he enunciated clearly, "you knew I was going to start setting up my office in the annex today."

Amanda sucked in a breath and tilted her head back to glare up at him. "I most certainly did not!" she insisted. Although she might have considered a practical joke had she realized he intended to pick up right where they had left off all those years ago. Matching wits and wills. The one thing she had never wanted to cede to the reckless instigator was victory of any kind.

Riley leaned closer, not stopping until they were practically close enough to kiss. "Listen to me, Amanda, and listen good. Playing innocent is not going to work with me. And neither," he warned, even more forcefully, "is your latest gag."

Amanda regarded him in a devil-may-care way designed to get under his skin as surely as he was already getting under hers. "I repeat—" she spoke as if to the village idiot "—I have no idea what you are talking about, *Doctor* McCabe. Now do you mind? I only have a forty-five minute break and I'd like to eat my lunch."

He flashed her an incendiary smile that left her feeling more aware of him than ever. "I'll gladly leave you alone just as soon as you collect them."

Amanda blinked, more confused than ever. "Collect who?" she asked incredulously.

Riley walked back to the door. Swung it open wide. On the other side was the surprise of Amanda's life.

If Riley had gone strictly by the stunned and baffled look on his former antagonist's face, he would have thought Amanda Witherspoon was entirely innocent in the commotion that had just gone on down in the hospital's main lobby.

But four years of nonstop high school rivalry had taught him that no one could plan and execute a ruse better than the beautiful woman before him. Amanda stared at the triple stroller, currently being manned by two college-age hospital volunteers—Riley's twenty-one-year-old sister, Laurel, and her friend, premed student Micki Evans.

Amanda's glance moved over the three children ensconced in holiday clothing. "I take it these aren't patients?" Amanda guessed finally.

Riley gave a reassuring smile to the three kids. He had no idea who they belonged to, but they were incredibly cute, nevertheless. The infant—Cory—had short dark hair and inquisitive eyes so dark blue he knew they would eventually turn brown. Amber, the toddler, was practically bald; her thin blond hair barely covered her crown. But she had an infectious smile and a sunny, easygoing personality. Chloe, the preschooler, had a mane of wildly curly light brown hair that stopped at her shoulders, and light blue eyes that radiated more natural mischief than Riley's ever had in his prime. Riley had tried talking to them, to get to the bottom of whatever was going on here—to no avail. The baby merely cooed, the toddler babbled happily but incoherently, and the preschooler was so stubbornly mute it appeared they were playing a game Riley was not in the mood for. Scowling, Riley turned back to Amanda. He could understand her wanting to pick up the jokes again, even if they were a little old for such shenanigans. His life had never been more enthralling than when they had been testing each other's wills and skills. But this ploy was, in his estimation, way over the line of acceptable behavior. And he was determined to make Amanda Witherspoon understand that.

Micki Evans piped up nervously, "Laurel and I found them outside one of the entrances when we were coming in to volunteer this morning."

"There was an envelope addressed to Riley attached to the stroller," Riley's younger sister, Laurel, quickly put in. "And for the record, I don't think you had anything to do with this, Amanda."

"Thank you," Amanda said.

"Well, I do," Riley groused. And he was damn furious about it. He didn't care how beautiful Amanda Witherspoon had become over the years. Or how sweetly sexy she looked in her pale blue nurse's uniform and white cotton sweater. She might appear innocent enough with her dark blond hair tucked into a casual ponytail at the nape of her neck, with sprigs of lighter blond hair escaping to frame her face in wispy strands. But Riley knew better. Her wide-set turquoise eyes radiated a spunk and daring that warned him not to be taken in by her soft feminine lips, stubborn chin and pert straight nose. Her fair skin might be lit with a glow that seemed to come from within, her cheeks a pale, becoming pink, but that did not mean she was the least bit trustworthy. Not when it came to him. Which was why, Riley schooled himself firmly, he could not let himself dwell on the new fullness of her breasts, the admirable slenderness of her waist, and the enticing curve of her hips. Never mind the lithe, graceful way she moved. Nor could he let himself wonder if her legs—now hidden by her uniform trousers—were as sexy and lissome as he recalled.

He was not here to woo her, but to call her to task.

Not that she looked ready to own up to anything she had done.

"May I read the note?" Amanda asked.

Curious to see how she was going to play this ruse out, Riley set his lips grimly and handed the red envelope over. Their hands brushed. He noted Amanda's hands were trembling slightly as she removed a Christmas card with a jolly old Saint Nick, adorned in cowboy hat and boots and holding a rope in his hand, featured prominently on the front of it. "I lassoed you a present," Amanda read out loud, before turning the page. Brow furrowed, she cleared her throat and continued reading out loud. "Dear Riley, Four-year-old Chloe, seventeen-month-old Amber, and four-month-old Cory need the kind of love only a daddy with a heart the size of Texas can give. Please do right by them and see they have a very merry Christmas. Santa."

Amanda's lips formed a round O of surprise as she looked up at Riley. "You have three children?" she asked in amazement. "I didn't even know you were married!"

If Riley had been in a charitable mood, he would have given her an Academy Award for her acting. He was not in a charitable mood. "I'm not married," he told her flatly.

Amanda's eyes widened. "Wow. I mean, I remember you as being sort of irresponsible and joking around all the time, but...wow," she stammered again.

Temper surging, Riley turned to his younger sister and her friend. "Would you mind taking the children to the playroom down the hall?" he asked in a low, clipped voice, doing his best to keep his emotions under control lest he upset the children.

"No problem," Laurel said with a nervous smile. She wheeled the triple stroller around with Micki's help, and they all exited.

Once again, Riley and Amanda were quite alone. "Guess you've been a little busy since you left Laramie," Amanda quipped as she picked up her sandwich, slid it back into the paper bag bearing her name, and placed it in the fridge.

Not that busy, Riley thought. "Those aren't my kids," he repeated firmly.

Amanda tilted her head at him. "Tell that to the kids' mother," she suggested skeptically.

Riley planned on that and much more. An outrageous act like this would not pass without retribution. He promised Amanda Witherspoon that. "Which brings us to the next point," he continued calmly, looking deep into her eyes. "What kind of mother would let you use her children to play a joke on me?"

Good question, Amanda thought. Only she wasn't playing a joke on Riley McCabe. Which could only mean one thing—he had to be playing a joke on her. The kind that would break all records in the history of their long-running feud. "Forgive me for trying to get *you* to do the right thing," she said with a shrug, aware staff were gathering in the hall just outside the lounge.

"So you admit you're behind this!" Riley crowed, ignoring the implication that the trio of children was his.

"I admit," Amanda countered, as she stalked away from him and out into the hallway, "you're a fool if you think you can get away with trying to publicly embarrass me. And furthermore—" she whirled around to face him once again "—had I known when I accepted a position as pediatric nurse here two months ago that you were going to show up here, too, I would have found some other small and charming West Texas town in which to live and work!"

Riley studied the indignant blush warming her face and neck. "If I were you I would admit I was bested and call a halt to this right now."

"Hey!" Amanda angled an accusing finger his way. "I'm not the one with three children spirited away to the pediatric floor playroom."

Riley lifted a dissenting brow. The air between them practically sizzled with sexual sparks. "Aren't you?"

Oh, no, Amanda thought as dread spiraled inside her. She knew that look. The look that said Riley was about to do something even wilder and crazier than what had already been done.

"Is it true?" Meg Lockhart-Carrigan, LCH director of nursing, finally piped up. She and her husband, Luke, had a brood of four. Meg looked Riley in the eye. "Are those children yours?"

"Actually," Riley smiled, wrapping an arm around Amanda's shoulder. "They're ours."

A gasp went through the hallway as even more staff, patients and parents gathered to witness the unfolding scene.

Amanda could feel the blood first draining, then rushing, to her face. *Damn you, Riley McCabe.* She clamped her lips together and spoke out of the side of her mouth. "Stop. Teasing."

"Who's kidding?" Riley said, clearly enjoying himself. He slid his arm down to her waist and hauled her against his length. "I've been trying to get this woman to marry me for ages now. She won't do it. Not even after the two of us had three children in secret."

Amanda's fists curled at her sides. If ever she had wanted to knock someone's block off, it was now. Her eyebrows climbed higher. "Riley, cut it out," she ordered sweetly.

Riley grinned back at her mischievously. "Only if you agree to make an honest man of me."

"Now that would be hard to do."

"Not really," he said softly, his low sensual voice doing strange things to her insides. "Someone want to call the hospital chaplain?"

"Maybe he could help," Meg Lockhart-Carrigan said, already reaching for the phone at the nurses' station.

"I always knew there were sparks between the two of you," someone murmured.

"I didn't know they were this hot!" someone else chimed in.

The chaplain bustled into the throng. "Someone call?" Reverend Bleeker asked.

"Yes. I'd like to know if I can marry Amanda Witherspoon here and now," Riley said.

Reverend Bleeker's brow lifted. He had known them both since childhood, had borne witness to their youthful tomfoolery. "Is there a reason you're in such a hurry?"

Riley shrugged his broad shoulders. With maddening nonchalance, he clamped a hand on her shoulder and turned her back to face him. "It's the only way I can think to put an end to the scandal."

Amanda stared at him, her throat dry. She had to hand it to him. He was playing out this crazy hoax to the end.

Reverend Bleeker looked at Amanda.

All too aware of the warmth of Riley McCabe's strong, capable fingers radiating through her clothing to her skin, Amanda stated just as decisively, "I'm sure there's another way."

"I don't know how when the lives of our three unclaimed children are at stake," Riley countered with exaggerated sincerity.

Amanda started counting to ten. Slowly.

"Unless, of course, you're afraid to marry me," Riley continued. Leaning closer, he goaded Amanda relentlessly.

She shrugged free of his light restraining grip and propped her hands on her hips. "Why would I be afraid?" she retorted, telling herself she was not going to get roped into any wildly exciting romantic drama with him.

Riley lifted his broad shoulders in an indolent shrug. His eyes lasered into hers. "You tell me," he taunted.

"Actually, Riley, I'd love to marry you, right here and right now, in front of all these witnesses," Amanda fibbed, determinedly matching him jab for jab. "But it wouldn't be legal without a license."

Reverend Bleeker cleared his throat. "Actually," he corrected calmly, "it would be quite valid—as long as the two of you entered into this marriage in good faith."

Amanda did her best to retain her nerve. "Meaning?"

"You could get married right this very minute, if you wanted," Revered Bleeker reassured them with an encouraging smile.

Amanda's knees began to wobble. She struggled to keep a poker face. "What about a blood test?"

Reverend Bleeker spoke as much to the crowd gathering in the hall of the pediatric wing as to the two of them. "None are required in Texas."

You're not helping me out here, Reverend, Amanda thought. "What about a license, then?" she asked, determined to find a face-saving way out of this mess Riley had gotten them into with his bravado. Not that she didn't deserve it, since years ago she had inadvertently pulled what had started out to be a peace offering and ended up being a very humiliating prank on him before she left town to go to nursing school in California, and he went off to college in Texas. She could hardly blame Riley if he didn't excuse her for embarrassing the heck out of him—she could hardly forgive herself.

"You have up to thirty days to apply for a license after you say your I Do's," Reverend Bleeker continued informatively.

Riley frowned, abruptly looking as concerned about the specifics of this mess they were suddenly in as Amanda felt. "Then what's that seventy-two hour waiting period all about?" Riley asked.

"That's how long it takes for the license to be valid, after the application is made," Reverend Bleeker explained.

And there was her out, Amanda thought. She wouldn't apply for a license. So the marriage would never be legal. Even if known prankster Riley goaded her into taking this ruse to the max. Which of course she hoped like heck he wouldn't. "Fine," Amanda said, looking at Riley and daring him to push her—and this farce—even one inch further, and see exactly what it got him. "Then let's do it!"

Riley had expected Amanda Witherspoon to back out way before now. The fact she hadn't, impressed him almost as much as it irritated him. Not about to be the one to cry uncle in this battle of wills, he merely smiled, took her hand and said to Reverend Bleeker, "I'm every bit as ready to go through with this as Amanda."

Although Amanda's pretty smile stayed in place, Riley thought he saw her will falter just a bit as he looked into her eyes.

"Would you like to go to the chapel?" Reverend Bleeker asked.

And do this before all that was holy?

"No," Riley and Amanda said abruptly in unison.

"Here is fine," Riley stated, amazed to find the Reverend not harboring objections of his own. Instead, the chaplain appeared as if he had expected something like this from the two of them all along.

"Yes, let's do it right here," Amanda concurred. She turned to Riley and batted her eyelashes at him coquettishly. "So long as you realize, Riley, that I won't obey."

As if he were that crazy and naive! He had known, even as a kid, that Amanda Witherspoon was as headstrong as she was beautiful. "All I ask is that you honor me." Riley used his grip on her hand to tug her closer still. Damn, but she smelled good. More expensive, grown-up, and sexy than he recalled her in her youth, even with the hint of hospital antiseptic clinging to her clenched palm. "You can do that, can't you, Amanda?" he taunted.

Amanda replied with a delicate shrug and kept her eyes

locked stubbornly with his. "Um. Sure." Her delicate brow furrowed. "I guess."

It was all Riley could do to keep from rolling his eyes as Reverend Bleeker opened the small prayer book from the inside pocket of his blazer. "Very well," Reverend Bleeker said with a great deal less reluctance than Riley would have expected, "if there are no further objections..."

Unfortunately, Riley noted, there weren't.

"We are gathered here today to unite Riley McCabe and Amanda Witherspoon in marriage...Riley, do you take this woman...?"

For everything she's worth, including, and especially, her pride. "I surely do." Riley gave Amanda a crocodile smile and with great satisfaction saw her falter, just a little, again.

"Amanda, do you take this man...?"

Amanda flashed Riley a dirt-eating grin, that told him she was not, and had never been, a pushover. "Oh, I absolutely do," she agreed in a voice dripping with Texas sugar.

"Since we don't have rings we will dispense with that part of the ceremony," Reverend Bleeker said.

Thank goodness for small miracles, Riley thought, as he pushed away the unlikely but nevertheless sweetly lingering possibility of eventually getting Amanda in his bed. He didn't want this "union of hearts and souls" feeling any more real than it already did before he could get the deservedly embarrassed and humbled Amanda to cry uncle and legally undo it.

Out of the corner of his eyes, Riley saw hospital chief of staff, Dr. Jackson McCabe rounding the corner of the hall. Obviously, his uncle had been informed of what was going on and the talented surgeon looked none too pleased. Right behind Jackson was Riley's stepmother, Kate Marten McCabe, who was the hospital psychologist and grief counselor. She looked irked and exasperated as all get out, too.

"Riley, you may kiss your bride," Reverend Bleeker said.

And figuring it had to be better than the rest of the options facing him, Riley did.

Chapter 2

Amanda had figured Riley McCabe would kiss her. After all, it was the defining touch to his ridiculous prank. One, she knew, all of Laramie would be talking about for years to come. One that put her last accidental joke on him to shame.

But as he wrapped his arms around her in a straitjacket of warmth, tugged her close and lowered his lips to hers in a kiss that she knew darn well was all for show, all she could think about was how wildly sensual it felt to have his mouth on hers. Not in the hot, openmouthed manner she would have wished, had he been kissing her for real, but in the carefully close-mouthed variety popular on stage and screen.

A whisper of desire swept through her, followed swiftly by a flood of tingling. Her toes curled in her shoes. Her knees went weak. And she wanted more than anything to be able to kiss him back, really kiss him back. And that was when, of course, he let her go. Looking for a moment as oddly shaken and disturbed as she felt.

Which was, of course, ridiculous, Amanda reprimanded

herself sternly, since all Riley had been doing was putting on a show for everyone around them who just happened to be there to unknowingly participate in this…sham!

As they stumbled apart, a cheer went up around them, followed by whistles and congratulations.

Riley dipped his head in acknowledgment, then took Amanda's hand firmly in his. Leading her through the fray, he dashed toward the elevator. Although Amanda had no desire to go anywhere with Riley right then, she did want to escape their audience. And that went double for Riley McCabe's stepmother, Kate, and the hospital's chief of staff, Jackson McCabe. Keeping a victorious smile she couldn't really begin to feel plastered on her face, she followed Riley into the otherwise empty lift.

As the steel doors closed behind them, Riley let go of her. Heart pounding, she leaned against the opposite wall, hands braced on the rail behind her. She glowered at him. "You know, I can believe you just seriously put a dent in *my* professional reputation. After all, you've had it out for me for years, Riley McCabe! But to use three unsuspecting little children and a hospital chaplain to do it…now that's low."

Riley punched in five and leaned back against the opposite rail. "I could say the same about you," he retorted evenly.

"You can't seriously deny you just set me up, but good!" Amanda admonished. "Pretending you and I were long-term lovers, with three illegitimate children to boot!"

Clearly aware he was annoying her terribly, he scanned her frame from head to toe, taking in the swell of her breasts and the curve of her hips before returning ever so deliberately to her face. He angled a thumb at his chest. "I don't deny employing my own particular brand of much-deserved payback on you just now."

"No kidding." Amanda continued to regard him accusingly. She had never been so embarrassed in her life!

"But I categorically deny setting you up," Riley insisted, as the elevator began to move and Christmas music filled the air.

Amanda felt herself flush self-consciously. She didn't know what her teenage nemesis was up to now, but she didn't like it one bit. And she especially didn't like the way he was continuing to look at her, as if he were imagining what it would be like to pick up where the chaste kiss had left off and make love to her here and now. Determined to irritate him as much as he was irritating her, Amanda blinked her eyes at Riley coquettishly. If he was pulling her leg, he was doing a damn fine job of it. "Then who did?" she inquired sweetly, wishing fervently all the while her heart would stop its telltale pounding and resume its normal beat. "Santa Claus?"

He tilted his head, gave her the kind of frankly male appraisal he had not been capable of in his youth. Back then she'd been dealing with a boy. Now he was all man. "Suppose you tell me. *Wife,*" Riley commanded in a soft, derisive voice that did strange things to her insides.

If there was anything Amanda hated, it was being held accountable for something she did not do. That had happened to her a lot in the days she had been at "prankster war" with Riley McCabe. "I told you," she enunciated clearly, as another shimmer of awareness sifted through her, weakening her knees. "I. Don't. Know."

Steadfastly ignoring her goading manner, Riley moved so that he was towering over her once again. "Well, then," he countered grimly, "that makes two of us, because neither do I."

Amanda felt her pulse skitter and jump as shock set in. "You're serious!" She swallowed hard, still struggling to take it all in. "Aren't you?"

He nodded. "This once, yes I am."

Panic surged inside her and her heart began to gallop. This was like a bizarre dream! "Then if you really didn't do this…

and I really didn't do it..." The blood drained from her face as she whispered tremulously, "Who did?"

Riley fell silent, shoved a hand through his hair, beginning to realize—as she was—the enormity of what had just happened. The elevator reached the top floor and the doors slid open. Riley took Amanda by the hand and led her to his office. It was in a state of disarray. Half-emptied boxes fought with diplomas ready to be hung on the wall. The only furniture currently in the room was a large desk and swivel chair.

"You promise me you don't know who those three kids are?" Riley asked yet again. He followed his question with a very sober, very probing look.

Amanda understood why he was having trouble believing her. There was little the two of them hadn't done to each other, back in their high school days. They'd covered every juvenile, teenage prank in the book, and then some, ending with Riley's managing to get a pet goat into her bedroom that had ended up eating the corsage from her senior prom, and her setting him up for what, she still suspected, had been the most humiliating, not-so-secret romantic rendezvous in his entire life.

"I would never use three innocent little children that way," Amanda reiterated emotionally. And she was beginning to realize, neither would he. Which left them where? she wondered. Another silence fell between them. They continued to survey each other, warily. "So who would have done something like this?" Amanda asked finally.

Riley's frown deepened. "I haven't a clue," he muttered.

"That Christmas card had your name on it," Amanda pointed out sagely. "Someone wanted those three children to end up with you."

"The question is why?" Riley mused, beginning to pace. He rubbed at the tense muscles in the back of his neck, looking more aggravated than ever.

Amanda hadn't a clue. She did know they were both suddenly over their heads. This was a situation for the professionals trained in such matters. "Maybe we should alert the authorities," Amanda suggested. "See what they can come up with."

Riley nodded his agreement, already reaching for the phone. "I'll put in a call to social services as well as my brother, Kevin. He's a detective with the Laramie County Sheriff's Department."

"And while we're at it," Amanda said, quickly thinking ahead, relieved to have something else to focus on besides the two of them, "we better talk to the hospital administrator, too, since the abandonment happened on hospital grounds."

Riley nodded in agreement and he and Amanda made the calls from his office. As soon as they had finished, they went down to pediatrics. Mercifully, everyone who had witnessed their "wedding vows" seemed to have dispersed, including Riley's uncle, Jackson, and his stepmother, Kate. Amanda knew she and Riley were going to have to face up to what they had done—foolishly goading each other into a joke marriage—but that would come later, she decided firmly. After they took care of the children.

"I was beginning to wonder when you were coming back," Laurel said as Amanda and Riley swooped into the pediatric playroom to claim the three children "left" in Riley's care.

"Or if," Laurel's friend, Micki Evans, added nervously. Unlike his little sister, who had a habit of getting in and out of all sorts of trouble, Micki was never one to cause anyone a moment's worry. Part of that was because Micki had been orphaned at fourteen, and only had a married older sister, who now lived in Colorado with her family, to rely upon. The rest, Riley supposed, was just personality. Laurel was dark haired and blue-eyed and so reckless and dazzlingly beautiful, guys couldn't take their eyes off her.

The petite Micki was red haired and freckled, and as serious about the future as she could be. The two young women were college roommates at University of Texas and best friends. Laurel had introduced her friend to Riley several years prior, and Riley had been mentoring the shy but studious Micki and helping her realize her ambition to attend medical school ever since. He'd even gone so far as to get Micki a summer internship in a Dallas hospital, where Riley had been on staff the previous summer, and then wrote a recommendation for her medical school applications earlier in the fall. Last he heard, she was still waiting to hear the result of her early-decision application to UT-Galveston med school.

"For all we knew, you two had left for your honeymoon already," Laurel said, only half joking, as she juggled the four-year-old Chloe on her lap.

Riley knew a veiled request for more information when he heard one. He had no intention of discussing his relationship with Amanda with his baby sister. "Amanda and I had a few things to discuss, about the kids," Riley said.

Micki was sitting on the sofa, with the infant Cory in one arm, the toddler Amber on the floor in front of her. None of the children were saying a word, yet seemed content as could be to simply hang out there. Which meant what? Riley wondered. Were the children used to being abandoned in strange places? Had this happened to them before? In their place, at their age, Riley would have been scared out of his mind. To the point that even Micki and Laurel, who were both great with kids and experienced babysitters, could not have calmed him. Yet these three children looked strangely accepting, almost numb.

"What's going to happen now?" Micki asked, as focused on detail as ever.

Riley hefted a diaper bag brimming with baby gear over his shoulder. "We're going up to my office to wait for the authorities and figure out what to do next."

"You're really concerned about them, aren't you?" Laurel marveled as they gathered up the children.

Riley knew his sister looked up to him, never more so than right now. For the first time in a long while, he didn't really feel he deserved it. "I'd be concerned about anyone in their situation," Riley said. "These three kids warrant better care." One way or another, before the day was done, he would see that they received it.

All three women looked uncomfortable at his blunt pronouncement. "Which is maybe why someone left the kids with you," Micki speculated after a moment as they crowded into the elevator. She maneuvered the stroller to the rear. "Because they knew what a good guy you were."

At the rear of the elevator, Amanda lifted a skeptical brow, but said nothing. It was clear she did not see him in quite the same way. Riley decided then and there to change her opinion of him. He didn't want Amanda thinking he was still the reckless, irresponsible, practical jokester she had known when they were teens. They were adults now. Hell, they were married—at least until they were able to correct their mutual foolhardiness. And they were going to have to work together at the hospital very soon. He wanted them dealing with each other from a position of mutual respect and maturity. The days of high emotion and impulsive behavior were past.

"Looks like your brother's here, at least," Amanda noted as the doors slid open and they moved out into the hallway once again. Riley followed her glance, catching sight of the tall, dark-haired man in the tan sheriff's department uniform and bone-colored Stetson. His youngest brother was an ace detective. Riley knew if anyone would be able to help them track down the origin of the children, Kevin would.

Kevin held the door for them, then followed them inside.

Finding a toddler wrapped around one of his legs, arms upraised, Riley reached down and picked her up. Aware how natural it felt to cradle the seventeen-month-old Amber in his arms, he asked, "Did you find out anything?"

"We don't have any reports of three children gone missing," Kevin stated grimly. Amber laid her head on Riley's chest. She put two fingers in her mouth and used her other hand to rub at the fabric of his sweater vest.

"I did, however, hear a report about two people getting married in a pretty big hurry, though." Kevin flashed them a teasing grin.

"Who told you?" Riley demanded irritably.

Immediately picking up on Riley's shift in mood, Amber frowned. It looked as if she might cry, so Riley widened his eyes and gave the little girl a great big smile to let her know it was okay. She relaxed in his arms once again, while Riley mentally reminded himself to watch his tone from here on out, lest he upset the kids.

Kevin touched the brim of his hat, pushing his Stetson farther back on his head. "It's all over town. And uh, just so you know, the news is sending pretty big shock waves through the family, too."

Riley could imagine. He hadn't faced off with Kate yet, but he figured he would have some more explaining to do as soon as his stepmother got hold of his father. When it came to family conundrums, Kate and his dad always handled things together. Which was probably why she hadn't chased him down thus far.

"Great," Riley murmured in an ultrasoothing voice at odds with the clearly exasperated content of his words. Out of the corner of his eyes, he caught Amanda's grin. "Now can we get back to the issue at hand?" he asked Kevin. "What are we going to do with the uh—you know?"

Kevin looked at Amanda, who had infant Cory in her arms, then back at Riley, who had toddler Amber in his arms, and over at Chloe, who was holding on to both Laurel's and

Micki's hands for dear life. Kevin asked, "None of you have any idea who they are?"

At that, Chloe moved even closer to Micki and Laurel. The curly haired angel might not have said a word yet, but Riley was certain she hadn't missed one bit of what had been going on. The four-year-old absorbed words and actions like water into a sponge.

Riley shook his head in answer to Kevin's questions, while Amber sucked her thumb and laid her nearly bald head against his shoulder. "Aside from first names, no," Riley said, patting the toddler gently on the back.

Amanda looked serious now, too, as concerned and worried as Riley was beginning to feel. "I wish I did," she vowed, cradling Cory close to her chest. "But I can't remember ever seeing these children around the hospital or the community."

As Amanda was talking, social worker Felicia Winters joined them.

Amanda brought her up to date on everything that had happened thus far.

Felicia frowned. The plump gray-haired woman had worked for the county for nigh on thirty years. Her experience showed in the weathered lines of her face. "We have a real problem. There's no foster home available until mid-January, at the very earliest, that would allow us to keep them all together."

Big tears welled in the four-year-old's eyes. Noticing Chloe's distress, the toddler began to cry. Soon the infant and Chloe both joined in the cacophony of sound.

"You can't split them up," Amanda said to Felicia, over the din.

Riley agreed that would be too cruel, after what the children had already been through. "Their remaining security is tied to staying together," he said.

Felicia shifted the clipboard in her arms. "Believe me, I don't want to separate them but unless I get a suitable volunteer—a married couple—who can take all three children on an emergency basis, we'll have to place them in different homes."

At that, Chloe began to wail more loudly.

Amanda gestured for Riley to give her Amber, and swooped all three children into her arms simultaneously. "There, there, now," Amanda soothed firmly, patting them all on the back. "No one is going to make you leave each other. Riley and I are going to take very good care of you until we find your mommy and daddy."

Riley didn't know whether it was the conviction in Amanda's low, soothing voice or the tenderness of her touch that made the children calm down, but within a minute they were all quiet once again. She handed Chloe to Micki, Amber to Laurel, and Cory to Riley, then bent to rummage through the diaper bag and pulled out a bottle of formula. "Would you two please take the children down to the cafeteria for some lunch—and maybe stop by pediatrics on the way to warm this bottle for Cory—while we work on the specifics?" Amanda asked Micki and Laurel.

"No problem." The college coeds looked eager to leave the tense atmosphere of the room. Riley couldn't blame them.

"Riley and I will meet you there as soon as we are done here," Amanda promised, as Riley handed over the baby and then followed that with a crisp twenty-dollar bill meant to cover expenses.

"You-all take as much time as you need." Laurel smiled. "Micki and I can handle it." The girls put the children in the stroller and took off.

"You shouldn't have promised the children you and Riley would take them," Felicia Winters admonished as soon as they were alone again.

Riley hadn't intended to offer anything in terms of child care, and for good reason. He was a single guy, or at least he had been until an hour ago when his competitiveness and temper had gotten the best of him. He knew a lot about making sick kids well, and keeping children healthy, but nothing about how to take care of an infant, toddler and preschooler simultaneously. Furthermore, these weren't his kids. But the reaction of the children just now, coupled with Amanda's valiant offer, had changed all that.

"Amanda's right," Riley said. "The children are my responsibility. Whoever left them here today, left them with me." Like it or not, it was a task he couldn't abandon. "I'll take them."

"By yourself?" Felicia Winters blinked in surprise. Her expression turned skeptical. "Do you even have any experience with kids?"

Just the question he did not want to answer, Riley thought. "I'm a family doctor," Riley stated confidently. Looking over the petite Felicia's head, he saw the new respect in Amanda's eyes, found himself warming to it. "I can handle any medical issues that come up."

"Great," Felicia said dryly, as Amanda moved to stand right next to Riley, "but do you know how to change a diaper or make a bottle?"

"I'll help him," Amanda said, moving closer yet. "And I have plenty of experience with kids from newborn on up. I babysat my eight brothers and sisters as well as my nieces and nephews countless times."

Felicia exhaled. "I'd still feel better if I had a married couple."

"Actually," Kevin put in, looking eager to help, albeit in an ornery brotherly way, "Amanda and Riley are married as of noon today. In fact," Kevin continued with exaggerated seriousness, "they said their I Do's right here in the hospital's pediatric wing."

Thanks a lot, brother, Riley thought. He had been hoping not to bring their predicament into this. Too late, the county social worker was intensely interested.

Felicia looked at Amanda and Riley. "Is this true?"

Riley and Amanda nodded.

"So you're newlyweds—and you still want to do this?" Felicia asked in amazement. "Don't you have a honeymoon planned?"

Riley wished people would stop talking about that. It conjured up thoughts of hot, passionate lovemaking. And that was something that was definitely not going to happen between him and his temporary "wife." She'd caused him enough trouble already. If it weren't for her willingness to help him with the three abandoned kids he would have ended the farce of a union already. "Could we just go back to talking about the children?" he requested, making no effort to curtail his exasperation.

Felicia folded her arms in front of her and pressed her clipboard to her ample chest. "I'd prefer to talk about the two of you," she replied as Ted Keaton, the hospital's administrator, walked up. As always, the balding forty-something man looked as if he were in a hurry.

Caught up on what had happened thus far, the bespectacled five-foot-eight Ted said, "I can vouch for both of them. They're fine, upstanding people. Otherwise, they wouldn't work at this hospital. I didn't know about the romance." Ted paused to check the pager vibrating at his waist before turning it off. "Apparently, very few did, but that shouldn't make a difference, should it?"

"Not as long as it's a stable home situation," Felicia allowed.

"It will be," Riley promised quietly. He looked over at Amanda. She nodded her agreement, obviously as willing to put their personal issues aside as he was, in order to see Amber, Chloe and Cory's needs were met.

Felicia frowned before cautioning sternly, "If I agree to this, neither of you can bail out on me. I'd need your word you'll take care of the children until, at minimum, December 26."

With his brother on the case, there was no way it was going to take that long to find out where the kids really belonged, Riley thought. He looked at Amanda and shrugged. "You have it," Amanda and Riley said in unison.

The matter settled, Kevin left to file his report with the sheriff's department. Felicia Winters told them she'd start processing the paperwork and went on to her next case. As the hospital administrator was departing to answer his page, the phone on Riley's desk rang. He picked it up, listened, not liking what was being said on the other end of the connection. Finally, he exhaled. "We'll be right there," he promised.

"Right where?" Amanda asked curiously as Riley replaced the receiver on the base.

Beginning to feel as stressed out as Amanda now looked, Riley scowled and said, "The chief of staff's office. My uncle Jackson wants to see us." And that, Riley knew, could not be good.

"All right. Someone start explaining what's been going on here today," Jackson McCabe demanded as soon as the door was shut behind them. The talented general surgeon and devoted family man supervised Laramie Community Hospital's medical staff as smoothly as Riley's grandfather, John McCabe, had. Upsets like this were not encouraged. And as a new hire, with a previous reputation for playing way too many practical jokes, Riley knew it wasn't a conundrum he could afford to be caught in. Not if he wanted to be taken seriously as a family physician himself. Already regretting what his longstanding feud with Amanda Witherspoon had prompted him to do, Riley exchanged looks with Amanda. Neither knew exactly where to begin.

"Was the delivery of those three children a prank?" Jackson asked as Amanda eased into a chair.

Preferring to stand, Riley leaned up against a file cabinet. "Apparently not. Although we were both initially convinced that was the case."

Jackson rocked back in his swivel chair. "And then you blamed each other for their appearance?" he surmised.

Knowing this did not sound good, Riley folded his arms in front of him. He kept his voice even and matter-of-fact. "Yes."

"Whom do the children belong to?" Jackson asked as he picked up a pen and turned it end over end.

Delicate hands twined together in her lap, Amanda sat stiffly in her chair. "We don't know. The police and social services are working on it. Meanwhile, Riley and I have been granted temporary custody of them."

Jackson's eyes widened. "You're sure you want to do this?" he asked.

Riley and Amanda looked at each other again. Realizing this was the one thing they agreed upon, Riley and Amanda both said in unison, "Yes."

Jackson set his pen down. "I'm surprised social services allowed that."

Riley shrugged. He slid his hands in the pockets of his slacks, and continued to lean against the file cabinet. "They didn't have much choice. All the foster homes are full."

Jackson mulled this over. "Was Felicia Winters's decision based in part on the fact you're married?"

"Yes." Amanda flushed.

"So it's a real marriage?" Jackson's brow rose.

Amanda swallowed and said nothing.

"I'm not sure how to answer that," Riley said finally.

"So in other words it is not," Jackson confirmed with a deeply disapproving look at both of them and a long disgruntled sigh.

Riley shoved a hand through his hair. He wished he didn't know his uncle so well, and vice versa. "Let's just say it's complicated," he said finally.

"Complicated?" Jackson echoed, looking even more outraged as he pushed his chair back from his desk. "Try disingenuous, at the very least."

What could they say to that? Riley wondered. It was true.

Jackson stood and flattened both hands on the desk in front of him. "Okay, then, here is what you two are going to do," he told them authoritatively. "You are going to collect those three children, go home with the three of them, and work this whatever-you-want-to-call-it out on your own time in your own way."

"But I have a shift to finish," Amanda protested emotionally. She rose to her feet, as well.

"Not anymore, Miss Wither—Mrs. McCabe. You're on an emergency leave for a honeymoon," Jackson said firmly. "Effective immediately."

Riley stopped slouching and moved away from the wall. He agreed they should be verbally chastised for the ruckus they'd caused earlier in the day, but an enforced leave was too much. "Don't you think you're carrying this a little too far?" he asked his uncle patiently.

Jackson turned his glare Riley's way. "I don't think so. And oh, by the way, you're on an emergency leave, too," Jackson told him. "Unless one of you wants to clear up any lingering misconception and tell everyone that you heartlessly used those children to further the longstanding feud between the two of you? And that your wedding was some big joke scripted strictly for the entertainment of the parents and patients in the pediatric wing?"

Riley wasn't going to confess to that and neither was Amanda since it could cost them temporary custody of the kids. And, like it or not, for the moment anyway, the welfare of the three abandoned children had to come first, before their personal comfort, even before their careers.

"In the meantime, I want you two to realize that everything you do reflects on this hospital," Jackson scolded. "Patients will not take you seriously unless you take yourselves seriously. And that goes double for the rest of the staff. You're not wild and crazy teenagers any more. You're married. You have three children who—thanks to your speedy nuptials—now have a home to go to for the Christmas holidays, so I suggest you take them there. When you are ready to apologize and make amends, call and make an appointment with my secretary. Then, depending on what you have to say, we'll go from there."

Chapter 3

Riley knew a golden opportunity to prove himself imperturbable when he saw it; he did his best to look as if the meeting with the chief of staff hadn't ruffled him in the least.

Amanda, on the other hand, looked as piqued as could be as they left Jackson McCabe's office. Her fair skin was lit with a riotous pink glow that matched the hue of her full soft lips. Her long-lashed turquoise eyes were sparkling with indignation. She had taken her hair out of its low ponytail just before entering Jackson's office and combed it with her fingers. Riley found he liked the way her dark blond mane looked, tumbling down around her slender shoulders, as much as he loved the way she filled out her nurse's uniform. Not that he could afford to be distracted by any of that just yet. Not while they were still technically married anyway…

"That went well, don't you think?" Riley commented as they took the fastest route to the cafeteria.

Amanda turned and shot him a drop-dead look, letting him know they were definitely not on the same page. Not now.

Maybe not ever. "Just peachy. I always wanted to be put on administrative leave. Especially with you."

Okay, so maybe it hadn't gone so well. But griping and moaning about it wasn't going to change anything, Riley thought. The situation was what it was. The two of them were just going to have to deal with it. Given the fact his new "bride" slash partner in matrimony was not in the mood to discuss their punishment rationally, however, Riley decided a change of subject was in order. "Mind if I ask you a question?" he said casually, trying not to notice the provocative sway of her hips as she strode just ahead of him, trying her best to leave him in the dust.

Amanda exhaled, long and loud. She sent him another long-suffering glance over her shoulder. "If you feel you absolutely must."

Riley lengthened his strides to catch up. "Earlier, when we were talking to social services, why did you volunteer to help out like that?" He wouldn't have expected it from the Amanda he knew in high school. She never would have aligned herself with him, even momentarily, no matter what was at stake.

Amanda's shoulders stiffened. She refused to meet his gaze. "It wasn't for you."

Riley moved ahead to hold the door for her. "That much I gathered."

Her shoulder brushed his chest as she stepped past him into the stairwell. "It was for the children," Amanda continued as Riley shut the door behind them, closing them in the deserted passageway. Grabbing onto the railing with her right hand, she made her way carefully down the cement steps. "Their situation breaks my heart."

"Mine, too," Riley said, as he descended alongside her.

"And there's something else I noticed," Amanda said as they reached the first landing and circled around to the next set of stairs. She paused to regard him seriously. "In our line of work, you and I have both seen children who did not receive the care they should have had."

Sadly, Riley knew that was true.

Amanda swallowed and began climbing downward once again, slower now. "Those three kids do not act like children who have never known love."

Riley matched his strides to hers. Hands on her shoulders, he stopped her on the next landing, and turned her to face him. He surveyed the conflicted expression on Amanda's face that had appeared the moment they had both decided—impulsively, as usual—to jointly manage the guardianship of the children, even if it meant continuing their "marriage" a little while longer. "Meaning what?"

Amanda tilted her face up to his. "Someone out there obviously cares about them," she told him passionately. "Otherwise that person would not have left them with you, so they could have the kind of Christmas all children deserve."

"You think that person is going to come back for them?" Riley offered matter-of-factly, resisting what now seemed an ever-present urge to haul her in his arms and kiss her again. This time, without restraint.

Amanda nodded. "By December 26, if not sooner," she stipulated soberly. "When that person or persons shows up they are going to need our help. I want to be there when that happens. So," she released a long breath, and followed that with an equally telling look, before continuing in a determined voice, "if it means we stay technically married for the next week or so, before we undo what we so foolishly did a few hours ago, I figure we can soldier through."

Put it kindly, why don't you? Riley thought.

"So long as you understand," she went on firmly, as a fresh wave of color flowed into her cheeks, "this is merely a technicality to make social services—and the chief of staff—feel better about our situation."

Riley dropped his hands, stepped back. "So no sex, hmm?"

No thinking about what it would be like to momentarily let their defenses down, and let the past be just that, and discover what it might be like if they were as well-matched in the bedroom as they had been in practical-joke-administration.

Suddenly seeming to be able to read his mind all too well, Amanda declared flatly, "Not even a whisper of it."

Riley would have liked to say the thought of making love to Amanda had never crossed his mind. But it had.... During the kiss, he had wondered if the rest of her was as soft and feminine as her lips. What would she do if he gave passion free rein and crushed that sweet mouth of hers under his? Would she be as feisty and unrestrained in her lovemaking as she had always been in her mischief? And how much longer before he found out?

"So what now?" Riley's baby sister asked moments later from her perch in the hospital cafeteria, after Riley had explained to Micki and Laurel what had transpired with the authorities.

"We're taking the kids back to my place for the time being," Riley said.

"And then?" Micki asked as she put the empty bottle back in the overflowing diaper bag.

"We keep looking for their parents or guardians, right along with social services," Riley said.

Micki and Laurel exchanged uncertain glances.

"But not to worry." Amanda smiled reassuringly. "I'm sure we'll be able to manage the three of them between the two of us. And regardless of how long it takes to get things—um—settled—Riley and I will see the children have the very best holiday possible."

Both young women relaxed visibly. "We'll be around if you need extra help," Laurel offered.

"Thanks." Riley smiled at his sister's typically generous

offer. "But I think, right now anyway, that Amanda and I can take it from here."

They got the children's winter jackets, hats and mittens on. Then headed out, getting smiles and nods of approval from everyone they passed. Riley could tell from the way people were smiling at them that the rumor mill had been working overtime, and everyone thought the children were theirs. He considered correcting the misimpression, then decided against it. The truth—that social services and the sheriff's department were now involved—would get out soon enough.

"We've got a problem, Riley," Amanda said as he pushed the triple stroller out into the parking lot, toward his five-passenger SUV.

Actually, Riley thought, they had a bunch of them. He looked over at her in bemusement. "What's that?"

"We don't have car seats. And it's against state law to transport children in a vehicle without them."

"Good point," Riley murmured as he stopped just short of the driver's door. To his amazement, inside the vehicle, were two safety seats, and a booster seat. All properly installed on the backseat. He turned and looked at Amanda, not sure whether to feel relieved—that this major safety issue had been taken care of—or really aggravated. Truth was, he felt a little of both. He didn't like the feeling that some unidentified person was always one step ahead of him, manipulating and arranging. He was used to taking charge of his life, not feeling as if he was a victim of circumstances far beyond his control. "What the," he muttered in stunned amazement, loud enough for only Amanda to hear. "Who did this?"

Amanda stared at the rear seat. "I have no idea." She regarded him, clearly perplexed, then bent to lift Chloe out of the stroller. "Was your vehicle locked?"

"No," Riley admitted reluctantly as he picked up Amber. People in Laramie didn't have to lock their cars every second of every day.

Amanda set Chloe in her car seat, then turned to get baby Cory. "Maybe it was the same person who left the kids," she speculated.

More than ever, Riley wanted to know who that person was. "Do you know how to work these?" Riley asked, looking at the maze of straps and buckles on Amber's seat.

To his relief, Amanda did, and she leaned inside the vehicle to show him how.

Since it was located only a few streets away from the hospital, the drive to his house was accomplished quickly. Amanda took charge of baby Cory. Riley picked up Chloe and Amber and carried them both inside. All business, Amanda strode through the foyer, past the living room, to the kitchen. "We should probably do a quick inventory of your fridge and pantry and figure out what we're going to need to take care of them, and then go from there," Amanda said, over the infant's head.

"Good idea," Riley replied.

Amanda swung open the fridge and surveyed the contents—barbecue sauce and jelly, juice, milk, coffee, soda and beer. "Well," she drawled finally, shooting him a look, "you're definitely a bachelor."

Riley refused to feel embarrassed about the meager fare. "Give me a break. I just moved in a few days ago."

Amanda arched a delicate brow. "And yet managed to decorate the place from top to bottom?"

Riley followed her glance. The gray two-story frame house with the black shutters and doors was located in the historic section of Laramie. It had been built in the 1920s and lovingly maintained. "I bought it furnished, right down to the dishes and bath towels."

Amanda blinked. "You're kidding."

Did she really think he had selected the French chairs and settee in the formal living room, the gold-and-white toile drapes on the windows, and the antique Italianate dining room set?

Riley moved from the updated kitchen with cherry cabinets, stainless steel appliances and black marble countertops to the adjacent family room. The floor-to-ceiling windows brought in plenty of light. The brick fireplace made it homey, the large sectional sofa and entertainment armoire as comfortable as he needed it to be. This was the room where he hung out most of the time. The room, Riley couldn't help but note, that Amanda and the kids seemed to like the most.

"The woman I bought it from is a professional decorator and avid shopper," Riley continued, "and when I heard she was planning to auction off everything in here and start over in her new place, I made her an offer she couldn't refuse. Worked for both of us. I got a ready-made home and she got the funds to outfit her new place."

"Obviously, groceries didn't come with the deal," Amanda remarked dryly, walking back to eye his equally empty walk-in pantry.

"Sadly, no. Although I'm not sure that would have worked for both of us nearly as well, anyway. Mrs. Barker was heavily into macrobiotics and vegan. And I'm more of a meat-and-potatoes take-out kind of guy."

Amanda's glance briefly roved his tall, muscular frame. She seemed to find nothing to complain about there, Riley noted with pleasure.

"Heaven help us then," Amanda murmured as she propped the drowsy infant on her shoulder and patted his back until he uttered an adult-size burp.

"Want me to make a run to the grocery?"

Amanda nodded. "We're going to need diapers and formula and baby food—toddler variety—as well as foods suitable for a four-year-old."

Riley tried not to notice how maternal—and angelically beautiful—Amanda looked as she tended the children, even as he rummaged around for a paper and pen. Yet he sensed that she was still the same jokester she'd always been. A person couldn't change *that* much. He might be married to her—temporarily—but he wasn't in the market for a practical joker of a wife. No, when he married, he didn't want to be worried about what might be under his pillow or in his breakfast cereal. Nor did he want to have to be a continual court jester, there to provide maximum entertainment, the way he had been with Amanda years ago. Next time around...hopefully the last time around...he wanted to be free to be himself. Mature. Adult. Able to enjoy a good joke as well as the next person, but not constantly expected to deliver one. Their initial response to each other proved there was still plenty of "spark" between him and Amanda, in that regard.

"We'll also need plenty of whole milk, peanut butter, cheese and bread."

Riley had already forgotten the first few items on the list. He'd been too busy concentrating on Amanda, and his reaction to her. He jotted down what she had just said. "That sounds like a lot."

Amanda looked over his shoulder. "Or in other words," she guessed dryly, "too much for you to handle purchasing on your own."

Riley hedged, torn between pride and common sense. Grocery shopping usually took him a while, even when only a few things were on the list.

"Never mind, that look on your face is answer enough. Why don't we do some quick diaper changes and take Chloe to the bathroom, then all go to the store?"

That sounded like even more of an ordeal, Riley thought. Just getting them in and out of coats and car seats took a good ten minutes. "Shouldn't they nap or something?" he asked, beginning to understand what a huge task he had undertaken in volunteering to care for all three children at once.

Amanda's eyes glimmered with unchecked amusement. "Do they look sleepy to you?"

Anything but, Riley admitted reluctantly to himself, telling himself he was not going to get overwhelmed here.

"I think they'll be fine," she continued in a reassuringly matter-of-fact voice. "If not," she shrugged her slender shoulders affably, "we'll regroup, and come up with another plan. Besides, with the two of us there, it shouldn't take long."

The next few minutes were spent getting the children ready to go out again. Amanda put the sleeping infant back in the carrier and Riley carried the older children back out to the SUV. As Riley situated them in their safety seats, the two older children regarded him curiously. The four-year-old was seriously sucking her thumb, the toddler, her first two fingers. Neither was saying a word.

"So," Riley said, hoping now that she'd been around him a little more, Chloe would offer some helpful information. "Where are you kids from? Not Laramie, I know. If you were from around here, someone would have recognized you over at the hospital."

To Riley's mounting disappointment, she was as silent and uncommunicative as she had been when Kevin and Felicia Winters saw her at the hospital.

Riley could tell by the way Chloe was looking at him that she understood what he was asking, she just wasn't in a mind to cooperate with him. At all. Tamping down his frustration, his eagerness to get to the story behind the children's delivery to him, he tried again gently, "What's your last name? Where do you live? Do you have a dog? Cat? Grandma?" And who exactly was the Santa Claus in the note?

"They're not going to tell me anything, are they?" Riley whispered to Amanda, when the silence continued unabated.

"Give them time," she whispered right back, looking at that moment a lot more patient and understanding than Riley felt.

Time, Riley thought, was the one thing he did not want to surrender. It had only been a few hours, and already, he could feel himself beginning to feel somewhat responsible for the welfare of the kids. The McCabes were responsible stand-up kind of people who never turned their back on family or friends. Which meant that however these three kids had been delivered to his care, he had to see them through the Christmas holidays to safe harbor again. Period. He could not in good conscience do otherwise. Had they simply been pediatric patients of his, he could have kept a professional distance, while still caring for and about them. But he was assuming the role of "Daddy" here, however temporarily, a role that had much heavier emotional and psychological implications. And with Christmas Day still a week away...

What if the kids began to look at him as a parent figure instead of a guardian? What if they began to depend on him emotionally? Despite what the person or persons who had left them with him thought, Riley was not prepared to take on the three kids alone. Nor would it be fair to Amanda to ask her to help out indefinitely. Especially since Riley knew darned well that what worked in the short term might not be at all viable in the long run. No matter what happened next, Riley surmised grimly, the five of them were in one heck of a quandary.

"Wow. Three kids and a wife, all in one day. But then I guess you already knew about the kids, huh, Doc? I mean, there's no way you couldn't have," the young male clerk at the grocery store continued, suddenly looking as awkward and embarrassed as Riley felt.

Not about to get into the details of the children's abandonment while they were all right there, listening, Riley passed on the opportunity to correct the wrong assumption. The gossip mill would bring everyone up to date eventually. Soon everyone would know that the sheriff's department and social services were now involved.

Amanda looked at Riley. She was obviously thinking the same thing: it didn't matter what anyone else thought about them right now—they had to protect the children.

Riley turned back to the teenage clerk. "It's amazing. I'll tell you that." Hoping to discourage further comment, Riley turned his attention to the diapers and formula and baby food passing by on the conveyer belt.

Beside him, Amanda had her face nestled in the neck of infant Cory, while soothing Amber, who was buckled into the metal cart's toddler seat, with gentle strokes of her hand. Beside her, Chloe stood, an arm wrapped around Amanda's leg. As Riley paid for their purchases, he couldn't help but note how great Amanda was with the kids, and they with her. And he couldn't help but contrast the woman beside him with the Amanda he had known, years ago.

Without warning, his thoughts returned to the last prank she had played on him. It had been the night before he was set to leave for college, and she'd sent a note to him through mutual friends, telling him she was ceding victory of their four-year-long competition to him. Riley hadn't been surprised. Getting that pet goat into her bedroom without the cooperation or knowledge of any member of her family had been darned difficult. He felt he had won. Hands down.

So when she had sent him a note, asking him to meet her behind the bleachers of the high school stadium that night, saying she wanted to declare peace once and for all, he hadn't been averse to the idea. Something about the words she had written, and the way she'd been looking at him those last few weeks, had made him think—foolishly, he now realized—that Amanda had a giant crush on him. One that matched his secret crush on her. He'd gone to the rendezvous spot, and then waited and waited and waited. Predictably, Amanda had never showed, but unbeknownst to him, her friends had—

and they'd snapped photos of him waiting wistfully in the moonlight, bouquet of wildflowers in his hands—with the long-distance lens from the school photography lab.

The photos—and the story of his foolishness—had made the rounds of everyone in the senior class by the time Riley and Amanda had both left for their respective colleges the next day. It had taken years for Riley to live that fiasco down. And now there was—albeit not by either of their doing—another chapter to add to the list. He had never expected to be involved with her again, never mind in quite this way. Although, Riley noted, as he wheeled the cart out to the lot, and hit the remote to unlock his SUV, she seemed to be handling the situation a lot better than he was. To his irritation, the more uneasy he became about the task ahead, the more relaxed she became. Maybe because—unlike him—she really seemed to be in her element here, as she simultaneously tended to all three kids.

Appreciating the way she looked with her dark blond hair tumbling over the cranberry-red muffler she had wrapped around her neck, he murmured, "This kind of responsibility doesn't throw you at all, does it?"

Amanda smiled back at him, looking trim and pretty in her long black winter coat, as she helped Chloe climb up into her safety seat. "I wouldn't think it would rattle you, either, given the fact we both grew up in large, chaotic families."

Riley lifted Amber out of the cart seat and carried her around to the other side of the vehicle. "We only had six kids in ours." Five boys, one girl.

"Only six," Amanda teased as she buckled baby Cory into his safety seat, too.

Riley shrugged as he struggled with the three-point restraint on Amber's seat. "Compared to your family's nine kids…" Six wasn't a lot.

Making sure everyone was in safely, they shut the doors and returned to the cargo area to load their groceries. "And now, temporarily, you and I are mutually in charge of three," Amanda asserted, briefly looking as astonished about that as Riley.

Riley liked their new feeling of camaraderie. But then, people always pulled together in a crisis. "Which perhaps wouldn't seem so difficult if I had any kind of babysitting experience at all," he continued affably.

Amanda's shoulder brushed his as they tossed diapers in next to the cans of formula. "Not to worry, Doc. I'll teach you everything you need to know."

Aware being this close to Amanda was putting all his senses into overdrive, Riley forced himself to keep his mind on the task at hand instead of harboring fantasies of kissing her again. "You really enjoy being around kids, don't you?"

Amanda tipped her head back to look at him, but didn't move away. Obviously, she had no clue as to the direction of his thoughts. "I love it," she said softly.

"Which begs the question." Riley paused to search her face. "Why haven't you had any of your own yet?"

Riley saw her smile fade and her eyes go dark almost instantaneously. "The time has never been right," she said quietly.

Beyond that, she clearly did not want to discuss it. Realizing a change of subject was in order, Riley said, "The children seem to like you."

The sadness in her eyes fading only slightly, Amanda picked up a package of diapers and tossed it into the cargo area. Color filled her cheeks. "All children like me."

Abruptly, Riley felt as if she were pushing him away. The realization disturbed him. The last hour or so of mutual purpose had united him with Amanda in a way he had never expected. And it had made him realize something else. Something adult. He wanted to be closer to Amanda, to be able to look into her eyes and know their jokester past was just that, and she was as ready as he to move on to a more mature relationship. One that allowed them to talk intimately and honestly to each other, without always having to have their guards up. Right now, she was a mystery he wanted to solve. And the first step toward that would be to understand what was going on in that pretty head of hers and driving her actions. "You mean, because you're a nurse?" he asked.

To Riley's frustration, Amanda seemed to get even further away from him emotionally as she recited in a low, battle-weary voice, "Because I have the touch. I'm just a natural-born baby wrangler." She paused, her teeth raking the soft lusciousness of her lower lip. "It probably has something to do with growing up the second oldest of nine children. I spent my entire childhood helping take care of my younger siblings. It's only natural I would have picked up some skill at it along the way."

And now she thought he was using that skill—and hence, her—to his own advantage. Perhaps even being nice to her, just so she would help him. "I appreciate you helping me out here," Riley said.

Amanda sent him an even more skeptical look. "Sure."

Well, that certainly helped ease the tension, Riley thought dryly. But then he knew, as did she, that words were cheap. It was actions that counted. He would have to demonstrate to her that he had changed—just as he hoped she had—and that now that they'd put the mutual gags behind them, she could trust him again. And that was going to take time.

The two of them were silent as he drove back to his house. When they arrived, they discovered three large suitcases by the front door.

"Those wouldn't by any chance happen to be yours, would they?" Riley asked hopefully. Amanda shook her head, beginning to look as exasperated and wary as he felt. Feeling irked that the mysterious goings-on had not stopped, Riley parked and got out of the vehicle. He helped Amanda extricate all three children from their safety seats. Together, they headed for the front door. A quick peek inside the suitcases revealed the belongings of all three kids.

Amanda surveyed Riley over the tops of the children's heads. "You know what this is, don't you?" she commented softly. "Yet another sign that someone still cares, maybe more than that person would like to admit," she continued, speaking to Riley in a code the children were unlikely to be able to decipher.

Which meant that person or persons would eventually be back to claim them, thereby absolving he and Amanda of the responsibility for them, Riley realized slowly. Wondering why that idea wasn't as comforting as he would have expected, Riley helped Amanda get the children inside, then returned alone to unload the groceries. He was almost done when another car pulled up at the curb. Laurel and her friend Micki hopped out.

"I just thought I should warn you," Laurel told him hurriedly.

"Warn me about what?" Riley was about to demand when another car pulled up behind Laurel's and he saw the reason for his kid sister's concern.

Not surprisingly, Riley's stepmother, Kate Marten McCabe wasted no time in getting to the point.

"Perhaps Laurel and Micki could watch the children for a few minutes while your father and I talk to you and Amanda," Kate told Riley, in the same direct, no-nonsense manner she had used on him and his brothers when he was an out-of-control teenager, dealing with his grief over his mother's death.

"I think Amanda can be excused from this," Riley said. He looked from his petite blond stepmother to his tall, fit father. It was one thing for his parents to be treating him as if he were still a kid, another thing for them to be addressing Amanda that way.

"Amanda needs to hear what we have to say, too," Sam

declared. The owner of his own Dallas-based computer software company, he was as blunt and down-to-earth as he was successful.

"We'll just be upstairs, somewhere," Laurel announced discreetly. She took the infant. Micki picked up the toddler and took the four-year-old's hand. The five disappeared up the staircase. Seconds later, a door shut. Silence fell as Riley and Amanda sat down in the living room opposite Sam and Kate.

"I thought you two had outgrown pranks like this a long time ago," Kate said with a disapproving frown.

So had Riley. Until the moment he had dared Amanda to marry him and she had upped the ante and actually gone through with it.

"It was one thing when the two of you were toilet-papering each other's houses and soaping the windows of each other's cars, all through high school," Sam added.

Riley thought about all the times he had "fixed" Amanda's locker so everything she owned would come tumbling out, and the time she had "jammed" his so all sorts of feminine hygiene products would come flying out, when he finally managed to get it open. She'd bested him on that one, too. But he'd gotten her good, a couple times. Most notably when he had her believing her favorite rock star had just been spotted in Greta Wilson McCabe's Lone Star Dance Hall, conferring with Greta's friend, real-life movie star, Beau Chamberlain. He grinned, thinking not so much of her star-crazed antics, as the temper tantrum—directed strictly at him—that had followed. Amanda was one beautiful woman when she lost her cool....

"But you're adults now," Kate continued sternly.

"One would certainly hope so." Sam frowned. "Your actions today would seem to indicate otherwise."

Riley knew his parents were upset and disappointed in him. On one level, he was disappointed in his own behavior, too. He should never have let Amanda get to him that way.

Even if he had suspected—for one heated hour, anyway—that she was responsible for the appearance of the three kids. He should have let cool reason instead of his emotions prevail.

"And I'm sure your family would agree with me on that," Sam continued, all parental concern.

Amanda flushed, finally beginning to look as uncomfortable as Riley felt.

"Maybe they won't ever have to hear about it since they live in California now," Riley contended, doing everything he could to protect the woman at his side. "Especially if we're able to wrap it up soon and get the kids back where they belong, our hasty marriage will be declared null and void."

Amanda nodded and edged slightly closer to Riley. "I'm certainly not planning to tell my family about this," she echoed.

"You may not have to," Kate warned. "Your family still knows many people here in Laramie. And news like an impromptu marriage brought on by the appearance of three small children seldom stays quiet for long."

No kidding, Riley thought, in weary resignation. Word of their wedding in the hospital hallway had spread faster than a wildfire after a drought.

"We're going to sort this marriage thing out eventually," Amanda reassured his parents quietly.

"When the time is right," Riley agreed. Grateful his new "bride" was handling this uncalled-for intrusion so well, he reached over and briefly touched her hand.

"Meanwhile," Amanda continued with building confidence, "our plan is simply to care for the children to the best of our ability and wait for their parents or guardians to return." She shrugged and looked to Riley for emotional support. He gave it to her in spades.

"I mean, obviously the children have been well loved," Amanda continued matter-of-factly. "Sooner or later, someone has to show up to claim them and set the record straight...."

"And if they don't?" Kate asked bluntly.

"We'd obviously have to reassess our situation. But we're still days—maybe even weeks—away from that point," Amanda continued firmly.

"Did you mean what you said to my parents?" Riley asked Amanda seriously as soon as his parents had left.

Amanda released a short, impatient breath and continued to hold his eyes like a warrior princess in battle. "I didn't ask to be plopped into the middle of this mess, but I intend to do whatever is necessary to see these children's needs are met, even if it means voluntarily extending my leave from the hospital or taking vacation time. Although, obviously," Amanda continued fiercely, keeping her voice slightly above a whisper as she went to the kitchen to begin putting away the groceries they had brought in minutes earlier, "you and I can't stay married to each other indefinitely, Riley!"

Riley paused thoughtfully, then jumped on ahead. "Maybe we should."

Chapter 4

Amanda stared at Riley. She did not know how he could continue to look so cool, calm and collected after the events of the last four hours, especially when she felt so frazzled. She stepped closer so they were toe-to-toe. "Have you lost your mind?" she demanded, tipping her head up to his.

A slow, sexy smile crossed his handsome face. "Well, think about it," he drawled, in a husky voice that drew her even deeper into this escapade with him. "We're looking pretty foolish right now for having succumbed to our tempers and one-upped each other right into the state of holy matrimony. The chief of staff and my parents are right. If we back out we're going to look like a couple of reckless kids. On the other hand," he rubbed a hand across his close-shaven jaw, "if we stick with it, and pretend to give it a try—at least for a few months—our maturity would likely no longer be in question."

"Months!" Amanda echoed in disbelief. She couldn't pretend to be his wife for that long!

Riley rested his large, capable hands on her shoulders,

keeping her in front of him when she would have pivoted—and run. He shrugged off her concern. Continuing to radiate a distinctly male satisfaction, he smiled at her reassuringly. "Once we've established to the community we are not still a couple of 'reckless kids,' then we can always say we gave it a shot and get a quiet, civilized divorce."

He really had covered all the angles. Except perhaps the most important one. "I don't want to be divorced again."

Riley blinked, dropped his hands and repeated in stunned amazement, *"Again?"*

Aware her shoulders felt cold and bereft where the warmth of his palms had been, Amanda replied in an embarrassed tone, "I really don't want to discuss this, Riley."

"Well, I do," he retorted, an emotion she couldn't define in his amber eyes. Riley paused, clearly caught off guard by her revelation. "You could have told me you were married before."

Amanda flashed him a sassy smile she couldn't really begin to feel, considering the mess they were in. "And when exactly would that have been?" she returned softly. "Before or after or perhaps *during* the interlude where you claimed those kids were mine as well as yours, hauled me in front of the hospital chaplain and demanded I marry you and make an honest man of you?"

Riley grimaced, conceding her victory. "Okay, point taken." He shoved both his hands through his hair.

Amanda noted the disarray his angst had brought to his rumpled, sun-streaked light brown hair, and wondered if the shiny clean strands were as soft and touchable as they looked. With effort, she forced her attention back to the subject at hand. "I'm glad you agree."

Another loaded silence fell between them. "Aren't you going to tell me about it?" Riley asked eventually, his curiosity unabated.

Amanda shrugged, her hurt and humiliation over that period of her life now a distant memory. She wanted to keep it that way. "There's not much to tell," she told Riley matter-of-factly. "I fell in love with a newly divorced doctor some ten years my senior when I was fresh out of nursing school, and married him. Five years later, he decided he had never loved me after all and went back to his first wife, who was also the mother of his two children. And you know what the worst part of it was? I knew it was a mistake way before that, but because of the kids, and the way they had depended on me to mother them whenever they were with Fraser, I stayed on anyway."

"Are you still in contact with the children?"

"No." Amanda swallowed around the lump in her throat. "My ex and his wife asked me to step aside and allow them to put their family together again, without reminders of the time they had spent apart. So I did."

"That must have been really difficult for you."

Amanda nodded, glad she hadn't had to explain to Riley how much the whole experience had hurt her, or how wary she was of letting herself get into such an emotionally devastating situation again. "Anyway, since then I've been a little more careful," Amanda said quietly. She hadn't dated anyone with children. Or continued seeing anyone who didn't seem thoroughly smitten with her from the get-go. Until now, anyway. "So what about you?" Amanda pushed her thoughts away from herself. "Is this…whatever it is we are in…your first marriage?"

Riley nodded, serious now. "But I came close to getting hitched two years ago," he told her, the walls around his emotions already going up. If there was one thing Amanda could identify from bitter experience, it was a man holding her at arm's length. Determined not to let Riley shut her out the way her ex had, she studied him. "I have the feeling there's more to this story." A reason why he had brought up his near miss to matrimony. "What haven't you told me?"

A troubled light came into Riley's eyes. His voice dropped a notch. "I've been thinking. There's no way on this earth Evangeline could have given birth to either the older or younger children and had them be mine. I saw her every week during the six years we dated—she was never pregnant. But the toddler was conceived about the time Evangeline and I broke up."

Worry swept Amanda that this situation they were in was all too real and potentially heartbreaking. "You think she might have had the baby and not told you about it?"

"It doesn't seem likely. But neither does the delivery of three children on my doorstep, so to speak." Riley paused, and looked all the more distressed. "What if one of the children is mine?"

Then Amanda was going to be the odd woman out again. But not about to admit to Riley that was how she felt, she forced a commiserating smile. "Then I'd say Evangeline has a heck of a lot of explaining to do."

"I agree." Riley looked Amanda in the eye. "Which is why I think the sooner we talk to her the better."

Aware they still had a lot of groceries to put away, Amanda went back to emptying sacks, while Riley attended to filling the fridge and cabinets. "Where is she?"

"Dallas. She's a physician at the hospital where I did my residency."

"Are you going to call her?"

Riley stood with a jar of baby food in each hand. "I think under the circumstances that this is a discussion better had face-to-face."

Amanda didn't know whether to be relieved or disappointed. "So, you want me to stay here with the kids?" she asked.

"No." Riley put the last of the supplies away, then turned to face her. "I want you and all three of the kids to go with me."

* * *

"So how do you want to do this?" Riley asked three and a half hours later as he parked in front of a contemporary seven-story condominium building in a trendy neighborhood of Fort Worth, Texas.

"I was thinking I'd just take Amber in and get their reaction to each other first."

For reasons she didn't want to examine closely, Amanda preferred not to meet the woman Riley had nearly married who might have borne his child.

"I'll just sit here with Chloe and give baby Cory his bottle," Amanda volunteered.

Unfortunately, no sooner had Riley left the car with Amber and disappeared into the lobby of the building, than Chloe began to cry. Her tears sparked wails from baby Cory.

"Riley and Amber will be right back," Amanda soothed.

To no avail.

Chloe became even more hysterical at the idea of being separated from one of her siblings.

With a beleaguered sigh, Amanda decided there was only one thing to do. Join 'em.

Riley had let Evangeline know he was en route to see her. When he had spoken to her briefly on the phone, she had reluctantly agreed to give him five minutes of her time if he met her at home this evening. Since they hadn't exactly parted amicably, Riley knew that was a major concession on her part.

Still, nothing could have prepared him for the sight of his ex-lover clad in one of the sexiest and most revealing negligees he had ever seen. Cut down to her navel in front, several inches below the waist in back, the black satin fabric clung to her hips and thighs before ending at midcalf.

Barefoot, with her inky-black hair tousled, she looked as if she had just crawled out of bed.

Taking a look at the toddler cradled in his arms, she frowned. "I hope you're not expecting me to babysit."

"Not unless Amber is your baby, too," Riley said.

Evangeline let out a peal of laughter that echoed in the elegant hall.

Behind Riley, the elevator doors opened on the sounds of two crying children. Amanda hurried toward him, staggering under the weight of the child in each of her arms.

Seeing Amber, Chloe wailed even harder. She held out her arms to her baby sister, who, seeing Chloe and baby Cory crying, began to sob, too.

"Darlin'," a low male voice called from behind Evangeline. A sexy, twenty-something stud wrapped only in a sheet, a cowboy hat tipped rakishly on his head, swaggered out to join them. "What's going on?" the young man asked.

Behind Riley, other apartment doors began to open. Irritated looks were thrown their way.

Evangeline rolled her eyes. "Come in here before I get a noise violation!" she demanded, ushering everyone inside her luxurious home.

Everything was white—furniture, drapes, rug. Even the Christmas tree that stood in the corner was a white-flocked artificial tree.

"What's this about?" the man continued, perplexed. "Who are these people?"

"A long and amusing story, I am sure." Evangeline patted her young lover on the arm. "Wait for me in the bedroom, hon. This won't take long."

"All right." The stud detoured to the bar, where he grabbed a bottle of wine. "But if you're not back in five, I'm coming back out to get you!" He disappeared around the corner.

Now that the children were reunited, they had all stopped crying.

"Well?" Evangeline looked at Riley.

Riley took Chloe from Amanda and cradled the four-year-old in his other arm, so Amanda was only holding the infant, Cory. "These three children were left for me at Laramie Community Hospital," Riley explained.

"What does that have to do with me?" Evangeline asked with an accusing look. She looked irritated that he had bothered her. "They're not sick, are they?"

"They seem to be in fine health. The note stated that they needed me to be their daddy."

Evangeline paused to compute that information. Her precisely plucked eyebrows lifted in inquisitive fashion. "Why?"

Riley abruptly released his breath, his frustration mounting. "That's what I'm trying to figure out."

Evangeline tilted her head at him. She was still beautiful but also one of the most emotionally contained people he had ever met. Next to Amanda's fire and warmth, well…it was difficult for Riley to imagine what he had ever seen in Evangeline, aside from her considerable skills as a physician in a specialty most avoided, and the lack of emotional demands she placed on him at a time in his life when he had been so busy studying and learning he hadn't been able to handle any.

"Are you trying to tell me you cheated on me?" Evangeline continued.

"No. I'm trying to tell you that if one of the children is my child that you're the only possible mother, and only of Amber here." Riley gestured to the toddler cradled in his left arm. "Obviously, the time frame for four-year-old Chloe and baby Cory don't line up for us."

Evangeline looked at Amanda. "How do you line up in all this?" she asked suspiciously.

Amanda flushed. "I'm, uh, sort of temporarily, but not really his wife." The pink in her cheeks deepening, she waved off further inquiry. "It's a long and ridiculous story."

Evangeline burst into peals of laughter. "Oh, Riley, this one really takes the cake!"

Her reaction irritated the devil out of him. "You think I'm joking?" Riley demanded coolly.

Pity colored Evangeline's regard, as she shook her head at him. "I think you've had time to regret changing gears with me, and know the way you got into my life in the first place was through your very clever practical jokes on people. But I am not falling for this one, Riley McCabe." Evangeline shooed them all toward the door, disclaiming, "And I am not ever falling for you again."

"Kids asleep?" Riley asked Amanda an hour later.

Because it was too late to drive back to Laramie, they had checked into a three-bedroom suite, complete with kitchen, at an extended-stay hotel that was geared for families. Working as a team, they had fed and bathed the kids. While Riley gave Cory a bottle and put him down, Amanda tucked the older children in bed.

Amanda nodded. "Before I even finished the first story."

Riley peeked into the adjacent bedroom. Chloe was curled up in the double bed, the younger two were snoozing in portacribs lined up against the wall. As always, as long as the three could see each other, and knew they were together, they seemed content.

Reveling in the peace and quiet, Riley poured Amanda a cup of coffee and brought it to her. He sank down beside her on the sofa. There was a good six inches of space between them. They weren't touching in any way but it still felt intimate. Riley wasn't as opposed to that feeling as he figured he should be. "Sorry about what you witnessed earlier," he said, figuring they should talk about what had happened, rather than let it be the elephant in the living room all evening. "I had no idea Evangeline would be…entertaining."

"And then some." Briefly, Amanda looked as embarrassed as Riley had been to find his ex in such a compromising situation. Amanda sipped her coffee, avoiding Riley's eyes. "She's a very sexy woman."

Riley slouched down into the cushions and stretched his long legs out in front of him. "As well as a damned fine oncologist."

Amanda turned slightly to face Riley, her shoulder nudging his in the process. He noted with pleasure she made no attempt to draw away. "And practical joker, too?"

Riley thought he saw a fleeting glimpse of jealousy in Amanda's eyes. Aware he had jumped to conclusions and been wrong about Amanda's interest in him before, he pushed the tantalizing notion away and concentrated on answering Amanda's question instead. "No. Evangeline never played any jokes on me. She just enjoyed the ones I played on others." He paused, reflecting. "Her medical specialty is so emotionally grueling, the only way she survives is by blowing off steam during her time off."

Maybe because she was a nurse herself, Amanda seemed to understand how draining taking care of cancer patients could be. "So Evangeline is just living life to the fullest."

"Exactly," Riley acknowledged, knowing for a while that was all he had wanted to do, too—live his life in the moment, while having as little non-work-related responsibility as possible.

Amanda turned toward Riley even more, her bent knee brushing up against his thigh. She studied him intently, looking deep into his eyes. "What did you do to 'change gears' with her?"

Riley shrugged. "I asked her to marry me."

Amanda's soft eyes widened. "In a joking way—or serious?"

"I was serious," Riley admitted ruefully, recalling just how naive and shortsighted he had been about the dilemma facing them. "I thought it was time. I'd been out of residency a year. I wanted a family. Neither of us was getting any younger."

Amanda smiled and tucked a strand of dark blond hair behind her ear. "I hope you put it a little more romantically than that."

Riley tore his eyes from the soft spill of silky hair over her shoulders, only to find his glance at the even softer and more seductive curves of Amanda's breasts. She was wearing a red turtleneck sweater, with appliqués of Santa's workshop sewn on the front, jeans and a pair of red Western boots. Damn but she was pretty, he thought, even with her hair tousled and her lipstick long gone. He wondered if she knew how worked up he got just sitting next to her like this. Swallowing, Riley took another gulp of coffee. "That's about how I said it." He shifted restlessly in his seat, to ease the pressure starting behind the fly of his jeans.

Amanda ran a hand through her hair and rested her bent elbow on the back of the sofa. The unconscious movement gave him an even better view of her breasts. "I gather she turned you down."

Aware it was all he could do to avoid taking Amanda in his arms and really, truly kiss her this time, instead of pretending to do just that for the audience gathered around them, Riley nodded in acknowledgment. "And then she dumped me," he said matter-of-factly, recounting a disappointment he was long over. Nevertheless, it was nice to see the sympathy and understanding in Amanda's eyes, to know she felt for him, whatever he had been through. "Evangeline said we had come together for mutual fun and pleasure and she wasn't equipped for anything else. She could see that I was more than ready to settle down and have a family with someone, but she wasn't interested in kids or marriage—shc had all she could handle with her oncology practice."

Amanda reached over and covered his hand with the softness of hers. "How did you take that?"

Enjoying the warmth of skin on skin, Riley turned his hand over, so his palm was against hers, their fingers loosely entwined. "My ego was hurt." He curved his hand tighter around hers.

"And…?" Amanda leaned closer still.

Drinking in the alluring clove and cinnamon scent of her perfume, Riley shrugged again. "Deep down I was relieved. I think I always knew she didn't love me, as much as she liked spending time with me, and I don't think I ever loved her, either. 'Cause if I had I think I could have given up on the idea of kids and marriage and been content to just be with her. I think if I had loved Evangeline the way I should have, the two of us would have been enough."

"So now what?" Amanda withdrew her hand from the comfort of his. She looked as spellbound by him as he was by her. "You want to take the kids back to Laramie?"

"Eventually," Riley allowed, surprised at how protective he already felt toward the three little children. "But first I want to visit the family health center where I practiced for the last three years," he told her.

"More ex-girlfriends?" Amanda asked dryly.

Riley thought but couldn't be sure that he saw a glint of jealousy in Amanda's pretty eyes. He shook his head. "No. I'm a one-woman kind of guy, always have been." He looked deep into her eyes and winked. "I figure you should know that."

"I guess so, since I'm temporarily married to you," she bantered back, copying his comically exaggerated tone, some of the tension easing from her slender frame. "But back to why you want to go there…"

Riley covered her hand with his. "I'm hoping someone there will know who might have deserted the children."

Amanda lifted a curious brow as her fingers twined with his. "You think they might belong to a patient?"

Riley regarded Amanda, feeling a unity of purpose that was oddly soothing, as well as an indication of what a good team they made. "Maybe," he allowed quietly. He shrugged, his natural compassion coming to the fore. "It would make sense if the person responsible for the three kids was going through a rough time and thought they couldn't handle being a parent and looked to me—a family doctor—to take them in and care for them."

Unfortunately, a visit to the clinic early the next morning yielded nothing. None of the doctors and nurses there had recognized any of the children, and a search of the patient database yielded no matches either. Amanda was as disappointed by the lack of results as he was, and Riley thought about what to do next all the way back to Laramie.

As soon as they returned home, he put in another call to his brother Kevin. "Any news on the law enforcement front?" Riley asked hopefully.

"No," Kevin returned unhappily. "And no parents of three—male or female—have been reported missing either. We'll keep searching, but if we don't discover anything soon, you may want to go public with your search for their parents."

Riley guessed where this was going. "You mean call in the media."

"It is Christmas," Kevin countered hopefully. "And it's the sort of story national newspeople love."

Riley frowned and rubbed at the tension gathering in the back of his neck. "Stories like that also bring out every nut around."

"And you want to protect them from that."

"As well as whoever left them with me. Obviously, the kids' parent or caretaker had to be really desperate, and for whatever reason, that person trusted me to protect Chloe, Amber and baby Cory."

"I admire your tenacity even if I don't envy you the days ahead," Kevin said. "But I'll do my best to keep searching."

"Thanks, Kevin." Riley sighed.

"And in the meantime, you keep an eye out for any clues

to their identity, too. Try to get the four-year-old to open up and start talking," Kevin advised.

Easier said than done, Riley thought, as he cut the connection and put the phone back on its charger base.

"No word, hmm?" Amanda said.

Riley shook his head and looked at Chloe. She was curled up on the chaise lounge next to the living room window, fast asleep, her thumb in her mouth. Thankful he had bought this house with all sorts of comfort items he would never have thought to buy for himself, he went over and tucked the chenille blanket around her little shoulders. A wave of tenderness swept through him, as potent as it was unexpected. Although Riley loved kids and was used to caring for them, he wasn't accustomed to feeling such a strong parental pull. Yet there was no denying that the need to protect these children was as fierce as anything he had ever felt. The only thing that had ever come close to rivaling it was the attraction he felt for Amanda Witherspoon. He just hoped that the first wasn't destined to end as unsatisfyingly as the latter.

"Kevin thinks that the kids will help us figure out where they are from."

"Assuming we can get Chloe talking." Amanda smoothed Chloe's curls from her forehead and tucked the blanket in around her. She bent to kiss her cheek, then straightened, anxiety in her eyes. "She hasn't said a word yet," Amanda worried out loud.

Riley was concerned about Chloe's silence, too. He took Amanda's hand and led her across the room to the hearth. Behind the heat-tempered doors, a fire crackled. "Chloe probably hasn't spoken," Riley theorized, "because she is so traumatized by whatever happened to force the three kids' sudden abandonment."

Terrible possibilities filled both their minds. Amanda teared up. Before Riley knew it, he had put both arms around Amanda's shoulders and drawn her into a comforting hug. "I just can't imagine anyone leaving them at the hospital that way unless he or she were really in dire straits," Amanda said hoarsely, her face pressed against his chest. "The children are just so sweet and adorable."

And then some, Riley thought as he stroked a hand through Amanda's dark blond hair. He whispered back, "Never mind splitting them up."

Amanda tipped her face up to his. She looked so vulnerable. His heart filled with compassion and something else—something sweet and satisfying—he wasn't sure he was quite ready to identify. Hands splayed across his chest, she murmured fiercely, "We can't let that happen."

"No, we can't," Riley agreed, just as firmly. "We're just going to have to keep them with us until we discover who they really belong with."

"And yet," Amanda paused, distraught, "if we do that, they're going to depend on us," she cautioned, moving away from Riley once again. "Not just physically, but emotionally, as well."

Riley knew the dangers of that. They couldn't provide security for kids who had already been through heaven-knows-what, and then just rip it away. An action like that would leave them heartbroken, at the very least, and, at the worst, permanently mistrustful. It would be just as cruel to treat them in a methodical, uncaring way. "I know."

"They need a mommy and a daddy, Riley."

And Riley wanted to be there for them, in exactly that way. Surprisingly, Amanda seemed to yearn for that opportunity, too. Riley hadn't asked to be in this situation. Perhaps, neither had Amanda. Yet over the last twenty-four hours, the situation had evolved in ways neither had expected or could turn away from. He approached Amanda, hands outstretched. "Look, I know you nixed staying married to me simply for the sakes of our reputations and careers."

Her chin took on that stubborn tilt he knew so well.

Amanda folded her arms in front of her, emotional armor back in place. "A decision I still think is the right one." She regarded him steadily. "Marriage is serious business, Riley."

He wasn't going to argue that. His mind moving ahead to what was best, not just for him or Amanda, but all of them, Riley pointed out calmly, "And yet we are married, Amanda." Up to now he had been fighting that fact, trying to ignore that aspect of the situation. But after a night spent tossing and turning alternately worrying about the children and fantasizing about her, Riley was beginning to wonder if that approach was even practical. Maybe instead of pretending there was no chemistry between them they should take the alternate path, explore it to its fullest, see where it led.

Amanda's fair cheeks flushed. "Married in name only," she reminded him.

Riley shot her a seductive smile, even as he cautioned himself not to move too fast, lest he jeopardize any passion they might feel in the future. "For now."

She whirled away. "Don't even think about seducing me."

"Why not?" Riley stepped in front of her and held his ground. He angled a finger at the region over her heart and continued with smug male satisfaction, determined to open her mind up to the possibilities the same way his was. "You're obviously thinking about it, or you wouldn't have brought it up."

Amanda tossed her head. Silky dark blond hair flew in every direction. "Only because you're looking at me that way," she accused, planting her hands on her hips.

Aware this was definitely not a conversation to be had in front of the kids, even if they were sleeping, Riley grabbed her hand and drew her into the adjoining dining room. He backed her up against the wall. "And what way is that?" he chided, liking the spark coming back into her turquoise eyes, the sassy, challenging spark she used to have whenever she looked at him.

Amanda looked at him warily. "The way that says you want to have your way with me."

Riley flattened his hands on either side of her, and leaned in even closer, until they were almost, but not quite, touching length to length. The playfulness that had livened up their youth was back, full force. "That is way too many ways in a sentence," he teased.

Amanda rolled her eyes, but to Riley's delight, didn't attempt to move away. "You know what I mean," she lobbed right back.

"I do." Riley straightened reluctantly, knowing he couldn't remain that close any longer without hauling her into his arms and kissing the socks off her. He regarded her steadily. "And I also know what I want—if the worst occurs and we aren't able to reunite these kids with their real parents, or get them back to their previous home."

Amanda paused. Her tongue snaked out to wet her lower lip. She regarded him with utmost caution. "And that would be—?"

"For all of us to become a family," Riley announced.

Chapter 5

Amanda swallowed. How was it possible that Riley McCabe had tapped into her secret Christmas wish for herself—the one she had foolishly penned in her "note" to Santa, that had been slipped, along with all the other letters from all the other pediatric patients and parents and staff, in the North Pole mailbox next to the Christmas tree in the pediatric playroom? Riley McCabe couldn't possibly know she had whimsically asked Santa for a husband and children of her very own….

Unless he had somehow seen her letter to Santa.

But that was impossible, wasn't it?

Whatever the truth of the situation, there was no clue on Riley's handsome face. "You can't be serious," Amanda allowed finally.

"Oh, but I am. Suppose no one comes to claim them. Or suppose someone shows up and says they can't or won't take care of them any longer, and they are 'giving' the kids to me, so to speak. I couldn't begin to do this alone."

Amanda did not doubt the truth of that. Struggling not to

notice how good Riley looked, how handsome and ruggedly at ease, she fastened her gaze on the strong column of his throat, and the tufts of swirling dark gold hair visible in the open collar of his button-down shirt.

Hand to his chest, she pushed him back, knowing if there was a point to be made this was the very best way to make it. "So hire a nanny."

Riley's amber eyes lit up. He leaned closer, his warm breath whispering across her ear. "You can't hire someone to love these kids, Amanda. It doesn't work that way." He paused to let his gaze rove her dark gold hair and the features of her face. "A mother's instinct is something a woman either has or doesn't have, and let's face it," he complimented her huskily, "you have it in spades."

Amanda tried—and failed—to remain impervious to his praise.

"Chloe, Amber and baby Cory have already been abandoned once." He paused to give her a guilt-inspiring look. "They don't need to be abandoned again. And the only way to ensure that they feel as loved as they deserve to be is if they have a mommy *and* a daddy in their life."

Without warning, Amanda recalled that Riley had lost a parent once, shortly before he and his dad and his four brothers moved to Laramie when Riley was fourteen. Her heart went out to him. "You really identify with these kids, don't you?" she commiserated softly.

Riley nodded. "I know what it feels like to lose a mom. I can't imagine being left with no one."

Amanda bit her lip. "They'd have you."

"A dad's important," Riley agreed candidly. "But there are things guys can't give that only women can. A certain… I don't know, softness and tenderness. Bottom line, women have a different way of looking at things than men do, and kids need both kinds of comfort." He tucked a strand of hair behind her ear before slowly, reluctantly, dropping his hand.

"You're already giving them love and tenderness, Amanda." Riley searched her eyes. "They want to be with you."

Amanda couldn't deny that. She and the kids had bonded instantly. But she was good with all kids. To the point she had never met one she couldn't soothe. "They also deserve two parents who love each other deeply." A strong and loving marriage, her folks had often told her, was the foundation of every healthy, happy family. Amanda didn't see how you could have that when the union was fashioned strictly for convenience.

Riley challenged her with a look that was sexy, self-assured and faintly baiting. Amanda blushed. Being in such close proximity to him had left her feeling unaccountably jittery and excited inside. Unless she got hold of those feelings, who knew what might happen between them as the days and nights wore on.

"There are all kinds of love," Riley continued amiably.

Was Riley trying to tell her, just as Fraser had, that she wasn't physically lovable in an exciting or passionate way? That she lacked the siren gene that drove men wild? Having already endured one marriage that was lacking in the "bedroom," Amanda was not ready to sign on for another. And just because a mere kiss from Riley had thrilled her to pieces, did not mean that he felt the same. Men, she had belatedly discovered, were capable of viewing lovemaking as a physical release, instead of the blissful joining of hearts and souls she had always dreamed it could be. Amanda didn't want to find out Riley viewed relations between a man and woman as unemotionally and practically as her ex.

"We've been rivals." He traced the curve of her cheek with the pad of his thumb. "Why not friends and coparents, too?"

Amanda felt her knees weaken even as her heart began to pound. "Because if and when I ever hook up with a man again, I want it all, Riley," she told him fiercely. She dropped her glance to the strong column of his throat, visible in the open V of his shirt. "Physical passion. Deep abiding love. Laughs. Tenderness. You name it. I would think you'd want the same."

"I do. I just don't see why—with time—we couldn't have it all."

Amanda felt herself flush with an inner heat she could not contain. "I don't think real love works like that, Riley." They were vulnerable here. Both of them. They had to remember that.

Riley gave her a thoughtful once-over. "And I don't know why you're so determined to put the brakes on our undeniable attraction to each other without first figuring out where it might lead."

Easy, Amanda thought, as she swallowed around the sudden constriction in her throat and struggled to get air into her lungs. She didn't want to get hurt again and her feminine intuition was telling her Riley McCabe could break her heart, if she lowered her guard, even slightly. "We don't even know where the situation with the kids is going to lead," she continued.

"True, but I like to keep my options open," Riley returned meaningfully. "So should you."

Amanda glanced up at the ruggedly handsome contours of his face, appreciating his strength and determination as much as his irrepressible spirit. Independent in nature, she enjoyed being on her own. But single life could get lonely. Dull, even. With Riley as her partner, she knew she'd never have to worry about either again. And that was something to consider. Her days had been filled with work and little else since her divorce. Twenty-four hours with Riley and she felt as if she were living every moment to the fullest. It was a good feeling. One she didn't want to let go. She still needed some insurance against another failed romantic relationship. She needed to know he would be understanding and supportive either way. "And what if I decide an experimental fling with you is not what I want?" Amanda asked quietly. Would it cost them their newly blossoming friendship?

Riley lifted his hand and gently touched her cheek. "Then I'll respect that. And we'll go our separate ways, none the worse for having spent this time together," he promised, just as the doorbell rang.

Riley arched a brow, looking as annoyed by the intrusion as she felt. "You expecting someone?"

"No." Frowning, Amanda answered the front door and saw the family member she least wanted to see.

Riley recalled Priscilla Witherspoon. Amanda's older sister had been the same age as his brother Will. His older brother had been a jock, prone to trouble, while Priscilla was an uptight bookworm, who now had a Ph.D. in quantum physics. Last he heard, Priscilla had been teaching at Stanford and living in California with the rest of Amanda's family.

"Honestly, Amanda, you could have let someone in the family know where you were," Priscilla began as she walked into the foyer. She was wearing a long tan raincoat and sensible shoes. Her dishwater blond hair was cut in an unflattering style that framed her thin face. "We've been calling and calling, ever since we heard the news about your latest 'mishap' with Riley McCabe from old friends here." Priscilla pushed her horn-rimmed glasses closer to her eyes and looked at the three children napping in the living room. "I must say it didn't surprise me to hear you had been sowing wild oats, Riley McCabe, but Amanda, I thought you knew better than to get involved with one of Sam's sons." Priscilla pursed her lips at Riley. "Especially this one."

Amanda pressed her index finger to her mouth. "Shh. Let's go in the kitchen," she whispered. "So we don't wake them."

"Well?" Priscilla demanded when they had retired to the rear of the house. She handed Riley her coat and he hung it on the decorative coatrack next to the back door. Looking as fashion challenged as ever in a red cord shirtdress and lime-green cardigan, Priscilla folded her arms in front of her and regarded Amanda with mounting exasperation. "What do you have to say for yourself?"

"I don't have to defend myself or my actions to you," Amanda said as she began to make coffee for the three of them.

Bravo, Riley thought, turning away to get out a cardboard bucket of holiday cookies they'd picked up at the market.

Priscilla regarded Amanda with concern. "You do if you don't want Mom and Dad and the rest of your siblings coming out here to talk some sense into you, too. Right now, I'm the emissary from the family, but it won't be just me for much longer unless you tell me something reasonable I can take back to them."

Riley noted Amanda was apparently too stubborn to explain anything to her interfering older sis, so he did it for her. "Three children I had never seen before in my life were abandoned to my care for the Christmas holidays. I am not the biological father of any of them. Obviously, I can't care for them alone so Amanda is helping me while we search for their real family."

Priscilla appeared only partially appeased. She narrowed her eyes suspiciously. "What does any of that have to do with the two of you getting married in the hallway of the hospital yesterday?"

Amanda winced and rubbed her temples. "It was a joke," she said.

Priscilla snorted derisively. "No one in the family is laughing, Amanda."

"Nor are the McCabes," Riley cut in amiably, hoping to divert some of the unwelcome "pressure" away from Amanda. He put his arm around her shoulder. "But that's life, Priscilla. What strikes one person's funny bone may seem completely humorless to someone else." Take this talking-to, for instance. He failed to see anything amusing about it at all.

His attempt to reason with Priscilla failed.

She glared at her younger sister. "I hope you have already taken steps to have it annulled."

Sparks of temper gleamed in Amanda's eyes as she poured mugs of coffee for all three. "Actually, we haven't."

"But you will," Priscilla pressured.

"Maybe." Amanda became even more tight-lipped as she set the cream and sugar on the center of the table with a resounding thud. "And maybe not. Frankly, I haven't decided what I want to do, and neither has Riley."

Shock warred with disapproval on Priscilla's face. "Amanda, you cannot seriously be thinking of continuing with this farce! Riley McCabe has always been the worst possible influence on you."

"Gee thanks, Priscilla," Riley said, helping himself to a couple of Christmas cookies.

Priscilla declined his wordless offer of a confection with a lift of her hand. "Well, it's true. Before you and your brothers moved to town, Amanda was a perfect little angel. She never got into trouble. She always did what she was supposed to do."

That didn't even sound like the woman he had married. Riley positioned himself next to Amanda, every protective instinct quickly coming into play. "Sounds boring," he announced lazily.

"Maybe to a bounder like you," Priscilla retorted archly. "But Amanda never played practical jokes on anyone, before or after you, Riley McCabe! Which leads us all to think—then and now—that you hold some sort of special power over her."

"Special power!" Riley echoed, not sure whether to be insulted or just amused. Beside him, Amanda rolled her eyes.

"And you continue to be a very bad influence on our

Amanda, Riley McCabe!" Priscilla charged, even more disapprovingly.

Riley had to admit there was some truth to what Priscilla was saying. He hadn't ever matched wits and wills with anyone else the way he did with Amanda. Never found himself going over the line, to the point where his emotions were guiding his actions, rather than his intellect.

"Hello! I'm still here," Amanda interjected as she helped herself to an iced butter cookie, too. Temper flaring, she glared at her older sister. "I am my own person! A mature adult who is perfectly capable of making her own decisions and living her own life, without the helpful advice of my family."

Priscilla scoffed. "There's nothing adult about a pretend marriage, Amanda. I assumed you would have learned that in your last go-round."

Riley winced as the color left Amanda's face. Darn that Priscilla. Amanda's older sister had drawn blood. Slowly and deliberately Riley put his coffee down. He wrapped his arm around Amanda's shoulders. "No one speaks to my wife like that," he warned, ready to throw Priscilla out bodily if need be.

"Amanda knows I didn't mean any harm," Priscilla declared with a frown. "I am just trying to talk sense into her." She gave Amanda an imploring look. "Let's go back to your apartment where we can talk in private, honey."

"No. Anything you want to say you can say in front of my husband." Amanda pressed intimately close and wrapped her arm around Riley's waist. Her head was resting on his chest. Riley knew it was just an act designed to get under her sister's skin, as much as Priscilla was getting under Amanda's, but he had never felt anything so good. So right. Maybe there was more to this marriage, and his relationship with Amanda, than he had realized....

It was Priscilla's turn to rub her temples and try again.

"Look, Amanda," she said in a much softer tone, "I know how hard it has been for you since the divorce, especially since Fraser and his ex have refused to allow you to be part of your former stepchildren's lives. But you have eight nieces and nephews in California that would love to have you participate in their worlds. You could live with anyone in the family, look for a new job, babysit or nanny to your heart's content, and maybe eventually even find a new boyfriend." Priscilla glared at Riley, then turned back to baby sis. "Someone more suitable. Someone who doesn't think life is a joke."

"Hey, I never said that," Riley cut in, tightening his grip on Amanda all the more. He had a serious side. People, who had known him back when he was a reckless, fun-loving kid and hadn't been around to see his transformation into a responsible human being and family doc, just refused to see it. He had hoped coming back to Laramie as an adult, after such a long absence, would give him a fresh start. He could leave his jokester rep behind. The appearance of the three kids and his reaction to Amanda had blown all that. Once again he was trouble with a capital *T*.

"No, you just acted that way," Priscilla returned haughtily.

Amanda lifted her chin. Her soft lips compressed stubbornly. "Riley wasn't joking just now when he asked me to stay and bring up the kids with him," Amanda said, coming to Riley's defense as stalwartly as he had come to hers.

Priscilla paled. "You can't seriously be considering it," she breathed, distraught.

"Actually, Priscilla," Amanda paused to let the impact of her words sink in. "I think I just agreed."

"Sure you should be sleeping with such a bad influence?" Riley asked drolly several hours later as he joined Amanda in the master bedroom and shut the door behind him.

Amanda was already clad in a pair of flannel pajamas that were the definition of sweet and innocent girl-next-door. And yet somehow they were damn near the sexiest nightclothes he had ever seen. Maybe because of the way she filled them out. Her dark blond hair was all tousled, her cheeks pink with agitation, her turquoise eyes glittering with fiery lights. She looked beautiful and kissable and ticked off as all get-out, and Riley couldn't say he blamed her. He wasn't happy about her sister's visit to them, either.

Riley crossed to the comfortable reading chair where Amanda was sitting, feet propped up on the ottoman in front of her, baby Cory cradled in her arms. They had discovered the previous night if they woke the four-month-old infant and gave him a diaper change and a bottle of formula at midnight, he would sleep until six or seven the following morning. It also helped to keep the bedroom lights low. Hence, only one bedside lamp was on. It illuminated the suite with a soft, romantic glow.

"I mean, I could thoroughly corrupt you or something even more than I already have," Riley teased, wanting to see more of the normal zest for life back in Amanda's eyes, instead of this roiling resentment.

Amanda finished giving the first half of the bottle and shifted the drowsy Cory onto her shoulder for a burp. "It's necessary—" Amanda stated firmly.

"Said Eve to Adam," Riley interjected pointedly, trying not to notice how the weight of the baby had pulled the fabric of her pajamas off one shoulder, exposing the shadowy hollow and the lusciously soft curves of her left breast. With effort, Riley returned his gaze to Amanda's face. It was a peculiar feeling, discovering they were both in the same boat. Riley was used to them being completely at odds with each other. To suddenly find they were facing the same dilemma—how to handle their families' mounting censure in addition to caring for the three kids together gave Riley a feeling of solidarity with Amanda he had never expected to have. And that, plus the increasingly intimate nature of their enforced cohabitation, was giving rise to all sorts of fantasies he knew he shouldn't entertain.

"I want to get my family off my case," Amanda continued as Cory, responding to her pats on his back, let out one—then two—man-size burps. Both of them grinned at the sound. "Which is why I invited my sister to spend the night with us before she flies back to California tomorrow," Amanda told Riley seriously, looking so darn sexy at that moment he wanted to cross the room and take her in his arms and forget everyone and everything else. "Because I want her and the rest of my family to know that their days of pushing me around and telling me what to do are long over. I'm an adult. I make my own decisions. Ones that work for me and not them. Even when they make it clear they don't approve!"

Okay.... Glad we have cleared that up, Riley thought sarcastically to himself, a little disappointed he was being used that way but not exactly surprised. He had known from the moment his new wife had issued the invitation to her meddling older sister that Amanda had an agenda. He had just been hoping—foolishly, he saw now—that it hadn't all been to demonstrate her independence. But rather to open the door to romance, as well.

"And second, you and I are not really going to be sharing the sheets," Amanda said as she shifted baby Cory in her arms and moved gracefully to her feet.

Riley glanced back at the king-size bed that had been inspiring fantasies—however unrealistic—ever since he'd learned they would be hitting the sheets together earlier that evening. A fact that had incensed Amanda's meddling sister Priscilla to no end.

"You intend to sleep on the floor?" he teased, treading closer, aware of how much pleasure simply ribbing her brought. Although that was nothing compared to the intoxication he felt drinking in the alluring cinnamon and clove perfume she wore.

"No, silly." Amanda shifted baby Cory to Riley's arms and handed him the bottle, so Riley could get his baby-fix in, too. "I intend to devise a Great Divide."

"This, I've got to see." Riley settled down with baby Cory in his arms. He had held children dozens of times. Tiny patients. New members of the McCabe clan. But none of them had affected him the way these three kids did. He didn't know if it was the notion that they were meant to be with him, at least for now, the fact they were all so sweet and personable, or simply that they desperately needed parents to love and protect them. All he knew was that when they looked to him for comfort, food, shelter and every other necessity of life, he felt like a dad. And it was the best feeling he had ever had.

Well, maybe a close second best, Riley amended. The best thing he had ever felt was having Amanda in his arms, kissing him back, sending all his senses into overdrive. He had known her lips would be soft and warm and womanly. He hadn't expected her to taste so sweet, nor her lips to move in such a deeply sensual, evocative way. That one reluctant, ever so public kiss had conjured up the need to take that dangerous emotion and the white-hot bolt of desire and see exactly where it led them. Hopefully to bed. Not that, judging by her restrained expression, she intended to allow him to kiss her again anytime soon. Riley sighed, watching as she took a blanket from the cedar chest at the bottom of the bed and rolled it into a long cylinder. She then drew back the covers and tucked it between the two pillows.

"Nice," Riley said. Noting baby Cory had finished his bottle, he put him on his shoulder to burp. "But I fail to see how shoving a rolled blankie between our sheets is going to get your family to approve of our living situation." And that was exactly what Amanda wanted, whether she admitted it or not.

"Obviously, that isn't going to happen," Amanda said dryly. "But just the fact we're caring for the kids together, have been married, and are now sharing a bed is going to make it obvious that we are taking our quandary seriously and trying to lie in the bed we've made, so to speak."

"So perhaps that will encourage them to end the interference."

Riley rubbed Cory's back until another resounding burp filled the room. "Either that, or it'll have your parents even more upset and on the first plane out here, reading us both the riot act for acting so irresponsibly." From what he remembered of the elder Witherspoons, they were even more demanding and critical than Priscilla. Riley couldn't see them backing off in their demands. More likely, they would simply keep badgering Amanda until she caved.

Amanda's slender shoulders stiffened as she bent over the bed, placing the barrier just so. "There's nothing irresponsible about taking good loving care of these three children while we hunt down their parents," Amanda declared, taking the sleepy baby from Riley. Her expression so tender and loving it filled his heart, she laid the sweet infant down on the bed and swaddled him in a flannel blanket that would keep him warm and cozy through the night. Finished, she carried baby Cory to the borrowed crib in the children's room across the hall and settled him onto his back. His blue eyes shut, and his rosebud mouth worked as if still drinking the bottle before finally falling still once again.

With Riley beside her, Amanda checked on the other two children. Chloe was sleeping on her side, her teddy bear clutched in her arms. Amber was on her tummy, her knees drawn up beneath her, her diaper-clad bottom extended into the air. Amanda turned her gently, to a more comfortable position and tucked the soft blanket around her. She barely stirred. Riley took her stuffed animal and put it right beside her. They looked a moment longer, then left as quietly as they had come. Amanda noted the light in the guest room was off, which probably meant her sister was already asleep.

Appearing as relieved by the reprieve from Priscilla's nonstop lecturing as Riley felt, Amanda led the way back into the master bedroom. As soon as the door was shut, Amanda walked back to Riley. Hands on her hips, she looked him square in the eye and picked up where their conversation had left off. "I've been thinking, Riley," she told him soberly.

"Me, too," Riley quipped. *About taking a risk and kissing you again...*

"We established that I didn't play a prank on you and that the kids weren't left by your ex or any of your former patients in Dallas, but we really didn't take our search in the other direction. Is there anyone else—aside from me—who might feel he or she owes you a practical joke of this magnitude? Someone you've outpranked in the past, perhaps?"

Interesting point, Riley thought, and one he had yet to consider, probably because he'd been so focused on Amanda all along. He thought about it, then shook his head. "I see where you're going with this." He stripped off his shirt and walked into the adjacent bath. He left the door open and Amanda lounged in the doorway, watching, as he layered mint-flavored toothpaste onto his brush. He brushed his teeth, rinsed and spit. Aware this situation was beginning to feel almost too intimate, he wiped his mouth on a towel, then straightened, towering over her. "But this isn't the kind of joke a guy would play on another guy," he stated soberly.

Amanda knew she was reaching. In her heart of hearts, she sensed that the kids had been left out of desperation. Just as she realized she had to stop making this "marriage" of theirs suddenly feel so real. She needed to remind herself of his jokester past. Remind herself that Riley never had been the kind of guy she would pick to get involved with seriously. Because if she let herself think that way, if she let herself be seduced into thinking she could trust him, not just with her heart, but her long-held very secret romantic fantasies about him—or worse, gave in to the palpable sexual attraction simmering between them—she could be in a lot of trouble here.

Big-time trouble. The kind of trouble a woman like herself did not recover from once the impetuous fling ended. And any involvement with Riley McCabe would likely end the moment the three children were removed from his care after Christmas.

"Trust me," Riley continued, simultaneously reading her wariness and looking irked that she had brought up the prankster side of him once again. "It's nothing any of my buddies would do."

Amanda edged closer, trying not to notice the stretch of satiny smooth skin over broad shoulders and muscular pecs, the washboard flatness of his abs, and lower still, where the arrow of dark gold chest hair disappeared into the waistband of his jeans. Was it her imagination, or was he beginning to be as aroused by their proximity to each other as she was?

"What about a woman, then?" Amanda directed her glance away from his beautiful body, back to his warm amber eyes. Was there someone else in his life uniquely intriguing in the way she had always been? Someone who had filled the years between his teenage rivalry with Amanda and his love affair with Evangeline, a woman he hadn't yet thought about?

"I don't play practical jokes on women." Riley returned the towel to the rack. He swaggered back into the bedroom and toed off his boots.

Amanda followed, heart pounding, aware their "marriage" had never felt more intimate or genuine than it did now. Which was ridiculous, she reminded herself sternly, since their union was merely a temporary solution to a very complex problem. "What do you call me then?" she demanded resolutely, keeping her eyes focused on his face.

"You," he tapped her playfully on the nose, "are the exception to the rule."

Amanda warmed beneath his teasing touch despite her strict admonition not to fall victim to his considerable charms. "And why is that?" she challenged softly. Letting him know with a glance that she had no intention of succumbing to the nonstop attraction simmering between them. No matter how much she wanted to discover what lay behind the fly of those snug-fitting jeans. Or just how he would kiss her if they had no audience.

"I don't know." He threaded a hand through the tousled layers of her hair. His glance roved her face and he looked as if he wanted very much to kiss her. For real, this time. "Maybe because you had a way of getting under my skin from the very first," he told her softly. "Maybe because you were such a good rival. And maybe just maybe because I've always had a little bit of a crush on you—" his voice dropped a seductive notch "—and just couldn't admit it to myself, until now."

His confession shook her to her soul. The next thing Amanda knew, his head was lowering over hers. If the first time he had kissed her had been unbelievably chaste, the second was passion defined. Before Amanda had a chance to do more than draw in a quavery breath, his arm was around her waist, tugging her close, and their lips were fused in a kiss that was more intimate and searing than anything she ever could have imagined. As his tongue tangled with hers, desire swept through her in hot, effortless waves. She felt so many things. Surprise. Heat. Want. Need. He tasted so good, so undeniably male. And as the fiery kiss continued, she found herself lost in the miracle of it. She had waited a lifetime to be kissed and held like this. She had waited a lifetime to feel like this. As if no one else, nothing else, existed in this moment of time but the two of them and the yearning deep inside them. And yet as he lifted a hand to unbutton her pajama top, his warm strong hands slipping inside her top to claim the silky softness of her breasts, panic engulfed her once again.

Fearful of making another mistake, of falling for a man who would never love her the way she yearned to be loved, Amanda finally tore her lips from Riley's and called a halt.

"No," she said breathlessly, turning her head to the side, "we are not doing this just so I can get back at my family!" There were better ways to accomplish that, she knew.

"I agree," Riley said emphatically, picking her up in his arms and laying her down on the bed. "Our families have nothing to do with what is going on between you and me right here, right now." Riley stretched out beside her, tucked a hand beneath her chin and turned her face back to his. He looked deep into her eyes. He lowered his head, kissed her again, consuming her with his mouth. Lips, teeth, tongue, he used them all to maximum advantage as his hands returned to claim and caress her breasts. He was hard, relentless, irresistible in his pursuit of her. And still he kissed her, his lips warm and sure as he took every ounce of feeling that had been building between them for years and years, and used it to his advantage.

The kiss ended and his lips forged a burning trail down her neck, across her collarbone, the slope of one breast, then another. Amanda arched against him as his mouth circled each nipple, bringing them to taut aching peaks. Passion swirled and dipped around her, drawing her into its mesmerizing depths.

"What's happening now has to do with you and me," he told her as he made his way slowly back to her mouth. He threaded his hands through her hair, kissed her again, with even less restraint. He dragged her so close their bodies were almost one. Her senses spun as he sucked her bottom lip and touched the tip of her tongue with his own, then stroked his hands down her body once again. His warm palm slid lower yet. "This is about how we feel, Amanda. And what we want, which is to make love to each other, here, now."

Was that what she wanted? Amanda wondered shakily as Riley continued to inundate her with kisses and the overwhelming security of his tall, strong body? To make love without being loved? Realizing what was about to happen, what she had encouraged him to do, Amanda placed both hands on Riley's chest and pushed him away from her. "No," she said firmly, as the sensual mist faded and her sanity returned. "I don't care how good it feels," she told him fiercely, looking him straight in the eye. "We are definitely not doing this."

Chapter 6

"Are we going to talk about this?" Riley asked, as Amanda disengaged herself from his arms and rose from the bed.

"Isn't that my line?" Amanda replied as she plucked her pajama top from the floor and slipped it back on.

"We need to discuss why it happened," Riley continued, determined not to ignore the change in their relationship the way she so obviously wanted. "Where we go from here." He gave her a long, steady look. "We just very nearly consummated our marriage."

Amanda's hands trembled as she buttoned her shirt. "The reason we almost made love is we are living a fantasy life, pretending to be mommy and daddy to three children who are not ours. We need a dose of reality."

Reality, Riley thought, had been holding Amanda in his arms and kissing her without restraint, admitting that surrendering to their mutual passion had been what he had wanted from her all along. He closed the distance between them, not above using his superior size to inject some control into the situation.

"This mistake was just that," Amanda continued, plucking a brush off the bureau.

Riley tried not to take offense at that, even as he drank in her alluring cinnamon perfume.

Her hands trembled as she restored order to her hair. "And we made that momentary mistake because it's Christmas."

Riley lounged against the bureau next to her, his back to the mirror. He folded his arms in front of him. Reminded just how stubborn, strong-willed and defiant Amanda could be, he said, "I don't follow."

She lifted her chin, clearly trying for an air of cool challenge. "It's a well-known fact that romantically unattached people are lonelier and therefore more emotionally vulnerable during the holidays."

Riley arched his eyebrow deliberately. "So loneliness and a need for more holiday cheer drove you into my arms."

Amanda nodded. "And curiosity. I'm human. I like to have a little fun in the bedroom now and then."

Sure she was fibbing now, Riley demanded, "Since when?" The Amanda he recalled had been anything but interested in jumping from bed to bed. He sensed that was still the case, even if she wasn't quite ready to admit it to him.

Amanda crossed her arms stubbornly. "Maybe I've changed."

"And maybe you haven't." Riley put his hands on her shoulders and held her in front of him when she would have run away from what was happening between them. Again. "Maybe you only wish making love with someone could be an unemotional thing." Just as he had at one time when he had needed to protect himself from hurt and emotional demands he knew he would not be able to meet. That had all changed. He was tired of feeling so alone. He wanted the kind of emotional support and intimacy Kate and his dad, and all his married siblings, had. He suspected Amanda did, too.

Amanda blew out an exasperated breath and slapped both hands on her hips. She tossed her head at him, but made no move to extricate herself from his gentle, staying grip. "Since when did you know anything about me on such an intimate level?" she demanded, her lovely face gilded in the soft shadowy light of their bedroom.

Riley took her by the hand and led her toward the bench at the foot of the bed. The sudden cessation of their lovemaking left him feeling oddly bereft, and in some ways, lonelier than before. So maybe it was a good thing Amanda had pulled back at the last minute. If she hadn't, he might have really gotten in over his head. Picking up the threads of their argument once again, he said, "I know this. You spent more nights at home than most kids our age when you were in high school."

Amanda frowned, remembering. "I didn't have any choice about that." She sank down onto the padded seat. She looked down at her bare left hand that should have held a wedding band, proclaiming her as his new bride. "I was babysitting my younger siblings."

Riley regarded her empathetically. He sat down next to her and covered her hand with his. Delighting in the softness of her skin, he murmured, "I don't know how you did it, giving up nearly all your free time that way. I would have rebelled big-time."

Amanda's lower lip curved ruefully as she slanted him a sidelong glance, then stated in a low, matter-of-fact tone, "Ever stop to think my involvement with you was my rebellion?"

Riley paused, not sure whether that was a good thing or bad.

Her eyes sparkling at the memory of a very lively time in their lives, Amanda shook her head, continued almost shyly, "My parents hated my behavior when it came to you because it was so unlike me. And the more they tried to keep me home and out of trouble..."

Riley squeezed her hand companionably and looked her straight in the eye, remembering full well the ruckus they'd caused. "Not to mention, away from me," he interrupted softly.

"The more outrageous my jokes on you became," Amanda concluded.

Glad to recall a simpler time when one-upping each other was all that mattered, Riley wrapped a comforting arm around her slender shoulders. "I still haven't forgotten the time you turned all my science notes hot pink, right before semester exams. How'd you do that, by the way?"

She leaned against him, all the earlier contentiousness drained out of her. "Trade secret." She winked.

Liking the abruptly playful tone the evening had taken—it was a welcome relief after the stressful day—Riley shifted Amanda onto his lap and wrapped both his arms around her. "Come on. Spill." Riley prodded her with a look.

"We took all the paper out of your loose-leaf notebook and sprayed it with diluted fruit drink," Amanda confessed proudly even as she resisted cuddling against him.

Riley stroked a hand through the just-brushed softness of her dark blond hair. "Is that why the pages all had that sugary smell?"

Amanda nodded, still holding herself somewhat aloof.

Riley regarded her with respect, one accomplished practical joker to another. "Three hundred pages of notes must have taken a lot of time."

Amanda's eyes sparkled with merry accomplishment. "Yes, but it was worth it to see the look on your face when you opened your locker that morning and took out your science binder."

Riley chuckled softly. "Yeah, but I got you back by putting the green food coloring in your soda can." He recalled the excitement of those days. Always waiting, wondering, what she was going to do next…always plotting his next move. Knowing no matter what, he had to keep—and hold—her full attention.

Sort of like now.

Amanda shook her head in amused remembrance. She wreathed one arm about his shoulders, her fingers like silk against his bare skin, the other remained in her lap. "I had green lips for several days."

He stroked the pad of his thumb across the inside of her wrist, looked deep into her eyes. Knowing it was time their conversation took a serious turn once again, before she could avoid acknowledgment of what had just happened between them altogether, he continued softly, "And now you have a husband and a marriage you never planned on and dual responsibility for three kids."

Amanda stiffened, clearly as reluctant to get as emotionally entangled with him as ever. "It's more a convenient living arrangement than a marriage," she said defensively and moved to get off his lap.

Riley released her reluctantly. He stretched his long legs out in front of him and sat with his back against the foot of the bed. He watched as she stood and began to pace. "How do you figure that?"

She regarded him haughtily. "Because I have no intention of making our mistake a legal or in any sense a permanent one. Our marriage won't be a valid union unless we get a license before the thirty days are up. We both already agreed we have no intention of doing that."

Riley understood why Amanda was clinging to the initial agreement they'd made. She wanted to safeguard herself from hurt by not allowing herself to get emotionally involved with anyone again. He understood that. He'd done it himself. He also knew from experience that it didn't work. Avoiding meaningful emotional commitments only made you lonelier and more unhappy in the end.

He stood. More determined than ever to discover where this attraction of theirs was leading them, he took her weary, resisting body in his arms. "Forget the legalities of our predicament and the license, Amanda," he advised her gruffly. Cupping her chin in his hand, he lifted her face to his and scored his thumb across the softness of her lips. Ignoring the sudden wariness in her pretty eyes, he continued softly, "Let's talk about what's happening between us in this bedroom tonight."

Unfortunately, Amanda thought, that was exactly what she did not want to discuss. She tore her eyes from the bunched muscles of his chest and the whirling light brown hair that arrowed down and disappeared beneath the low-slung waist of his cotton pajama pants. "Mmm, no."

"No?" he asked, his sexy eyes glimmering mischievously.

Amanda closed her eyes against the memory of her response to the most masculine part of him. Her insides tingled as she recalled his kisses and what they had very nearly done. "I don't know you well enough to talk about what's so obviously on your mind, Riley McCabe!"

Riley threw back his head. A deep male laugh, rich with irony, filled the cozy silence of the bedroom. The look he gave her was direct, uncompromising, confident. "You're something, Amanda Witherspoon McCabe, you know that?"

Hearing him add his name to hers made her flush with pleasure. When he looked at her like that, he made her feel beautiful. And that, too, was dangerous. "I know you think so," Amanda said, trying desperately not to think about the quivers happening in her tummy or the hope rising in her heart. "But in the meantime, you need to understand that despite what just happened here tonight that you and I are just...friends."

Riley groaned and pressed his hands to his ears, before fixing her with a comically exaggerated look as he declared, "Worst words a guy could ever hear! Particularly—" he paused, his glance sliding over the tousled strands of her silky blond hair and softly parted lips "—when the words come from his wife of only one day."

"Pretend wife," Amanda corrected, trying not to notice how handsome and sexy he looked in the muted light of the bedroom. "Temporary wife."

Riley looked as if he wanted to change her mind about that. At least long enough to get her in his arms again and make love to her. But she knew that would be a mistake. Their situation was complicated enough without bringing sex into the equation or allowing herself to think their marriage was anything but a temporary solution for the benefit of the children mysteriously left in Riley's care.

Taking her by the hand, he led her toward the bed. Noticing the rolled-up blanket had been knocked right of center during their hot and heavy make-out session, Amanda leaned over and put it back.

"We've really got to get some sleep," Riley said.

"No argument there." Talking intimately with Riley was only going to lead to other things she knew she should avoid, even if she hadn't managed to do so thus far this evening. Aware her heart was pounding and there was a telltale fluttering in her middle, Amanda slipped into her side of the covers, turned her back to the middle, and shut her eyes. She half expected Riley to kneel beside the bed, like the Prince in the *Sleeping Beauty* story, press home his advantage and give her a good-night kiss. Instead, he switched off the bedside lamp, walked around the foot of the bed, and climbed in the other side. Leaving her to deal with her disappointment and desire. Even though she knew he was only doing what she had firmly stated she wanted him to do.

"And speaking of good ideas..." Ignoring the practical aspects of their situation, Riley removed the rolled blanket and tossed it aside. Behaving as if he knew instinctively what was in her heart and on her mind, he pulled her into the curve of his body to sleep. Amanda knew she should resist cuddling now the same way she had resisted it when he had pulled her onto his lap. But it had been so long since she had been held like this, if she had ever been held like this, so warmly and tenderly.

"I think I just figured out what I want for Christmas," he murmured in her ear.

Probably the same thing she already had wished for, Amanda thought, sinking luxuriantly into the strong solid curve of his body. *Thank goodness Riley would never see the note she had written and slipped into Santa's mailbox,* she thought, already drifting off to sleep. 'Cause if he did, she wouldn't have a chance at resisting him and the situation that could still very well break her heart.

"Leaving already?" Riley said to Priscilla Witherspoon the next morning as she carried her suitcase into the upstairs hallway.

Priscilla set her bags down and marched into the "nursery" where Riley was busy changing Cory's diaper. "If you were any kind of a gentleman at all, Riley McCabe, you would end this farce of a marriage and stay as far away from my sister as possible."

Riley laid Cory down on the waterproof changing pad on the center of the guest room bed. "Well, good morning to you, too," Riley drawled as he unsnapped the legs of Cory's cotton sleeper.

Arms folded militantly in front of her, Priscilla edged nearer. A dour expression on her face, she watched as Riley removed the sodden diaper, and pulled a baby cleansing cloth out of the plastic holder. Holding the infant's legs with one hand, Riley washed Cory's diaper area.

"We all tried to talk Amanda out of returning to Laramie

to work and live. She should have stayed in California, where she could be close to all her siblings and their families, as well as our parents. She doesn't need to do something like this to have children in her life. She can babysit for her nieces and nephews anytime."

So here was the rub. The real reason her family was so upset. "Was Amanda doing a lot of that, before she left?" Riley asked, pulling a fresh diaper out of the box and sliding it beneath Cory's bottom.

"As a matter of fact," Priscilla returned coolly, "she was."

Riley stared at the diaper. Realizing the tabs were facing the wrong way, he removed the diaper, turned it right side up and slid it back under Cory's bottom. "To the detriment of her own social life?"

Priscilla paced back and forth beside the bed. "Amanda didn't want a social life after her divorce."

Riley found that hard to believe. He scoffed as he applied a bit of zinc oxide cream to Cory's tender skin. Finished, he frowned at the residue still on his hand. Then cleaned it off with another diaper wipe. "Everyone wants a social life whether they're looking for romance or not," Riley informed her as he threw the crumpled cleaning cloth into the diaper pail.

"Not Amanda," Priscilla declared.

No wonder Amanda wanted to leave California, Riley thought.

Amanda popped her head in the door. She had Chloe by the hand, and Amber on her hip. "Need any help?" Amanda asked her sister.

Priscilla shook her head, all tight-lipped disapproval once again. "I can manage my bag."

Amanda tensed, looking from Riley to Priscilla. "Everything okay in here?" she asked warily.

"I was just telling Riley to take care lest he have the entire Witherspoon clan to deal with," Priscilla said tartly.

Riley flashed a pained smile as he buttoned up the legs of Cory's diaper and ended up with one extra snap on each end.

"Hence, I think he knows what he has to do," Priscilla finished.

Amanda looked as uncomfortable and eager to get rid of her nosy older sister as Riley felt. "The girls and I'll walk you out," she said.

By the time Riley had refastened the snaps on Cory's sleeper and walked downstairs, Priscilla was driving away. A tense look on her face, Amanda led the two girls over to the scattered toys on the family room rug. They sat down and began to play.

"What did she say to you?" Riley asked when Amanda walked over to the kitchen counter and plucked the breakfast dishes off the table.

Amanda shrugged her shoulders, a thoroughly dispirited look on her face. A remoteness he hadn't heard before crept into her low tone. "Apparently, my family sees similarities between my previous marriage and this one. They think I am just with you to have a chance at getting a ready-made family of my own. That without the kids, without the convenience of our living arrangements, and our 'marriage' giving me false security, I wouldn't even consider going along with you on this."

"And if what they think is true, what then?" Riley asked quietly.

"Easy." Amanda sighed. "They'll all be right there to say 'We-told-you-this-was-a-bad-idea.'"

Riley imagined that was all too true. Amanda's family had long blamed him for the disreputable turn in Amanda's behavior, whenever he was on the scene. It didn't, however, mean Riley agreed that he and Amanda were bad for each other. On the contrary, Riley felt he and Amanda brought out the vivaciousness in each other the way no one else did.

"That's one way to look at it," he said, taking her in his arms.

He held her close and tenderly brushed the hair from her face with the edge of his hand. "But suppose they're all wrong…."

If nearly making love with Riley the night before had felt real, Amanda thought, it was nothing compared to the sensation of standing in the kitchen, their lower bodies pressed together, his arms wrapped around her waist. She wondered if he had any idea how easily she could lose her heart to him. Not just now, but forever. "And suppose I believe in Santa Claus, too?" she challenged with a sassy toss of her head, reminding herself they were still in a very fanciful situation that could conceivably come crashing down around them at any second.

"Hey, take it from someone who knows," Riley teased, giving her a once-over that stirred her secret desire even more. "Santa's been known to grant a wish or two or three."

If only old St. Nick could make Riley fall in love with her in a way that would last forever! But no one could do that. Riley had to come to feel that way on his own, or they literally had no future together, Amanda reminded herself sternly. She had married one man who cherished everything she did for him and his kids, but did not—had not—ever loved her the way he should have. She wasn't going to make the same mistake again. No matter how much she was beginning to feel…maybe had always felt…for her former nemesis, Riley McCabe.

Regarding him in a chiding manner meant to discourage such ridiculously impractical notions, she began, "Riley…"

"Give us a chance, Amanda. Give this a chance." Riley's head lowered.

Amanda's traitorous heart filled with anticipation. The next thing she knew one hand flattened over her spine, bringing her close, the other was in her hair, tilting her face up to his. She had time to draw a quick excited breath, then his lips pressed against hers. Amanda tasted the masculine force that was Riley, felt his wildness in the unrestrained, sweeping motions of his tongue. She didn't want to surrender to him, but his will was stronger than hers, his embrace too full of sexual promise. With a low moan, she slanted her lips to better accommodate his mouth and twined her tongue with his. And even though she knew she should be resisting his incredibly tantalizing kisses, she couldn't seem to summon up the willpower to call a halt to the embrace, not when she was reveling in his tenderness and yearning was pouring through her in hot, potent waves. Amanda melted against him, acutely aware that she had never felt as sensual or been seduced quite so masterfully.

Riley had expected to kiss Amanda again. As soon as the opportunity presented itself and the mood was right. He hadn't figured she would respond quite so eagerly once her initial reservation was past. He hadn't expected her to mold her soft, slender body to his, wreathe her arms about his neck, go up on tiptoe and kiss him back passionately. Tormented beyond his wildest dreams—because now all he wanted to do was further the escalating desire and make her his—he drew back, breathing hard.

Amanda looked up at him, cheeks pinkening, her breathing as shallow and erratic as his. "The kids," he sighed, cursing his own restraint and bad timing. Had he known she was going to be this receptive to another kiss, he would have waited, picked a much better time. Like late tonight, after the children were all in bed for the night.

Amanda turned her head, noting at the same time as he that Chloe and Amber were still completely entranced by their play, and hence oblivious to the hot, passionate kisses between the two of them. A mixture of temper and chagrin sparkled in Amanda's eyes. "I thought we weren't going to make this mistake again!" she said.

Riley grinned, pleased by the indisputable fact she wanted him as much as he wanted her. "Hey," he protested in a lazy tone that brought even more indignation to her lovely eyes. "I never agreed to that."

"Well you should have," Amanda fumed, just as the doorbell rang and the two older children looked up from their toys.

"Saved by the bell," Amanda breathed. She gracefully extricated herself from his arms. "I'll get it."

Riley went to the door, too. His younger sister, Laurel, and her friend Micki Evans, were standing on the front stoop. Their noses and cheeks were red with the cold. Laurel held a fresh and fragrant evergreen wreath, strewn with red holly berries, in her hands. "Mom and Dad sent this over," Laurel said, helpful as ever. "They noted you didn't have one when they were here yesterday."

Micki smiled amiably as Riley and Amanda ushered the young women inside and shut the door behind them, to keep out the cold wintry air. "We thought you might need some help with the kids," Micki said as she stood beside Laurel in the foyer.

Laurel's voice dropped to a conspiratorial whisper, "We figured you might want to go shopping for a Christmas tree and presents and stuff."

Riley looked at Amanda. "Sounds like a plan to me."

"Me, too," Amanda replied.

"How long can the two of you stay?" Riley asked Micki and Laurel, aware the closest shopping mall and toy superstore was a good thirty minutes away, by car.

"As long as you need us to," Laurel said, already taking off her coat. "Micki and I are done with our final exams and home on break, so aside from the volunteering we're doing at the hospital, we're pretty much free to help you all the time."

"At least until Micki goes home for the holidays, too," Riley corrected.

Without warning, Micki got a pinched, unhappy look on her face.

"Actually," Laurel cut in as she wrapped a jovial arm

around her friend's shoulders, "I've invited Micki to spend the holidays with us this year."

"You're not going home to Colorado to be with your sister and her family?" Riley asked, surprised. He knew from previous conversations with Micki that she and her sister were extraordinarily close, and had been since they'd been orphaned, years earlier. To the point that Micki usually spent every break with her.

Micki tensed and looked as if she didn't want to discuss it. "Not this year," she said finally, looking away.

Sensing he had touched a nerve, albeit unintentionally, Riley changed the subject smoothly. He knew if Micki and her sister'd had a familial disagreement it was none of his business. Perhaps they'd patch things up on their own before Christmas actually arrived, in any case. "Any word from UT-Galveston medical school?" Riley asked Micki, changing the subject smoothly.

Micki grinned broadly. "Well, that's the other reason we stopped by." She literally exuded happiness. "I wanted to tell you that I got in!"

"Congratulations!" Riley said, genuinely pleased and proud of her.

"Thanks," Micki said. Tears of happiness glistened in her eyes.

Riley wasn't surprised the young woman was so emotional. He knew how much Micki wanted to be a doctor—it was one of the reasons he had written such a glowing recommendation for her.

Amber toddled over and wrapped her arms around Micki's legs. She looked up at her and babbled something unintelligible. Chloe moved toward Laurel and slipped in next to Micki. Standing between the two, Chloe wrapped an arm about each girl's knee and held on tight, still not saying a single word.

Laurel withdrew a piece of paper from her pocket and handed it to Riley, as concerned as ever about making everyone else happy. "Micki and I weren't sure what you guys knew about amusements for youngsters of a certain demographic, but we do because we've both done a lot of babysitting in recent years. So we sort of made a list of the t-o-y-s the k-i-d-s might like from S-A-N-T-A or you guys or whomever." She winked at Riley and Amanda. "It's a starting point, anyway."

As much as Riley hated to leave the three kids, even for a little while, he was glad for the time alone with Amanda. There was much they still had to deal with, to clear the way for them to pursue their attraction. He intended to see that happen. "Mind if we stop by the sheriff's department first and check in with my brother?" Riley asked as they headed toward Main Street, minutes later.

"I think it's a great idea," Amanda said as Riley turned his SUV into the parking lot. "The sooner we find out who the kids really belong with, the better."

Unfortunately, Riley and Amanda discovered to their mutual disappointment, Kevin did not have the answer yet. "We searched the database for missing kids nationwide," Kevin told them unhappily. "Nothing came up for any of them."

Amanda looked at Riley, the affection she felt for the children in her eyes. "I can't believe someone isn't missing the kids," Amanda murmured, tucking her hands in the pockets of her coat.

Feeling exactly the same way, Riley touched Amanda's shoulder reassuringly. "What about the note that was left with them?" Riley asked.

Kevin frowned. "There are fingerprints on it, aside from yours and Amanda's, but none that match anything in the system. Which means whoever left the kids with you does not have a criminal record."

"Well, that's good," Riley said, relieved. Aware Amanda

was suddenly looking a little pale, he held out a chair and she slipped onto the seat.

"Isn't there some other way we could identify them?" Amanda asked, her initial distress fading as she focused on the task at hand. "Somewhere else we could look?"

Riley was eager to solve the mystery, too.

"We're trying the social service and charity agencies in the Dallas-Fort Worth area now," Kevin said. "Circulating the pictures of the kids, seeing if anyone knows of a family in trouble who also might have somehow come across your path, Riley, because whoever left the kids with you knows of you in some not so obvious way."

"What do you mean?" Riley asked.

"It could be someone who lived at the apartment complex where you used to live, or someone who works at a restaurant or dry cleaners or grocery store you frequented. Or someone you ran across during one of your rotations during your internship and residency five, six, even seven years ago. And since Dallas is where you did your medical training and last worked, it seems the logical place to start."

"That's a lot of ground to cover," Riley remarked. "How soon do you think you'll have answers from all those places?"

"We'll hear back from law enforcement and social services in a couple of days."

"And if you don't find answers there?" Amanda asked, her delicate fingers worrying the strap of her shoulder bag.

"We'll gradually extend the search to the rest of the social welfare agencies in the state," Kevin said seriously. He went on reassuringly, "Plus, all the law enforcement agencies nationwide have now been notified, so should anyone report Amber, Chloe and Cory missing at any point in the future, those agencies will notify us immediately."

Amanda and Riley thanked Kevin and headed back out to the SUV.

"I don't know whether to feel elated or depressed," Riley said, opening her door for her.

Amanda snapped her safety harness while Riley climbed behind the wheel. "What do you mean?" she asked, appearing as if her emotions were as tumultuous and confused as his at the moment.

Riley frowned. "As much as I want the kids' family to be found, I don't want them going back into an unfortunate circumstance or being reunited with someone who doesn't want them, just because legally that's where they belong."

"Maybe whoever left them with you had good reason for doing what they did. Maybe they intend to leave the kids with you permanently, not just for the Christmas holidays. Maybe this was just a trial period or something. Kind of like a Christmas gift from the heart?" Amanda speculated, her soft lips taking on an optimistic curve.

Riley slanted Amanda an admiring glance. "You are romantic, deep down. Despite all your efforts to deny it."

"Hopeful," Amanda corrected, with an arch look, "that everything works out in a way that's best for all. In the meantime," she said, all business once again, "we better get on with the shopping."

The aisles of the toy superstore were packed with parents and shopping carts. En route, Amanda and Riley had narrowed the list of possibilities to two items per child, and two group gifts. A pink-and-white roadster-tricycle and a Talking Tammy doll for Chloe, a push-and-pull wagon and a Texas ranch toddler play set, complete with cowboys and animals, for Amber and a musical mobile and infant play gym for Cory. Riley added a huge tub of interlocking play blocks and several Educating Baby videos to the basket. He had just started for the checkout lines, when he went back and added a stack of storybooks—including several about Santa and the meaning of Christmas—that could be given to the kids and read now, to the cache. They made it another three feet, before he also added several wooden puzzles, which gave Amanda time to add a toy band and piano to the cart she was pushing. Riley grinned at her. "Do you think we're spoiling them?" he asked as Amanda selected three stuffed animals—a puppy for Chloe, a kitty cat for Amber and a teddy for Cory.

"I don't know. Maybe." Amanda appeared as if she was enjoying this as much as he. "But I so want them to have a wonderful Christmas, Riley."

"Me, too. And you know what that means?" he told her, enjoying the color in her cheeks and the sparkle in her eyes as they finally got in the long checkout line. "We've got to get a Christmas tree today, too."

An hour later, they were standing in the lot on the outskirts of Laramie. The local charity group had brought in Scotch pines that ranged from four to sixteen feet tall.

Riley grinned at her, looking happier than she had ever seen him. "You pick it out," he said.

Amanda knew this was all fantasy—the husband of her dreams and the kids she had always wanted, just in time for Christmas. But it was difficult not to get swept up into the dream nevertheless, if only for a short while. Doing her best to contain her emotions, she merely shrugged and said, "It's your house."

Riley took her gloved hand in his. "And you're my wife," he reminded her in a possessive voice. His grin widened playfully. "I have it on good authority that 'the wife' always gets the final say on decisions like this."

He was making her feel really and truly married to him. A dangerous proposition. Still tingling from the brief contact, she walked up and down the aisle of trees. The air was fragrant with the smell of fresh-cut pine and Christmas music played softly over the speakers mounted on tall, wooden posts. By Christmas Day it could well be seventy degrees outside, but for now the cold front sweeping the entire Southwest continued to immerse Laramie. Their breaths puffed in frosty circles in the damp wintry air. "How big a tree do you want?" she asked.

Riley shrugged. He tilted his head to study her, tucked a gloved hand just above her elbow. He came closer still, the warmth of his breath ghosting over her temples. "Show me what you want," he whispered. "It's yours."

Amanda blushed despite herself. She narrowed her eyes at him in exaggerated admonishment. "Getting a little racy there, aren't you, Doc?"

He waggled his eyebrows at her as they proceeded down the aisles at a leisurely pace, examining tree after tree. "Think so?" he asked cheerfully, looking more determined than ever to make her his—at least once—before this convenient marriage of theirs ended.

"For all the good it's going to do you," Amanda murmured right back, determined to be honest and let him know where they still stood. "Since—despite what my family thinks—I'm not one to repeat my mistakes." Except with Riley. With him, she was prone to letting emotion rather than cool reason rule the day. There was just something about him that brought out the reckless, restless, totally irresponsible side of her. Something about him made her want to throw caution to the wind and forget about putting on the brakes and make love to him, not just once, but again and again and again. And that would be a terrible move to make, since it would guarantee she would love him—and only him—forever. Regardless of how casually he felt about her and their current living arrangement.

Riley considered her for a moment, then leaned closer once again, bringing the tantalizing fragrance of his cologne with him. "What we started last night was not a mistake," he told her bluntly.

Amanda did not like the possessive look in his eyes or the presumption in his tone that said he was going to have his way with her again even if both their hearts got shattered all to pieces in the process. To have a dream just within your reach, and then have it yanked away, unfulfilled, was devastating, Amanda knew. She rolled her eyes. "Says you."

Riley chuckled as if he knew full well the reason behind her discomfort. He fingered the tag on a Christmas tree. "And so will you, one day soon," he told her gently, nudging the back of her hand with the back of his. He paused and looked deep into her eyes. "As soon as you admit we've got something special going on here. And agree to take it to the next step."

Suddenly, Amanda was having trouble getting her breath. "Third base?"

"Or fourth, if you need specifics." His voice dropped a seductive notch. "I want to make you mine, Amanda."

Amanda's pulse jumped. Leave it to Riley to lay it right on the line. "You mean have a fling," she said, marshaling her defenses and pivoting away from him.

Riley put his hands on her shoulders and gently turned her toward him. "Or a heck of a lot more."

"Depending?" Amanda asked.

"On how close you're willing to let us get," Riley replied seriously.

He was talking about joining more than their bodies now; he was talking about involving their hearts and minds. Unfortunately, as much as Amanda wanted to believe there was the possibility of a long-term future for them, bitter experience told her to be more than cautious where a man in Riley's situation, who simply needed a wife and mother for "his" children, was concerned. What seemed so right now might not appear all that perfect if the children were removed from the equation.

Slim Whittaker, the owner of the local hardware store and the president of the local Jaycees, came up to join them. "I hear congratulations are in order for you two," he remarked with a wink.

Amanda flushed self-consciously. Slim was in his sixties now, but she remembered darting in and out of his store a lot when she was a kid. Riley had done the same.

Riley let go of Amanda's elbow and shook Slim's hand. "No doubt about it," he said meaningfully, "I'm a very lucky man this holiday season."

As was she, in a way, since she had been dreading this holiday alone more than she could say. "Now if we could only pick out a tree," Amanda demurred, changing the subject smoothly.

"Well, let's see if I can assist you with that," Slim said.

Fifteen minutes later, a beautiful seven-foot Scotch pine was tied onto the top of Riley's SUV. "What are we going to do about the presents?" Amanda asked.

Riley paused. "You're right. We can't let the kids see them before Christmas morning. It would ruin the surprise."

Amanda thought for a moment, glad to have something practical to focus on. "We could store them at my place in the meantime and pick up some decorations for the tree, while we're there. Unless you have some?"

Riley shook his head. "I've never even had a tree," he confessed sheepishly.

Amanda did a double take. "Never?"

Riley shrugged his broad shoulders listlessly. "It always seemed like too much of a bother for one person."

Unable to resist teasing him, Amanda said, "Did you say 'Bah, Humbug,' too?"

"Ha, ha, Miss Merry Holidays." Riley made a face and Amanda laughed.

Having gotten the reaction he wanted from her, he sobered once again and asked curiously, "So, when did you start putting up your own tree?"

Amanda's gaze drifted to his hands. Strong, capable, masculine. She was in awe of how gentle they could be. "From the time I had my first apartment in nursing school. Heck, even in the dorm, I put up a little tabletop tree and put lights up around my room."

"Somehow that doesn't surprise me," Riley drawled, parking in the space in front of her townhome-style one bedroom apartment. They carried packages to the stoop. While Amanda unlocked the front door, he went back for more. By the time he joined her with the last of the children's presents, she had slipped off her jacket, and turned the lights on the tree in the center of her living room. The evergreen tree was beautifully decorated, with white lights, colored glass balls and candy canes. An angel sat on the top. A single stocking hung on the mantel. "We're not going to have to undecorate your tree, are we?" Riley asked.

"Oh, no. I've got lots of decorations. I collect them."

Amanda disappeared up the stairs that led to the loft-style bedroom and bath upstairs. She returned with a large plastic storage bin. She opened it up and began to sort through the decorations she had collected over the years. "Let's see here. I've got colored lights, garlands, lots of red and green and gold velvet bows, and a star for the top. Do you think that will do? It's all pretty kid-friendly stuff."

"I think it will be perfect." With a frown, Riley glanced at his watch.

"I know." Amanda smiled in commiseration, feeling as reluctant to leave the intimate setting as he. She got the decorations ready to go. "We've got to get a move on," she said, as the phone attached to his belt began to buzz. "We told Laurel and Micki we'd be home before three o'clock, and it's almost that now."

Riley lifted the cell phone from its leather holster and glanced at the caller ID. "Speaking of Laurel," he drawled humorously, then hit the speaker-phone function on his phone. "Hey, baby sister. What's up?"

"Riley, you've got to come quick," Laurel said urgently.

"Why?" Riley demanded, suddenly looking as alarmed as Amanda felt, at the anxious tone of his sister's voice. "Nothing's wrong with the kids? Is it?"

"Oh, no," Laurel quickly confirmed, to Amanda's and Riley's mutual relief. "It's Mom and Dad," she explained nervously. "They're on the way over here."

Riley frowned, still perplexed. "And that is cause for alarm because…" Riley prodded his sister gently, while still holding Amanda's eyes.

Abruptly, Laurel sounded near tears. "They're going to yell at me."

Chapter 7

"Since when have Mom and Dad ever yelled at you?" Riley asked, picking up the conversation with his distraught younger sister the moment he and Amanda walked in the door.

Laurel's lower lip trembled. She cast a look over her shoulder at Micki, who was playing with the two older children, while Cory sat beside her in the bouncy seat. "You know what I mean," she sulked, folding her arms in front of her, for a moment looking far less than her twenty-two years. "They're always so protective, and so darn nosy when it comes to my life!"

Barely able to contain his exasperation, Riley rolled his eyes. "I believe that's called being a parent."

Blue eyes spitting fire, Laurel continued to pout. She threw up her hands, all indignant fury. "When are they going to realize I'm an adult, capable of running my own life?"

This did not sound good, Riley thought. His parents did not lose their tempers with Laurel without a darn good reason. "What exactly did you do?" Riley demanded as a Jaguar sedan pulled up in front of the house.

"It's more like what I didn't do," Laurel mumbled. Peering out the window, she yanked open the front door and stepped out onto the front stoop. Riley took Amanda's hand, pulling her along with him and followed suit, shutting the door behind them. It appeared there was going to be some sort of showdown between his baby sister and their parents. Riley saw no reason to inflict it on Micki and the children. Amanda was a different matter. If she was going to be a part of his family, she needed to know what she was getting into. The McCabes were a close-knit bunch. If something needed to be said, it got said. Even if it hurt temporarily.

"You're not making any sense," Riley told Laurel as Kate and Sam marched determinedly toward them.

Laurel sighed loudly and shoved the wavy length of her dark hair away from her face. She looked at Amanda, who smiled at Laurel sympathetically, then turned back to Riley. "Mom and Dad saw my grades for fall semester."

"So what's the problem?" Riley asked, irritated by all the unnecessary drama in front of Amanda. "You're an A student."

"I thought we had a deal that you were going to be home to talk to us about this at three o'clock," Sam McCabe said as he reached the stoop.

Beside him, Riley's stepmother, Kate, looked equally upset.

Riley felt Amanda tense. He reached over and took her hand, not caring at the surprised looks that gesture generated.

"I was babysitting for Riley and Amanda's kids," Laurel said. She folded her arms in front of her aggressively as if prepared for battle.

Figuring a big brouhaha would help nothing, Riley did his best to ease the tension. "I didn't know anything about a family meeting or Amanda and I would have been here earlier and made sure Laurel was home on time," Riley said. "Although for the record, I think everyone is overreacting just a tad. What did Laurel do anyway? Get a B?" How big a tragedy was that? Geez. And he'd thought the Witherspoons were interfering and overprotective with their daughters!

"Try two Fs," Sam said grimly.

"What?" Riley and Amanda both did a double take.

"And two Cs," Kate added, equally concerned.

"Hey, let's not forget I got an A in my communications class," Laurel stated rebelliously.

"Unfortunately, that's not your major," Sam returned sternly. "And the grades in your area of concentration will determine what kind of job you can get upon your graduation in May. Employers are going to look at your performance in your business classes the last four months and wonder what in the heck has been going on with you."

"Do you-all really need to have this discussion here?" Riley asked in mounting exasperation. Wasn't this between Laurel and their parents?

Kate looked at Laurel with understanding. "Come home with us, dear."

Laurel moved so she was standing slightly behind and to the right of Riley and Amanda. "No." She regarded their parents stubbornly.

"At least give us an explanation then," Kate pleaded.

Laurel shrugged. "My grades are bad because I didn't have time to study."

"Why not?" Sam prodded.

"I was helping out a friend of mine who was in trouble," Laurel explained, stubborn as ever.

"For four months?" Sam asked disbelievingly.

"Yes," Laurel retorted, just as heatedly. "And for the record, if I had it to do all over again, I would—even knowing I was going to get such bad grades. Because that's just the kind of person I am!"

As her emotional diatribe concluded, Riley half expected his spoiled baby sister to say, 'So there!' and stick out her tongue, too. Fortunately, she did not.

"Is the friend still in trouble?" Kate interjected gently, using her skills as a gifted psychologist to inject tranquility into the volatile situation.

"Not so much," Laurel eventually allowed, a little less sullenly.

"Tell me the friend isn't male," Sam said, frown deepening.

Now that was like pouring gasoline on a fire, Riley thought. Thanks, Dad. Out of the corner of his eye he saw Amanda cast Laurel a sympathetic look. He followed with a warning look of his own. Laurel knew better than to talk back to their father.

"You've never liked any of my boyfriends!" Laurel returned furiously.

"Maybe because your boyfriends aren't on par with you," Sam agreed, not the least bit mollified.

Now that sounded like what the Witherspoons had to say about him, Riley thought.

Kate rolled her eyes as she stepped between father and daughter. "All right. Enough, both of you."

"Well, tell Daddy to stop being so mean to all my boyfriends," Laurel insisted.

"Well, start bringing home some that are worthy of you," Sam replied in the same contentious tone.

"How about we all just calm down and appreciate the fact that it's the Christmas season and we are all happy and healthy and here in Laramie together," Riley suggested.

Kate nodded in agreement. She turned back to Riley and Amanda in obvious relief. "Speaking of Christmas," Kate said, "the hospital has a favor to ask of you. It seems the person we had lined up to play old Saint Nick at tomorrow afternoon's pediatric party—as well as the person who volunteered to play Mrs. Claus on Christmas Eve—both have the flu. So, your names came up. I've got the costumes in the car. How about it? Either of you game?"

"Be happy to," Riley said, relieved at the change of subject.

"Me, too," Amanda said.

"In return," Riley continued, "Amanda and I would like you to do a favor for us."

"Name it," Kate said.

"Come in. Spend some time with the three kids. And tell us what you think…."

"They're obviously grieving," Kate concluded half an hour later as she helped Riley and Amanda prepare hot chocolate in the kitchen. In the living room, Sam had set the tree up in the stand and secured it to the ceiling with heavy-duty twine that would keep it from tipping over. Micki and Laurel were stringing it with lights, while Amber and Chloe watched intently, and Cory slept in the portable bassinet nearby.

Amanda got out the mugs and lined them up on the counter. "Well, that's to be expected, isn't it?" she asked Kate. "Since they're separated from whoever it is who normally takes care of them?"

"And yet," Kate pointed out, "the children aren't frantic, the way you would expect them to be if they had been ripped from their caretaker's arms, only a few days ago."

Riley went back to stand beside Amanda, so close their shoulders were touching. "You think the children should be crying under the circumstances."

Kate nodded, her expression solemn. "Amber and Chloe are definitely old enough to suffer from separation anxiety, but instead of sobbing constantly for their mommy and daddy, and running to the window and looking out, they just look sad and sort of resigned."

"Like the abandonment has been going on for a while?" Riley presumed.

Kate added marshmallows to the mugs lined up on the counter. "It's as if they are used to attaching themselves to whatever kind adult is handy. That's not a good situation. It doesn't bode well for what's happened in the past, or what might happen in the future."

Amanda reached over and took Riley's hand. He squeezed it, hard, letting her know whatever happened, they were in this together, and they would move heaven and earth to protect and care for those kids. It wasn't a task Riley would have asked for, but it was one he had been given this Christmas season and took very seriously.

Amanda squeezed Riley's hand in return. She met his eyes, letting him know with a single glance they were of one mind on this, then moved to get a tin of Christmas cookies.

"I'm especially worried about Chloe," Amanda told Kate. "Amber babbles constantly but Chloe hasn't said a word since she was left with us."

"And yet you can tell Chloe understands everything that is being said because if you ask her to do something, she knows what you mean and she's cooperative in the extreme," Kate observed.

Which meant what? Riley wondered. That Chloe was afraid of being abandoned? Again? And was trying to do whatever she could to prevent it from happening? The worry over what the kids had been through, and might still be facing, brought an ache to Riley's heart. Resolve to his gut. "What can we do to help Chloe feel better and start talking again?" Riley asked, no longer surprised by the fierce protectiveness he felt for the children.

"For starters," Kate advised, "make life as normal for the children as possible. Have Chloe and Amber do things that might seem familiar to Chloe, like help put the ornaments on the tree, once Sam has the lights all the way on, or bake Christmas cookies. Take the kids to the pediatric party tomorrow and let them sit on Santa's lap. Who knows? If it is exciting enough, Chloe may forget her grief and her anxiety and start telling us what's on her mind. Or at least ask Santa for the help she wants..."

"Want to help me put the star on the tree?" Riley asked Chloe.

Chloe looked at Riley shyly. Her wildly curling light brown hair bobbing, she nodded her head ever so slightly and put her tiny hand on a point of the star, next to his. Riley boosted her a little higher in his arms, and hoisted her so she was within reach of the top of the tree. Amber sat on the sofa, sucking her first two fingers while Amanda climbed onto the step stool positioned on the other side of the tree and helped guide the star in Chloe's hand onto the top branch. Chloe grinned, her light blue eyes radiating both satisfaction and excitement, as the star settled into place.

"It's pretty, isn't it?" Amanda smiled.

Chloe smiled back and gave another little head bob, but still didn't say a word.

Amanda went back to the sofa and lifted Amber so she could see, too. The toddler's brown eyes widened. She began to babble incoherently. Occasionally, they heard "pretty" but could not comprehend anything else of what Amber was saying.

Riley stepped back and plugged in the lights. The tree glowed with colored lights and pretty velvet ribbons. On the lower branches were child-safe figures—elves, Santa and Mrs. Claus, reindeer, snowmen and gingerbread men. All were within reach of the two children, and could be taken off and then replaced on the lower branches of the tree as much as the children desired.

"Pretty," seventeen-month-old Amber said again.

Chloe remained silent, but spellbound.

"I hate to say it, kiddos, but it's time for bed," Amanda

said gently. "So what do you say? Shall we go upstairs, get into our jammies and read a Christmas story?"

She held out her hands. Chloe and Amber each took one.

Happier than he could recall being in a very long time, if not ever, Riley went along to help tuck them in. Twenty minutes later, all three children were sound asleep. Riley and Amanda were back downstairs. The rest of the evening stretched ahead, intimate and inviting.

Amanda smiled, admiring their handiwork from the doorway of the formal living room. "I'm glad we got the tree."

"Me, too," Riley agreed. It looked as perfect in front of the bay picture window as the fire did roaring in the grate, on the other side of the room.

Riley walked over to add another log to the fire. "I just worry we might be going overboard," Amanda said after a moment.

Riley shut and locked the glass doors that kept the children safely away from the flames. He regarded Amanda, noting how beautiful she looked with her dark blond hair casually upswept, and her thin-wale cranberry shirt untucked. "Overboard in what way?" he asked as she neared.

Amanda ran her open palm down the side of her form-fitting black slacks. She raked her teeth across the softness of her lower lip. Worry lit her pretty blue-green eyes. "When we tucked them in just now, it felt like they were ours."

To Riley, too. "And that's a bad thing?" he teased, knowing where she was going with this, even as he wished she wouldn't.

Amanda swallowed hard, abruptly looking as if she might cry. "What if Kevin finds out whom they really belong to and that person wants them back?" she asked, stubbornly voicing the thoughts he refused to think. "What if this was all a way to give the kids a happy Christmas their own parents couldn't manage, financially or otherwise?" Amanda paused, shook her head. "I've been down this road before, Riley," she continued in a low, choked voice. "I've taken children into my heart, made them my own and had them ripped away. It hurts more than you could ever imagine."

Riley was beginning to—it had only been a few days, and already he felt as much a daddy to the children as Amanda did their mother.

"And even if no one comes to claim them or we discover their parents have permanently abandoned them," she continued, "there's no guarantee that social services would approve our request to adopt them, given the tenuous state of our marriage."

She had a point there, Riley knew. He wrapped his arms around her and held her close. "I'm concerned too," he told her tenderly, pressing a kiss on the top of her head. "I promise you we'll do everything we can to protect them," he murmured, rubbing a hand reassuringly down her back.

Aware they were getting used to touching each other this way, to behaving very much like a couple, he gazed into her eyes. "And we'll start," Riley continued determinedly, "by getting some expert legal advice."

"Thanks for coming over this evening," Riley told his aunt, family law attorney Claire McCabe Taylor.

"No problem." Claire allowed Riley to take her coat and hang it up. She ran a hand through her short auburn hair, and carried her briefcase into the living room, where Amanda already had coffee and cookies waiting. "I was working late tonight anyway. What's up?" Claire focused her intelligent dark green eyes on the two of them.

They all sat down. Amanda and Riley on the sofa together, Claire in the club chair opposite them. Briefly, Riley explained the situation while Amanda poured them all a cup of coffee.

"Okay, let me get this straight," Claire said, pausing to sip her coffee and take a few notes on the legal pad in front of her. She pushed her reading glasses farther up on the bridge of her nose. "When someone left Riley the three children, you both thought it was a practical joke. And you continued to think that when you said your I Do's in the hospital hallway."

"Right," Riley said, regretting that more than he could say. He knew now he should have believed Amanda when she first denied having anything to do with the appearance of the children instead of goading her into a prank-marriage both of them were still trying to live down.

"Has anything happened to change that?" Claire tugged at the hem of her discreetly tailored suit jacket. "Have you taken out a license or taken steps to make your union a real one in any way?"

"Are you asking if we have consummated our marriage?" Riley said.

"Not to put too blunt a point on it, but yes," Claire replied matter-of-factly, all lawyer now, "I am."

Amanda and Riley both flushed self-consciously. "Does it make a difference?" Riley asked, hoping it didn't. When he made love to Amanda, and he was determined now that he would, he wanted it to be for all the right reasons. Not as a means to an end.

"It depends." Claire sat back against the chair cushions, looking more concerned about the legal facts of the situation than the emotional ramifications. "If you two are planning to stay married, sleeping together certainly validates the union in the eyes of the court."

And it would certainly bring them closer, Riley thought. Which was exactly what Amanda seemed to fear.

Amanda's eyes darkened unhappily. "Even if we don't have a license?" she asked, avoiding Riley's eyes.

"You still have time to get one." Claire gave them both a pointed look. "And I would advise it if you want to stay married, just because it will makes things simpler in the long run, to have all the loose ends tied up. But," Claire stipulated clearly, "*not* having a license won't invalidate your marriage, since you have said your vows in front of the hospital chaplain and a myriad of other witnesses, are currently living together under the same roof and at least have the opportunity—if not the will—to consummate your union."

Make it as unromantic as possible, why don't you, Riley thought disparagingly, even as he knew this was exactly why he had called the straight-talking Claire over there to meet with them, so they would know exactly where they stood from a legal viewpoint.

"What happens if—at some point—we decide we don't want to stay married after all?" Amanda asked in a low, choked voice. Her hands were trembling slightly as she lifted her coffee cup to her lips. "Can we legally end it without getting a divorce?"

Riley understood why Amanda didn't want a second divorce. Her first had been difficult enough. What she didn't yet realize was that he was beginning not to want an end to their hasty union, either, albeit for totally different reasons.... He wanted to see where this attraction of theirs would lead. Find out if it was as powerful and inevitable as it seemed.

Claire studied them, then said finally with a great deal of lawyerly care, "The fact you two are continuing to live together certainly makes it harder to ask the court for an annulment."

"But not impossible?" Amanda concluded, zeroing in on all Claire hadn't yet stated with obvious relief.

Claire made a seesaw motion with her hand. "You'd need to have grounds, be able to prove that you did not enter this marriage in good faith."

"For example?" Riley questioned, not sure what she meant.

"If you were not of sound mind because you were inebriated," Claire explained. "Or were fooling around, playing a joke on each other. Although personally, I wouldn't go into a court of law and tell a judge that, because the judge would likely think the two of you did not respect the sanctity of marriage, and that could get you into trouble with the court." Claire paused. "So what's going on here? *Are* you two planning to stay married or not?"

Amanda and Riley looked at each other. Were they?

Tension sizzled between them. Try as he might, Riley could not figure out what was in Amanda's heart or on her mind. She seemed as confused about the situation as he was. He knew she was drawn to him, that she wanted only the best for the children. She also did not want to be hurt and the deeper their involvement with each other became the more potential there was for heartache, if everything did not work out as flawlessly as Riley hoped.

"Would our being married make a difference if we moved for custody of the children, if it turns out they don't have a home or other family to take care of them?" Riley asked.

Claire didn't even hesitate. "The state of your marriage will make a big difference, either way," she advised firmly. "Being part of a union that is a joke, even temporarily, would make you both look unreliable to the court. On the other hand, if you have a solid, committed relationship, and the children are doing well under your care and want to be with you, that will go a long way in your favor, should you request to adopt them."

Riley walked his aunt Claire out to her car. When he returned, Amanda was in the kitchen. She had the can of powdered formula and the jug of sterile water out and was busy assembling all the bottles for the next day. She looked rumpled and tired, and worried to her bones.

Riley felt exactly the same way.

He walked over to lend a hand by assembling the plastic components that went inside the bottle and kept baby Cory from imbibing too much air during feedings. "About what Claire said," Riley started.

"Your aunt is right about one thing," Amanda returned, before he could even attempt to persuade her that they had done the right thing in letting their growing feelings for each other practically lead them into bed. "We never should have gotten married the way we did with both of us thinking—erroneously, as it turned out—that it was all a practical joke that had gotten way out of hand. Had I even suspected," Amanda continued grimly," that our behavior could hurt our chance at an annulment later on, I never would have said 'I do.'"

"But we did say 'I do,'" Riley reminded her.

"And now," Amanda worried out loud, "we're living together, which only adds to the public perception that our marriage is a real one."

Sometimes it felt like one, Riley thought. To Amanda, too, it would seem. Was that what was really bothering her?

Riley took her hands in his. They were soft and silky and very feminine. "Claire didn't say our situation was hopeless, Amanda."

A distant look came into her eyes as she shrugged off his assertion. "Of course not. She's much too tactful to tell us what a mess we've made of our lives with our reckless behavior."

Taking in the tension in Amanda's slender frame, it was all he could do not to take her in his arms and kiss her until she went limp with longing. Keeping his eyes locked on hers, he continued, "But you obviously think we have done just that. Don't you?"

Amanda extricated herself from his grip and went back to putting the nipples and lids on the baby bottles. "I think our playing house this way has unnecessarily complicated our situation, and may get in the way of our getting a simple annulment as opposed to a divorce."

She sounded more the dispassionate attorney than his aunt had, Riley noted, as he helped her put the assembled bottles into the fridge. "And if you have to get another divorce you're going to feel like a two-time loser," he guessed.

Amanda shut the door with more force than was required. As she swung back around, she favored him with an unappreciative smile. "Be blunt, why don't you?" she said sweetly.

Riley backed her up against the appliance, not above reminding her that she was still his wife, still the woman—the only woman—he wanted in his life. He flattened his arms on either side of her, caging her in with the length of his body. He let his gaze drift over her in the same dispassionate way she was regarding him. "Is that the only reason why you don't want a divorce from me?"

Amanda's eyes sparkled and her deliciously full lower lip slid out in a kissable pout. She lifted her hands in an indifferent gesture and let them rest against his chest, carefully keeping him at bay. "What other reason could there be?" she challenged.

Riley sifted his fingers through her hair, loving the silky feel of it. The way her body shuddered and softened toward his, even as temper flashed in her eyes. "The difference in connotation between the two ways to end a marriage, perhaps?" he answered as she slipped beneath his outstretched arms and danced away from him. "A divorce indicates the people were married and they tried to make it work and failed. Whereas an annulment," Riley specified brusquely, "seems to imply they were never *really* married at all."

Amanda gave Riley a deliberately provoking look. Smiled with all the resolve of a born-and-bred Texas belle. "Which is why I would prefer to have one," she stated resolutely, as they continued their breathless two-step around the kitchen until her back was to the wall and he was in front of her once again.

"But it's not really true, is it?" Riley retorted, just as determinedly. Excitement building inside him, he struggled to examine his own emotions. "Especially when you consider we have been taking care of the kids together, have been behaving as husband and wife, slept in the same bed, and have nearly made love—"

Pretty color flooded her cheeks. "One night, Riley! And we did not finish what we started!"

Riley let his glance rove slowly over Amanda from head to toe, taking in her long, lithe legs, slender waist and generous breasts. "Only because you called a halt."

Her glinting eyes were hot with temper, her chest rising and falling with each breath. He braced a hand on either side of her and held his ground, all the while cautioning himself not to move too fast. His voice dropped another intimate notch. "If it had been up to me we would have risked it all then, and we still would."

Exasperation hissed through her teeth. She kept her gaze level with his as she continued to study him. "You're impossible."

Riley grinned and reminded himself to be the gentleman he had been raised to be. "I'm realistic." He looked at her sternly. "Bottom line, we want to take care of these kids, Amanda. Our best shot at doing that is by staying married. And if we're going to stay married, sex is going to have to come into the equation somewhere, given the fact we are both young healthy adults who clearly have the hots for each other. Even if you're too stubborn to admit it."

Amanda raised her delicate brow in pointed disagreement. "Whether we desire each other is irrelevant. We don't love each other, Riley!"

"That doesn't stop a lot of married couples I know," he insisted, determined that someway—somehow—they would handle this without sacrificing the passion they'd discovered but had yet to fully experience.

Amanda gave him a censuring look.

"Okay, bad joke," he apologized calmly, resisting the urge to take her all the way into his arms and kiss her, only because he was afraid she would take any move at this juncture the wrong way.

"Thank you." Amanda paused. "Besides, we haven't discussed every way of keeping the kids, assuming they have no other home or family. You could adopt them as a single parent, Riley, and hire a nanny or a housekeeper."

Riley knew that but the option did not appeal to him. He wanted to continue this arrangement the way it had started, with he and Amanda caring for the children together. "Where would you fit into their lives if I did that?" he asked softly, knowing she had to be as aware as he what a good team they made.

A troubled look came into her eyes. "I could still be their friend or mother figure."

Now who was kidding themselves! "And you'd be satisfied with that?" he prodded gently. A silence fell that told him she would not. She was simply looking for a way out of their increasingly complicated connection to each other. Guilt washed over Riley, for ever putting her in such a convoluted situation.

"Anyway," Riley continued, doing his best to put a practical spin on their situation that Amanda could accept, "a housekeeper slash nanny is out. I've already been there, done that, the year after my mom died." He had never had a more miserable existence. Nor had the rest of his family. He would not inflict it on the three innocent babes sleeping upstairs.

"That's right," Amanda recalled thoughtfully. The tension in her slender shoulders eased once again. "You and your siblings had a whole series of nannies before your dad moved you all back to Laramie."

"Ten of 'em, in six months, and they were all awful." Riley pulled a ladder-back chair out from under the table and sank into it. Taking Amanda by the wrist, he guided her gently onto his lap. "If Kate hadn't agreed to step in and help out for a few weeks—as a favor to my grandparents—I don't know what we would have done."

Amanda settled more comfortably on his thighs and wreathed her arms about his neck. "Look, just because your dad hired some bad nannies doesn't mean that there aren't any good ones out there."

Riley supposed that was true. It wasn't the point.

"You really want to put these three kids through a trial-and-error process while we search for the perfect Mary Poppins after all they have already been through?" He swallowed hard around the sudden lump in his throat. "Do you really want to deny them your tender loving care?"

Amanda raked her teeth across her lower lip. It was obvious to Riley how much she already loved them. "I guess that doesn't make sense," she admitted finally.

"You're darn right it doesn't," Riley agreed without hesitation.

Worry lit her eyes. "But neither does pretending to have a real marriage just to be able to adopt the kids!"

Riley shrugged and, his mind already racing ahead, asked point-blank, "Who says we have to pretend?"

Chapter 8

"The fact we're not in love with each other?" Amanda guessed, citing the most obvious deterrent to their staying hitched that came to mind.

"But that doesn't mean we will never be in love," Riley argued in a low practical tone. "When Kate Marten moved in with my dad and my brothers and me, she and my dad didn't even like each other. In fact, the two of them irritated the heck out of each other."

Amanda tapped her chin in a parody of thoughtfulness. "I see that similarity."

Riley ignored her droll remark. His amber eyes took on a persuasive gleam. "Plus, Kate was engaged to be married to some other guy."

Amanda drew in a bolstering breath. She had feared all along the intimacy of their situation would be too much for them. She had counted on the kids to serve as distraction, chaperones and all-around energy sappers. Instead, their mutual love of the children was drawing them inexplicably closer. Which meant it was up to her to keep a cool head. Amanda favored Riley with an artificially bright smile. "Except I'm not engaged to someone else."

"Yes, that is one thing in our favor," Riley acknowledged in the same droll tone, before turning serious and shifting her closer, once again. "The point is," he continued gently, searching her eyes, "both Kate and my dad cared about all of us kids. And that shared concern brought them closer and closer, until there was no longer any denying the fact that the two of them had fallen in love with each other and wanted to spend their lives together, taking care of us."

Amanda swallowed around the sudden lump in her throat and tried not to think how handsome Riley looked in his sweater-vest, pin-striped button-down shirt, and faded jeans. "You think because it happened to them it could happen to us?" Despite her efforts to keep her emotional distance, she could feel herself being drawn in.

"Yes. But even if it doesn't happen in that same way, I think you and I and the kids have what it takes to make a happy family. Think about it, Amanda." Riley cupped a hand over her knee, the warmth of his palm spurring her heart to beat a little faster, even before he gave her a companionable squeeze. His eyes darkening with possessive intent, he shifted his grip from her knee to her hand and affably continued making his case. "You and I have always gotten each other and known what makes each other tick, otherwise we never could have kept our long-running practical jokefest going all through high school."

That was certainly true, Amanda thought, feeling the warmth and tenderness of his comforting presence all the way to her soul.

"We share a common concern and affection for Chloe, Amber and Cory. We both want to be their parents, if it turns out they are as 'genuinely orphaned' as they appear." Riley ticked off his reasons, one after another. "We share a love of medicine and healing others. We work well together as a parenting team. Plus—" he paused to let the weight of his words sink in "—we both decided—separately, but at the same time in our life—that we wanted to return to our roots and make our home in Laramie."

These were all good reasons. At one very naive time in her life, Amanda had imagined they were all reason enough to make a marriage last. A heart-wrenching loss of the husband who never really loved her, the kids she had come to call her own and a painful if matter-of-fact divorce had taught her otherwise. She wanted it all. She wanted to know, if she ever committed herself heart and soul to a man again that he would love and cherish her and stick with her through thick and thin. She did not want to live the rest of her life waiting for Riley to figure out, as her ex-husband had, that he really loved and wanted to be with someone else.

"And then of course," Riley teased in a low, risqué voice, "there is the sex. I think we've got real potential there, too."

There it was, the trademark orneriness, the inability to be serious for more than five minutes at a time, that she had been expecting from Riley all along. "I knew you were going to bring that up," Amanda declared hotly. She wished she didn't want him to kiss her again, but she did. And judging by the way he was looking at her, he wanted to kiss her again, too. She tried to get up off his lap.

He wouldn't let her. So she tried again. And this time he did let her go. "I know we haven't actually made love yet—at least not all the way," he said as he followed her to the adjacent laundry room, "but I think when we do it's going to be amazing."

Amanda flushed self-consciously despite herself. She opened the lid of the washer and began transferring wet baby clothes into the dryer. "Plus we get each other, Amanda. And we share the same sense of humor. Many an arranged marriage has started—and succeeded—on much less." Riley stood close enough to be able to see her face, but not so near he was in her way. His voice dropped a compelling notch. "Given the right conditions, the love between a man and woman can grow as easily and completely as the love we already feel for the kids."

Wordlessly, Amanda shut the dryer door and switched it on.

She took a load of pastel bath towels and receiving blankets and stuffed them into the well of the washer.

Riley picked up the pink-and-white bottle of laundry detergent specially formulated for young children's tender skin and removed the cap. "I know there are no guarantees, Amanda," he said as he filled the measuring cup to the line and handed her that, too. "There never are when it comes to relationships." He paused as she poured in liquid detergent, handed the lid back to him and added fabric softener to the dispenser. "But don't you think we at least deserve a real chance at making this work—in every way—instead of arbitrarily setting limits on our feelings that may not hold in any case?"

Amanda set the dials and hit the on button, then turned, resting a slender hip against the machine. She folded her arms in front of her, doing her best to hide the hurt and disappointment she felt, at having been proposed to in such an unemotional way. "I think you missed your calling," Amanda returned dryly, wishing fervently that Riley could love her the way she was beginning to love him, with all her heart and soul. But he didn't and she needed to force herself to remember that before she found herself becoming a "convenience" in lieu of a "wife" once again. "You should have been a salesman," she told him admirably, pretending a joking ease she couldn't begin to really feel. "Because with a silver tongue like that you could probably sell anything."

Riley ignored her attempt at levity. He let his glance rove her face before returning with laser accuracy to her eyes. "Does that mean you agree?"

"It means..." Amanda drew a deep breath and forced herself to hold her ground, even as she protected her heart, and the hearts of the three children involved. "I am seriously confused." *And so seriously in lust with you, Riley McCabe, that I can't stand it.*

Something flashed in Riley's eyes. He began to relax. "You don't have to decide anything now," he reassured her softly, lounging back against the opposite wall. He slid his hands in the pockets of his jeans and continued talking to her as casually as if they were discussing the weather. "All you have to do is leave yourself open to the possibility that this current conundrum of ours might actually turn out to be the best thing that ever happened to us."

And what if it was just another road to heartache and misery? Amanda wondered.

Riley straightened, a confidence-inspiring smile on his face. "We can do this, Amanda," he told her, abruptly leaving all traces of the reckless side of him behind. "We can make our marriage a real one in every way if we remove the self-imposed limits and just allow ourselves and our imaginations free rein."

Figuring he had pushed as hard as he dared for one night, Riley said good-night to Amanda and let her go on to bed—alone—in the guest room while he stayed up late with Cory, giving the infant his last bottle of the night and rocking him back to sleep, before turning in himself at midnight.

He figured he almost had Amanda agreeing with him, but by morning he could see her guard was up once again. Which meant he was going to have to use every weapon in his romantic arsenal to get her to open up her heart to him as readily as she had already done with the three kids. Riley figured, with a little help from family and friends, he could do it. Because now that he knew what he wanted—a relationship with Amanda every bit as strong and enduring and unexpected as Kate and Sam's—failure simply was not an option.

In the meantime, he and Amanda had the task of playing Santa and Mrs. Claus for the kids in the hospital. Riley was going to be up first. He knew it was a long shot, but he hoped the Christmas ritual would spark something in Chloe, help her start talking again. He wanted the little girl to feel secure enough to speak again. Riley knew Amanda harbored the same hope. Hence, their spirits were high as Riley, Amanda and the three kids met up with Micki and Laurel at the pediatric ward the next afternoon, in advance of the big event. Instead of their usual pink-and-white volunteer aprons and white shirts, both young women were dressed like Santa's elves.

Laurel winked at Riley and swiftly gave him the info he needed. "Santa is going to be joining us in the pediatric playroom for our staff and patient Christmas party at two this afternoon."

Riley glanced at his watch. That gave him approximately thirty minutes to get dressed. "I'll be in my office, taking care of something," he said.

Micki stepped into his path. "Before you leave, you have to write a letter to Santa," she interjected with a smile.

Riley took the holly-green paper and envelope they handed him. He looked over at Amanda. She looked pretty in a trim black wool skirt, white turtleneck and dark green Christmas cardigan, embroidered with gaily wrapped gifts, decorated trees and candy canes. Opaque black tights made the most of her slender, showgirl legs. "You, too," he said.

Amanda smiled and ran a hand through her straight and silky hair, pushing it away from her slender shoulders. "I already mailed my letter to Santa weeks ago," she said with a mysterious grin.

Noting the pinkness of her cheeks, Riley wondered what she had asked Santa to bring her. But figuring she wasn't about to tell him, at least not here and now, he held the paper so only he could see and quickly filled in his yuletide request. Finished, he slid the paper into the envelope and sealed it. "Put it in the mailbox." Laurel pointed to the box on the post next to the Santa's Workshop in the corner.

Riley walked over and slid it into the slot.

Still wondering what was in Amanda's letter to Santa, he kissed the kids goodbye and squeezed Amanda's shoulders. Ignoring the mixture of caution and desire in her eyes that had been there ever since they got up that morning, he brushed his lips against her temple, too, then headed to the parking garage to pick up the garment bag containing the borrowed Santa suit and went on up to his new office space.

It was just as he had left it the other day, with diplomas half-hung, and boxes of belongings scattered among the utilitarian office furniture the hospital had supplied.

Feeling a little blue that chief of staff Jackson McCabe hadn't yet seen fit to reinstate him and Amanda, Riley switched on the office intercom. "Silver Bells" filled the air as he stripped down to his boxers and T-shirt and pulled the pants up over his legs. The first thing he noticed was that the pants were way too short, the second was that the waist was about a foot and a half too large for his belly. A fact that would have been no problem, had the wide black belt been notched to fit him, but it was cut to wear with the pants.

Riley searched through the rest of the costume. There was no stuffing for his waist. He picked up the phone and asked the hospital operator to page Amanda Witherspoon. Seconds later, her voice came on the line. "Amanda speaking."

Warming at the sound of her sweet, melodious voice, Riley replied, "Hello, Amanda. This is your husband speaking."

A slight pause in which she seemed to be thinking a moment. "What's up?" she asked finally.

"If you're not that busy, could you bring me a pillow?"

She laughed, a soft silky sound. "Is this a trick question?"

Riley sighed and took another look at the pants hem hovering just below his calves. Good thing those boots were nearly knee-high. Or should have been knee-high if he weren't so tall. "The only trick involved is how I'm going to keep these pants up without something to hold them up. And since I can't exactly run around the hospital half-dressed without spoiling the surprise for the kiddos…"

"I'll be right there." Click.

Suddenly feeling a little happier and a lot more optimistic, Riley sat down to wait. To his pleasure, Amanda wasn't long in getting there. She breezed in, two pillows in hand. "Just in case we need to make you a little rounder than one pillow will allow," she said.

"I thought these suits came with special padding," Riley said.

Her expression softening compassionately, she tossed him one fluffy white pillow. Riley caught it one-handed. "Maybe whoever wore it last didn't need the extra, um, girth," she speculated cheerfully.

"Good point." Glad he had her help, Riley slid the padding into the front of his pants. The pillow kept going until it hit the seam at the base of the zipper.

"I think you're going to need to put the jacket on before we can secure it, since the belt goes over the jacket." Her expression as serious as the task of creating a viable St. Nick for the kids, Amanda handed Riley the coat. As Riley released his grip on the waistband of his pants and dutifully slipped the jacket on, his pants and the pillow both fell down to his knees. Amanda's soft laughter filled the air.

Had they been anywhere else, had Riley been able to take advantage of his unexpected disrobing and make love to her then and there, or at the very least get in a few passionate kisses, he wouldn't have minded the situation one bit. As it was, he just felt ridiculous. "Oh, man, this is just not going to work," Riley said, embarrassed. Though he didn't necessarily mind being indisposed around Amanda, being so around the kids and their parents and staff and having a wardrobe malfunction was another matter indeed.

"Sure it will, we just have to figure it out," Amanda said confidently. Her lips curving determinedly, she searched through the garment bag and pulled out two suspenders. "For starters, these will help," she said, holding the black elastic aloft.

Riley looked skeptical. "It will keep my pants up, but it won't keep the pillows in place."

Amanda grinned. "Give me a chance to work some magic here."

While Riley held his pants at waist height, Amanda stepped behind him and snapped on the suspenders, front and back, then helped adjust them so they fit over his shoulders. She slid two pillows in front of him. They filled in the space created by the extra fabric at Riley's waist. Riley looked and felt ridiculous. "I look about nine months pregnant," he quipped, trying not to think about what her nearness was doing to him. "Which wouldn't be bad if I were a woman and expecting, but..."

Amanda studied him while he thought about kissing her again. "Maybe we should put one in front and one in back," she said. No sooner had she tried it, than she clapped her hand over her mouth and burst into giggles. "Um, no."

"A little too roly-poly?" Riley asked, wondering even as he spoke how it was possible for her to get prettier every single time he saw her. Amanda had been a real looker when she was a teenager, but that was nothing compared to how gorgeous she was now.

She shook her head, explaining merrily, "A backside that's just too oddly shaped."

"Well, we wouldn't want that," Riley drawled.

"Let's try this," she said, and put the pillows side by side on his chest, instead of one on top of each other. The fluffy white cushions wrapped around his sides, but kept the girth more barrel shaped and hence like Santa.

"Now if we can just figure out how to keep the pillows from slipping around," Riley lamented.

Amanda snapped her fingers. "We'll use surgical tape!" She went into the supply cabinet in one of the exam rooms, and returned to the private office where Riley was dressing.

Now they were talking, Riley thought. "So what did you ask Santa for Christmas?" he asked Amanda curiously as she secured the pillows around his midriff. He had to admit he liked it when she put her hands on him like this and acted all wifely. Maybe because such moments gave him a glimpse of what it would be like to really be married to her, heart and soul.

She slanted him a flirtatious look. "If I tell you, it won't come true."

"Sure it will," Riley declared with a wink, "since I'm Santa."

She straightened, the silk of her honey-colored hair brushing against his chin, and flashed him a lofty smile. "Not the real one."

Riley liked matching wits with Amanda. It made him feel as if he was in one of those old Tracy-Hepburn movies Kate and his dad liked to watch on TV. "There is no real Santa," he said.

"Sure about that?" Amanda taunted with exaggerated certainty. She moved away from him, offering him a great view of her stunning backside as she put the tape and scissors away.

Riley followed her lazily. He put his hands on her shoulders and brushing the silky curtain of hair aside, gave in to temptation and pressed a fleeting kiss on the nape of her neck. Her skin was silky and warm. "I can give you whatever you want, you know."

She quivered at his questing touch and turned to face him. Splaying both hands across his chest to hold him at bay, she tilted her head at him and gave him one of those imperious looks that made him want to haul her against him and kiss her until all pretense between them faded and she went weak in the knees. She shook her head at him in an indifferent gesture. "I don't think that would be prudent, do you?"

Riley wrapped both arms about her waist, regretting the layers of cotton that kept them from really touching, middle to middle. "Since when have you ever wanted to be prudent, Mrs. McCabe?"

"Since forever," Amanda said.

Riley grinned. The one thing Amanda was not was a good fibber. Smiling his satisfaction, he looked down at her tenderly, amazed at how much he liked seeing her like this, eyes sparkling feistily, her deliciously full lower lip sliding out in a kissable pout. "Then how about you give me what I want?"

Her eyes shimmering with an unmistakably aroused light, she regarded him in a deliberately provoking manner. "And what would that be, Doctor McCabe?"

You, Riley thought. "This." Riley planted one hand at the base of her spine, the other at her nape. Hauling her as close as the pillows would allow, he dipped his head and, ignoring her soft gasp of surprise, delivered a searing kiss. To his deep contentment, Amanda did not even try to draw away, and he let all he wanted come through in another long, deep kiss.

With an immediacy that stunned him, she confirmed her acquiescence with a soft sigh. Her fragrance waltzed through his system, inundating him with the sweetness of desire. He shuddered as her tongue swept into his mouth, hotly and voraciously, and she threaded her fingers through his hair, bringing his mouth closer still. Her passionate response was all the encouragement he needed. With a low groan, Riley twined his tongue with hers, drinking in the sweet peppermint taste of her lips, and the sweetly feminine fragrance of her skin and hair, making no effort at all to disguise how much he wanted and needed her, and was beginning to realize now that he always would. He wanted to be a husband to her in every way. Starting now. Today.

She groaned as his hands moved to her breasts. "Riley..."

"That's it." He cupped the soft weight in his hands, felt his own body—and hers—tauten in response. He sensed the need pouring out of her, mingling with the desire and the temper. "Say my name," he whispered huskily against her throat. Unable to help himself, he delivered another stolen kiss, this one sweeter, more drawn out than the last. His need to be close to her as overwhelming as it was inevitable, he tipped her head up to allow him greater access, and kissed her long and hard and deep. Soft and slow.

"This is not what you were brought here to do this afternoon," Amanda protested, even as she kissed him back, more tenderly and rapaciously than before.

Eager to please her, knowing it couldn't be done here, now, Riley reluctantly broke off the kiss and lifted his head. "You're right," he told her, still struggling between his desire to protect her and his desire to make mad, passionate love to her, damn the consequences to their lives, their careers. Desire thundering through him in waves, he stepped back, very much aware what the self-imposed restraint was costing him. "We shouldn't start something we can't finish here and now."

Amanda pressed a hand to lips that were wet and swollen from their kisses. Her eyes glowed with a soft, ardent gleam, even as sanity returned and she hitched in a short, worried breath. "Or ever, if we're going to be bluntly honest."

Riley wasn't that gallant. He sensed, in the end, she wouldn't be, either, as a passion like this was too strong, too powerful, to resist. But for the moment, he realized reluctantly, there were other yuletide promises to keep and wishes to fulfill. So they'd just have to concentrate on that.

Amanda was not surprised the kids in the pediatric ward welcomed "Santa" with shouts of glee and excited smiles. The holiday was always a particularly emotional time for their young patients. Being in the hospital just made it more special. And, gold-rimmed Santa glasses disguising his lively amber eyes, Riley did not disappoint.

"Ho, ho, ho, and what would you like from Santa this year, little boy?" he asked the six-year-old patient, who was still recovering from an automobile accident.

"A pony," the child said enthusiastically.

Amanda watched his parents wince.

"'Cause I want to ride it," the little boy continued, settling as comfortably on Riley's lap as the plaster casts on his arm and his leg would allow.

Riley removed the pipe from the corner of his mouth, then asked in a low, thoughtful voice, "Do you have a barn for the pony to sleep in and a grassy pasture where the pony can eat?"

The little boy shook his head.

Riley stroked his beard. "Hmm. Well," he allowed in a gravelly voice that could very well have belonged to the legendary St. Nick, "a real live pony needs both to be happy. But a stuffed toy pony—now that can stay in your room and even sleep in your bed at night. Would you like that?"

"But I want to ride it!" the little boy pouted.

Riley tilted his head, considering. "Santa's workshop has toy riding ponies," he allowed finally. "The kind that you rock back and forth on. Is that what you mean?"

The little boy nodded. His parents relaxed into smiles. This, apparently, was something they could handle, giftwise.

"Well, I'll talk to the elves and see what I can do," Riley said. "In the meantime, you keep on taking your medicine, and do what the nurses and doctors and your folks tell you to do, okay?"

The little boy nodded. He wrapped his uninjured arm about Riley's neck as the photographer took their picture. "I love you, Santa," the child whispered.

Riley smiled as he patted the child's thin shoulders. "Love you, too, son."

Next up was an appendectomy patient, still sore from surgery, who wanted a dollhouse. Then a four-year-old recovering from a tonsillectomy, and an eight-year-old who was undergoing chemotherapy. Finally, it was Cory, Amber and Chloe's turn.

Cory went first. As soon as the infant looked up at Riley's beard, he burst into tears. "Santa" was unable to comfort him, even when he whispered in the infant's ear. Perhaps spooked by her baby brother's reaction, Amber cried, too, and squirmed to get off Riley's lap the moment she was set down. Finally, it was Chloe's turn. Suspicious and uncooperative, she sat with her arms folded in front of her and refused to acknowledge "Santa's" presence, even when Amanda, Micki, Laurel and some of the other "helper elves" coaxed her to do so.

Amanda could tell Riley was bummed about it, and remained so through the rest of the day. By the time they had put the kids to bed for the night, she'd had enough of his pensive mood. It was so unlike him.

"How much longer are you going to continue worrying about what happened today?" she asked as the two of them met up in the family room to clean up the play area. She knew the rest of the day had been difficult for all of them. The kids had wanted Amanda, not Riley, and remained out of sorts all the way to bedtime. It hadn't mattered how Riley had tried. He had remained a persona non grata to the kids, who seemed to resent the fact he hadn't been there to comfort them, along with Amanda, when they had needed him.

"I'm not worrying," Riley declared as he picked up colorful interlocking blocks and tossed them into the plastic carrying case.

Amanda rolled her eyes as she bent over to pick up the storybooks, lent to them by the extended McCabe family. "Ha!"

she said as she organized them and put them into a neat stack on one of the end tables.

Riley scowled as he got down on all fours to retrieve the blocks sticking out from beneath the bottom of the sofa. "Well, maybe I am feeling a little disappointed the kids did not sense they could trust me, costume or no."

And therefore, Amanda guessed, been happy to sit on Santa's lap and confide all. Instead, unlike the rest of the children in the pediatric ward who had greeted Riley's Santa Claus enthusiastically, all three of the children in Riley's care had given him their own version of the heave-ho. "That booming baritone you were using and your costume probably just scared them." She slipped off her black suede flats and wiggled her stocking-clad feet in the carpet. "After all, you were wearing two pillows, a beard, wig and glasses!"

Riley took a moment to admire the view of her legs from down there, before shifting his gaze to his knees. "Kids have a sixth sense about who they can trust and who they can't. That's obviously why they naturally go to you more than me," he ventured with a disgruntled sigh.

Amanda couldn't argue that; the parenting, post-Santa, had been a little one-sided. Not because Riley hadn't been available, but because for whatever reason the three kids had wanted her. And only her, for the rest of the day. To an embarrassing degree. Furthermore, she was as frustrated by the current situation as he was. Doing her best to soothe his wounded feelings and ease the concerned look in his eyes, Amanda said, "They were probably still just a little freaked out by seeing Santa."

Riley winced as he tossed a toy school bus into the storage bin. "I think you just made my case for me."

"Maybe they had never seen a fat man in a hat and beard before," she theorized helpfully, noting Riley did not feel as confident caring for the three children as prior circumstances dictated.

"And maybe," Riley retorted sharply, then softened the effect of his words with a commiserating smile, "all kids need a mother's love more than a father's, especially at times when they are upset or sad or scared, or simply not feeling all that secure."

Able to see he was mentally kicking himself for what he perceived as his failure on the parenting front, Amanda faced him. "Are we talking about Amber, Chloe and Cory?" she asked gently, knowing there had to be more here than what was visible on the surface. "Or you and your siblings after your mom died?"

Riley lifted his shoulders in an indifferent shrug. A brooding look was on his face. "Dad tried, but he just wasn't much comfort," he allowed brusquely.

Amanda could see Riley was worried about following in his father's footsteps. Worried about parenting the kids on his own. Worried about somehow not being up to the task if the kids remained in his care. But she didn't want to be his wife—or their mother—just for that reason. And she feared that was where this assessment on his part was leading. "That was your father's fault, not yours," she stated firmly.

"Whereas Kate—a stranger—was a huge help to us," Riley continued with a sigh.

No surprise there, Amanda thought compassionately as she trod closer. She knew what it was to doubt yourself, feel you had failed, or worse, impulsively gotten yourself into a situation you should have avoided at all costs. It wasn't fun. "Kate's a psychologist and a grief counselor, Riley. And a very talented one at that," she soothed with a sympathetic smile. "Of course she could help you more than your dad. Kate wasn't grieving your mother. You and your sibs and your dad were. And as for the kids, they wouldn't have responded to me any better had I been the one wearing the Santa suit today."

Riley lifted a skeptical brow. "Care to put that to the test when you wear the Mrs. Santa suit on Christmas Eve?" he challenged mildly, a hint of the old sparkle coming back into his eyes.

Not if it proved the theory he was currently espousing, Amanda thought. Hands spread wide, she inched even closer, and looked at him with exasperation. "It's not a fair comparison, Riley. That will be three days from now. The children will have a lot more time with us, between now and then, than you have had with them thus far and that will in turn give me an unfair advantage over you."

"Meaning what?" Riley scoffed, deliberately weighing every word she said. He took her hand lightly in his. "That you think they'll not just warm to your Mrs. Claus the way they didn't warm to my Santa, but will probably even tell you what they want for Christmas? Not that Cory can do anything but coo yet or we're likely to understand Amber's babbling, mind you."

"But it's the attempt that counts." Amanda guessed where he expected things to go. "Especially if Chloe were to pick that opportunity to speak for the first time."

Riley's fingers tightened over hers. "Right," he said.

Reveling in the warmth of his tender touch, Amanda offered playfully, "And if they want to run in the other direction when they see me in my costume? What then, Riley McCabe?"

He gave her the lazy once-over. "Then I owe you anything you want for Christmas, Mrs. McCabe."

Amanda's heart rate kicked up another notch. She liked the sexy turn the conversation was taking almost as much as the sound of his low, husky voice. "And if they don't, what then?" Amanda asked.

"Then *you* owe *me* anything *I* want," Riley murmured, his eyes glowing with a determined sensual light as he took her all the way into his arms.

"And what would that be?" Amanda asked, splaying both hands across his chest.

"Guess," Riley lowered his mouth to hers. His lips were warm and firm against hers, sweetly coaxing, loving. And in that moment, everything stopped. The world narrowed to just the two of them. Amanda had waited a lifetime to be kissed and held like this. She had waited a lifetime to feel like this, she thought, as she wreathed her arms about his neck and threaded her fingers through his hair. And she'd be damned if she could stop it. She kissed him back thoroughly, loving the way his tongue stroked hers, once and then again...and again.

Amanda had never been a particularly sexual person, but Riley McCabe made her feel white-hot. All woman. As in need of the emotional comfort and physical reassurance he offered as she was eager to give it, in return. She moaned low in her throat and drew closer yet, swearing as her knees gave way as swiftly as her will to resist. Their coming together like this had been inevitable. She had known that from the very first, which was why she had fought so hard against it. Because she had known making love with Riley would change her forever. As he continued kissing her persuasively that no longer seemed like such a bad thing.

The next thing Amanda knew, Riley was drawing her over to the large sectional sofa. He shut off the lights in the room, stripped off his clothes in the moonlight filtering in through the drapes, then wordlessly helped her out of hers. Another shiver of excitement swept through her. "Beautiful, so beautiful," he breathed as he took her in his arms again and kissed her as if he were in love with her and would be for all time. Aware she had never felt desire like this before, fearful she never would again, she clung to him, returning his caresses eagerly. He guided her down to the sofa, turned her onto her side, facing him and stretched out beside her. Amanda's heart raced as his mouth moved on hers in a kiss that was shattering in its possessive sensuality. His manhood pressed against her inner thighs, hot and hard, as he molded her breasts with his hands, circling the aching crowns, teasing the nipples into tight buds of awareness. Coupled with his wanting, it was enough to drive her toward abandon. She arched against him, murmuring her need low in the back of her throat. "Riley—"

He chuckled softly, pressing his lips against her throat in a series of hot, wet kisses. "We're getting there in due time, I promise." He kissed her again, then his mouth was moving to her ear, the nape of her neck, sending her into a frenzy of wanting once again. Engaging every sense he made his way slowly down her body, patiently exploring, fulfilling every wild and wanton fantasy she had ever had. Shifting from passion to tenderness and back again, until there was only the driving need, only this moment in time, the throbbing of his body and hers. Amanda hitched in a breath, aware he was making her feel so warm and safe, even as she was trembling and falling apart.... "Riley, oh Riley," she whispered as he filled her heart and sent her soaring.

For Riley, their coupling had been years in the making. Aware she had never looked more radiant than she did at that moment, color blushing her cheeks, dark golden hair tumbling over her bare shoulders, he tunneled his hands through the smooth strands and moved upward to once again capture her soft, parted lips. Yielding to him with the sure sensuality of a woman who had secretly been his to take for years and years, she clasped his shoulders and trembled as he kissed her, their bodies taking up a primitive rhythm, until there was no doubting for either of them how much they needed each other, needed this. Not that Riley was really surprised. Amanda had been his obsession all four years of high school. And she had remained in his thoughts every year thereafter. He had told himself he could handle coming back to Laramie, knowing all the while that she was living here again, too.

Now, as she surrendered herself to him completely, the soft

whimpering sounds in the back of her throat a counterpoint to the lower, fiercer sounds in his, he realized that Amanda was precisely the reason why he had come back.

Not, as he had first thought, because he wanted to be taken seriously by those who had known him in his teens.

But because there had been something unfinished between them, he realized as he shifted her over onto her back, parted her knees and stroked the delicate insides of her thighs. Because she had haunted his dreams and made him feel alive.

Never more so than right now, Riley noted ardently as he moved to make her his in the most intimate way possible and she arched to receive him. Unable to delay their joining a second longer, he stretched out over her. He slid his hands beneath her, lifted her to him, driving deep, kissing her hotly all the while.

Until that moment, Riley hadn't recognized the difference between making love to someone, versus simply having sex. Now, he knew, and he realized, as both shattered and reached for the edge of oblivion, he would never go back again.

This was what he wanted. What he had always wanted. Amanda.

In his arms. In his bed. In his life.

"I can't believe we just did the one thing we're not supposed to do!" Amanda lamented as soon as they'd both had a chance to catch their breath. Extricating herself from Riley's embrace, she moved away from the sofa and began hurriedly getting dressed all over again.

Riley would have preferred to stay naked. Unfortunately, he knew she wouldn't be comfortable unless he were wearing something, too. She needed to relax if they were going to have the conversation they needed to about what had just happened between them, so he reluctantly pulled on his boxer briefs and slacks. He shrugged on his shirt and, leaving it open, walked over to stand beside her. He was stunned by the swift change in her mood—from passion to regret—and yet he wasn't. Deep down, he had known she wasn't as ready for this as he was. Yet he had seduced her because he had seen that as the quickest path to Amanda's heart.

Trying to inject some levity into the situation, to lighten the mood between them, Riley quipped, "What I can't believe is that it took us so long to do what we're not supposed to do." Especially since both of them had a long colorful history of doing just that.

Amanda threaded her fingers through her hair. Her palms trembled as she pushed her silky mane away from the flushed contours of her face. "You wanted this to happen all along," she accused, looking as near tears as he had ever seen her.

Riley knew he was supposed to feel thoroughly chastised, but he didn't. She might think they had just gone too far, too fast. He didn't. "You want the truth?"

"Of course!"

Her increasingly emotional state made it easier for him to remain calm. Riley shrugged. "Then yes," Riley admitted frankly, "I did."

Exasperation hissed through her teeth. She balled her fists at her sides and looked at him as if she didn't know whether to slug him or kiss him again. "Riley, we just had sex," she told him miserably. "We consummated our marriage!"

Riley knew it hadn't been simple sex. That left you physically drained but feeling nothing inside, not wanting or needing more. Knowing he had to touch her again, he took her stiff, resisting body into his arms, and sifted his fingers through her hair. "So what?"

"So it makes things a lot more complicated."

"I've got news for you, Amanda. Things were already complicated and they're going to get more so."

Amanda pushed herself away from him. "Not if I have anything to say about it," she remarked, giving him a killer look. "We made a mistake, Riley. It doesn't mean it has to happen again."

Riley grinned, and though he was very tempted to prove her a liar here and now, thought better of it as she picked up her shoes and stormed toward the stairs. "We'll see about that," he promised lazily.

Amanda swung around to face him. She planted both hands on her hips and glared at him, her eyes gleaming like polished stones. "What is that supposed to mean?" she demanded.

Riley sauntered closer, not stopping until they were nose to nose. He studied her closely. Her lips were still swollen from their kisses. Her full, luscious breasts were rising and falling with each rapid breath she took.

Her hair was tousled and sexy. She looked so ripe and ready to go back to bed, in fact, it was all he could do not to let his baser instincts get the better of him and seduce her all over again. "It means we both know now exactly what it is we've been missing." He paused to let the weight of his words sink in, then continued in a soft serious voice that promised them a future every bit as exciting and satisfying as their first bout of lovemaking had been. "I'm not going to forget," he told her frankly. "And neither, Amanda, are you."

Chapter 9

The phone rang at shortly after five the next morning. Riley groaned and reached for the receiver. "McCabe here," he muttered drowsily.

"Hi, Riley. This is Meg Lockhart-Carrigan. Sorry to wake you so early, but is Amanda there, by chance? I tried to get her at her apartment and there's no answer."

"Hold on." Riley looked up to see a sleepy Amanda coming out of the guest room across the hall. He motioned her in and passed the receiver over to Amanda.

She perched on the edge of his bed, still rubbing her eyes. Riley noted Amanda looked none the worse for their night spent apart, whereas he'd been so lonely for her he'd had a hard time falling asleep.

"Hello?" She listened intently.

Knowing it must be important if the director of nursing at Laramie Community Hospital was calling at this time of day, Riley switched on the bedside light. He surveyed her patiently as he lounged against the pillows, waiting for her to finish.

Amanda was clad in an old-fashioned pink-and-white-striped flannel gown that had a high collar and a row of buttons down the front. Tiny pleats brought the soft fabric close against her breasts. Beneath her sternum, the fabric was loose and flowing. She looked as pretty and sweetly satisfying as their lovemaking had been. It was all Riley could do not to take her in his arms and make her his all over again.

"No. It's not a problem," Amanda was saying as she brushed the hair from her face. "Does this mean…? Right. I understand." Disappointment permeated her low tone. "No. Of course. We'll talk about that later."

In the bassinet at the end of the bed, Riley heard Cory begin to stir. He went to get the drowsy infant. "What's up?"

Amanda picked up her brush and ran it through her hair on her way to the bathroom. "One of the nurses on the day shift for pediatrics has come down with food poisoning. Meg asked if I could come in at six-thirty for the patient status report, and work from seven to seven today. I said okay."

"Does this mean you're off administrative leave?" Riley asked as he gently laid Cory down on the bed. He unsnapped the legs of his sleeper and took off the damp diaper.

"Unfortunately, no." Amanda's tone went from matter-of-fact to tense and out of sorts in an instant. "Meg made it clear that this was just an emergency request. To be reinstated, you and I still have to get our situation straightened out and talk to her and Jackson McCabe."

Riley knew Amanda was as frustrated by their predicament as he was. And yet, she knew, as did he that there were no easy solutions, save making and keeping their marriage a real one. Something she was not yet inclined to commit to, although Riley still had hope this would happen, sooner rather than later, despite her generally cautious approach. "You're upset to still be on leave?"

Amanda shrugged and avoided his eyes as she reached for the uniform—since laundered—she had been wearing the day they had gotten the kids and been married. "The only time I haven't worked as a nurse, since earning my B.S.N., was when I was married to Fraser and taking care of his kids."

Riley put a clean diaper on Cory then discovered he needed a dry sleeper, and T-shirt, too. "Was that what you wanted?"

Amanda stepped into the bathroom to dress. Completely oblivious to the impact her slender curves were having on him, she spoke around the door that blocked her from his view. "I would have preferred to pull two or three twelve-hour shifts a week, and spend the rest of the time mothering, but Fraser didn't agree that was wise, so…I put my own ambition on hold. And stayed at home."

Riley finished dressing Cory, and noting the room had gotten a little chilly overnight, wrapped him in a blanket. "If we're able to adopt the kids, as we both hope, I think you should be able to work, too."

"Right now that's a pretty big *if,* Riley." Amanda accompanied Riley to the kitchen. She took a bottle out of the fridge, added a premeasured amount of water to the baby warmer, put the bottle in and switched it on. Finished, she turned to Riley and held out her arms for Cory. Burying her face in the infant's dark hair, she pressed a kiss to his crown, cuddled him close. "I know the circumstances don't really seem to warrant this opinion, but I still think whoever left the kids with us really loves them and is going to change his or her mind and want them back, once the holiday has come and gone."

Riley was afraid of that, too. It didn't mean he was going to hold back on anything while he waited to find out what December 26th would bring.

"All the note specifically asked you to do was see the kids had a merry Christmas. It did not ask you to keep them permanently."

"The part about them needing a daddy to love them seemed to imply that."

"I agree. And that's the way I want to read the situation, too, but we have to keep in mind—for all our sake's—that this may not be the case," Amanda cautioned.

Noting the bottle warmer had switched off, Riley removed the bottle and tested a drop of formula on his wrist. Finding it to be just right, he handed the bottle to Amanda. She sank into a chair, while he set about pouring Amanda some juice and making her a couple of slices of toast. "Well, regardless how this eventually turns out, or what happens, the kids still need all our love, Amanda. And the promise of a safe and loving future, no matter who they are with. Us, or other family."

Amanda sighed as she lovingly cuddled the infant in her arms. "I want that for them, too," she said wistfully. "But no matter what happens, I still need a job to go back to, and a life. So, in that sense," she admitted, her lips taking on a troubled slant, "maybe this request from Meg, along with the conditions she and Jackson McCabe have put upon either of us going back to work full-time at the hospital, is just the reality check we need."

"Tell me you need our help this morning and you'll be saving my life," Laurel said, three hours later, when Riley opened the front door to find his baby sister and Micki standing on the front stoop.

The evening before Riley couldn't have imagined he would be able to handle all three kids by himself all day, but the children seemed to have gotten over their pique with him. It was as if their post-Santa discontent had never happened.

Being able to parent as efficiently as he and Amanda did together, however, was another matter entirely. Chloe and Amber had been up since six, but thus far Riley had managed only breakfast for all three, clean diapers for the two younger sibs and an assist in the potty for Chloe. However, no one was crying and everyone's hands and face were clean, so Riley considered that a victory, albeit a small one. "You heard Amanda got called in to work?" he asked.

"No. I'm just trying to duck another lecture from Mom and Dad," Laurel said. Shivering in the brisk morning air, she rushed past into the house, Micki on her heels.

The friends smiled as Chloe and Amber padded out into the foyer, in their footed sleepers. The two little girls beamed up at the two pink-cheeked college coeds. It was almost as if, Riley thought, the four of them spoke a language he had yet to master—female!

"What are Kate and Dad lecturing you about?" Riley asked, shifting Cory to his other arm.

Laurel heaved a huge sigh. "The same thing." She threw up both hands, the moment she took off her coat, and looped it over the rack in the hall. "My poor grades. Dad still wants to find the person responsible for distracting me from my studies, like that's going to help anything. He's been quizzing Micki every chance he gets for info on my latest guy friends."

Micki made a face, looking as though she wanted to be anywhere but Laramie while all this was going on. Riley felt for the premed student. Always so serious about the direction she wanted her life to take, Micki never seemed to get in any trouble at all. He only wished he could say the same thing for his impetuous baby sis. Riley took Micki's coat and hung it up, too. "*Was* it a boyfriend's fault?" Riley asked Laurel, point-blank.

Laurel gasped in dismay. "Not you, too!"

Looking increasingly uncomfortable with the private, familial direction the conversation was heading, Micki took the hands of Amber and Chloe and slipped off into the family room, where an Educating Baby video was playing on the television. She sat down in the middle of the toys spread out over the rug and was soon joined by the other two.

Laurel held out her arms, and Riley handed Cory over. He walked into the kitchen to get another cup of coffee for himself. "Maybe if you told Kate and Dad the whole story, they would understand why you did what you did and ease up on you," he suggested.

Cuddling Cory nonstop, Laurel followed Riley into the sunlit kitchen. "Oh, they would not."

Riley paused to offer his guests coffee. When they both refused, he poured himself a cup and put the pot back on the warmer. "Are you still involved with this person or persons?" he continued his inquisition.

Suspicion tautened her features. "Why does that matter?" Laurel demanded, even more upset.

Riley prayed for the patience he didn't usually have for Laurel's self-generated predicaments. "I think it would be reassuring to the folks to know the crisis—whatever it was—that caused your grades to nosedive last semester is over. So—" Riley lifted the mug to his lips "—is it over?"

Laurel shrugged and held Cory all the closer. "Sort of."

Riley lifted a brow.

"Well, I hope so," Laurel amended hastily. "At least I *think* it is."

"That's not very comforting, Laurel."

"It's the best I can do at the moment," Laurel announced airily. "And anyway, it'll all work out eventually even if I *haven't* found a permanent solution to all the problems quite yet."

If only he had that kind of confidence about his own situation with Amanda and the kids, Riley thought.

"My doing poorly first semester is no reason for me to spend the spring in Laramie," Laurel continued haughtily.

Riley paused. "Mom and Dad want you to do that?" he asked in surprise.

"Yes," Laurel tossed her mane of dark hair, "and all because I won't promise them I won't help this friend of mine anymore!"

"Well, maybe they're right, maybe this friend of yours is a bad influence on you," Riley speculated bluntly.

Laurel's voice dropped to an accusing whisper. "And maybe my friend isn't any more of a bad influence on me than Amanda Witherspoon is on you, big brother!" Seeing she had struck a nerve, Laurel backed off, slightly. Then asked slyly, "How are things going between you and that new wife of yours, anyway?"

Was there no end to his family's nosiness? Riley wondered. "None of your business."

"Did you hear that Micki?" Laurel yelled into the adjacent room. "Riley won't tell me what's going on with Amanda. That means he's sweet on her."

Riley shook his head, sipped his coffee, said nothing.

"You are, aren't you…?" Laurel persisted, edging closer. Her dark blue eyes glittered with excitement that reminded Riley how young—and naive—Laurel still was. "Will you stop matchmaking for me and my wife and worry about your own problems?" he asked, making no effort to hide his exasperation.

"Why, when yours are so much more interesting?" Grinning, Laurel shifted Cory to her other shoulder. "So what did you get your wife for Christmas and when are the two of you going to give it up and start wearing wedding rings?"

Yet another question his family shouldn't be asking. Riley gave her a quelling look. "When we feel like it."

Pique turned the corners of her lips down. "At least tell me that you've gotten Amanda a Christmas present," Laurel said.

He said nothing.

"Riley." Disappointment echoed in Laurel's low voice. "How can you expect to woo Amanda into staying married to you if you don't even cover the basics?"

Because he was wooing Amanda in other more important ways by making love to her and making her his, Riley thought. Not that his approach seemed to be working all that well in retrospect. When Amanda had left for the hospital this morning, she had just about seemed "reality-checked" into leaving this tenuous life they were building for themselves. And all it had taken to make her feel that way was a little admittedly precipitous lovemaking with him and a few honest but direct words from the hospital's nursing supervisor. Being back at the work Amanda loved—even temporarily—would probably only cement those feelings.

Aware the college girls were waiting for his confession, Riley said drolly, "I hate to break it to you two hopeless romantics, but it will take more than a present to make Amanda want to stay married to me."

Micki joined them. She looked as curious now as Laurel. "Why do you say that?" she asked softly.

Riley had been thinking about that all morning. Amanda did not have a mercurial personality. She was at heart as steady, practical and efficient a woman as he had ever seen. Except where he was concerned. He alone seemed to have the ability to drive her crazy and push her to do things no one else could even hope to see. Part of that was the sizzling physical attraction between them they were just now acknowledging. The other half was the combination of suspicion and one-upmanship their "war of pranks" had built up over their teenage years. That four-year contest had lain an underlying foundation of distrust between them that Riley was having a hard time erasing.

"It's complicated," he muttered finally in frustration.

"Tell us!" Laurel practically shouted since she was so irritated with him.

"It's because of a lot of stuff that happened when we were kids," Riley explained finally. And because, bottom line, Amanda didn't quite trust him or her feelings for him, or his for her, any more than she trusted that the children might very well be permanent fixtures in their lives if no one came back to claim them. It was because Amanda kept waiting for the other shoe to fall, just as he sort of secretly was. It was because this all seemed a little too good to be true. It seemed like a TV movie about Christmas, rather than their own actual lives. Hell, it seemed like a dream from which he never wanted to awaken.

"So? Can't you go back and fix it?" Laurel persisted.

"Yeah," Micki put in, unable to see what the insurmountable problem was, either. "Why don't the two of you just agree to go back to the point where everything went terribly wrong and start over from there?"

The first thing Amanda noticed when she walked in the front door at seven that evening were the five Christmas stockings attached to the fireplace mantel. The second thing she noticed was Laurel and Micki sitting in the living room with all three children, reading bedtime stories, instead of Riley. She slipped off her coat and hung it on the rack next to the door.

"Riley's not here," Laurel volunteered.

"He had to go out for a while," Micki added.

"But there's something upstairs on your bed," Laurel continued.

"He said you should look at it right away," Micki agreed.

Amanda went in and kissed and hugged each of the three children. They all looked happy to see her, but content to be where they were, too.

"Long day, hmm?" Laurel said.

Amanda nodded. It wasn't the work that had worn her out so much as the endless questions about Riley and their marriage and what the future held for them. Smiling and pretending to shrug off such serious questions had taken its toll on her. The truth was, she wanted to know where they were headed, as well. Was Riley in the process of falling in love with her the way she was falling in love with him? Or was it more a convenience and casual sex sort of thing?

"Well, maybe what Riley left for you will cheer you up," Laurel stated slyly.

"Only one way to find out," Micki agreed.

Her interest definitely piqued, Amanda walked upstairs to the master bedroom. She had half expected the bunches of mistletoe hanging from every conceivable arch and doorway. The stuffed goat standing on the center of Riley's king-size bed was something else. The goat was surrounded by a circle of green plastic Easter grass and what looked like a half-eaten prom corsage. Hanging out of the goat's mouth, was an envelope.

Stymied and smiling in bemusement, Amanda picked up the envelope and took out the note inside. It was yellowed with age. And bore her juvenile handwriting, not his. It said,

> Okay, smarty-pants, you win. I can't compete with a goat. Nor do I want to. I've always had the hots for you and tonight I'll prove it to you. Meet me behind the high school bleachers—home side—for a make-out session you'll never forget. Your rival, XXXOOO, Amanda.

A line had been drawn through *Amanda* and *Riley* had been substituted. By his signature—and it was definitely his signature, she would recognize that handwriting anywhere—was a crudely drawn heart with an arrow through it, and a Christmas wreath.

"Very funny, Riley McCabe," Amanda whispered as she sat down on the bed and stroked the stuffed goat's whiskers. So they were back to playing pranks on each other again. The question was, what did *she* do next?

Riley stood, waiting in the cold. Beyond the Laramie high school stadium, he could see the Christmas lights blinking in the dark, starry night. Eight o'clock, he figured Amanda'd had enough time to get home, talk to the girls, see the goat and the note, change clothes and head this way. The cell phone in his pocket vibrated. He plucked it out and answered on the second ring. "This better be good news," he warned.

"Operation Win Her Heart is well under way," Laurel reported merrily.

A wave of relief flowed through him, followed swiftly by impatience. "Did Amanda say she is coming to meet me?"

Laurel scoffed. "Well, no. But she did say she was going out and might be kind of late, and asked us to stay until one of you showed up again."

Now, that sounded promising, Riley thought, eager to pick up where they had left off the evening before. Though not necessarily here, out in the cold. "Are the kids in bed?"

"Yes," Laurel replied smugly. "Sleeping soundly, I might add."

Riley looked out at the parking lot, which was empty save for his SUV. A mixture of disappointment and unease flowed through him. "You're sure Amanda didn't give you a clue what she was going to do?" She couldn't have taken the goat and the note the wrong way…could she? Oh, hell, what if those particular symbols of their tempestuous past had made her mad instead of eager to see him?

"I thought you had this all worked out," Laurel persisted.

Heaven knew Riley had tried. He heard rustling noises and muffled voices on the other end of the connection, as if Laurel was covering the mouthpiece with her hand, while she talked the situation over with her coadvisor to the lovelorn.

The transmission cleared up again. Laurel's petulant voice came through clear as a bell. "I knew you should have let us help you with whatever you set up for her, Riley! Who gives the woman they love a stuffed goat, anyway?"

Who indeed? Riley wondered. Had he been nuts to think he and Amanda could go back? Pick up where things had taken a really wrong turn and make them right again? So they'd have a foundation of trust beneath their relationship, instead of wariness and mutual double crosses.

"Whatever you do, when she does show up, don't try to be funny," Laurel advised in a low serious tone. "Because she didn't look like she wanted funny when she left here."

Great, Riley thought. Since funny had generally been his strong suit with the ladies.

"Be romantic," Micki chimed in, even more helpfully.

Footsteps sounded on the paved path behind him.

Riley turned, saw Amanda coming toward him. He was used to her being gorgeous, but she blew him away tonight in a red chenille turtleneck sweater, sheepskin-lined suede jacket, skintight jeans and bright blue-and-red Western boots. Her silky-straight hair was loose and flowing, framing a face that couldn't help but make angels sing. "Gotta go." He cut the connection, folded the phone in half, and put it back in the pocket of his leather bomber jacket.

"Talking to your little helpers?" Amanda teased, her long legs eating up the ground between them. She stopped just short of him.

Riley's pulse jumped as he took in the sophisticated cinnamon fragrance of her perfume.

"If you mean Micki and Laurel…"

She sent him a look that was at once skeptical and amused. A little too wary and cool. As if she had gone all the way back to high school, to the beginning of their relationship with each other, when she had to keep her guard up and her sense of humor at the ready at all times. He swore silently to himself.

Amanda tipped her head up and searched his eyes. "They seemed very eager for us to get together tonight."

Maybe because they knew how much was riding on this, Riley thought. As well as how very bad I am at telling this woman what I feel. "I guess you got my note," he said inanely at last, wondering where all his own devil-may-care-cool had gone.

"Actually," Amanda corrected as she came one step closer, "it was my note to you." The lights in the parking lot illuminated the area behind the bleachers. It was light enough for him to see the regret in her eyes, dark and deserted enough to still feel somewhat intimate and cozy. She paused, confusion reflected on her face. "You kept it all these years?"

He took her hand, and walked along the back of the bleachers, all the way to the other end. "It was in my high school yearbook."

"And it never occurred to you to take it out?" Amanda said, as they moved across the front, to the middle of the bleachers. "Why didn't you throw it away?"

"I don't know." Riley led her toward the top of the bleachers, where the view of the Christmas lights in town was best. "At first I was just so furious at being taken in by such an obvious ploy to humiliate me." He settled on the cold metal seat, his back to the home team press box.

Amanda settled close beside him. She propped both boots on the bench below them. "You thought I was serious."

Riley shrugged and took her leather-gloved hand in his. "I'd had a secret crush on you for what had seemed like forever." He figured he might as well confess. Maybe if he bared his soul to her, she would start believing she could trust him. He turned and gave her a sidelong glance. "It stoked my ego to think the same might have been true for you. Then, when I found out it wasn't..."

"Actually," Amanda interrupted, "it was." Her thigh brushed up against his as she turned toward him, too. "I had a secret crush on you, too, Riley." She shook her head, recalling. "Why else do you think I kept up the practical joke war?" Color came into her cheeks. "It was the only way I knew to get and keep your attention."

Her confession sent his spirits soaring. "You had that, all right," he told her. So much wasted time. So much they still didn't know and understand about each other. "So what made you write that note to me in the first place?" he asked her curiously.

"The goat." Amanda took his hands in hers. "And the fact we were both heading off to college and might never see each other again, since my family was also moving to California. I knew by fall break that 'going home' to me would mean hopping a flight to San Francisco, whereas you would still be driving home to Laramie to see your family."

Riley struggled to understand the episode that had caused such pain. "So you wanted one final chance to humiliate me in front of your friends?"

Amanda ducked her head, embarrassed. "I didn't think my friends knew about it. I wrote the note to you in secret! And told everybody I knew that I was done playing pranks on you. And I meant it. Unfortunately, my girlfriends didn't believe it for one red-hot minute and they followed me here to the stadium that night, camera in hand. I was about to run off to meet you behind the bleachers when they ambushed me, and figured out enough about what was going on to put two and two together. I was so embarrassed, and afraid I was the one about to make a total fool out of myself by throwing myself at you, that I saved face and let them think I had meant to stand you up all along." She swallowed hard, shook her head, and Riley could have sworn there were tears shimmering in her eyes as she said thickly, "It broke my heart to see you standing out here, all alone."

It had been no picnic for Riley, either. The hurt and humiliation of that one night had stayed with him for years. "Where were you?" he demanded gruffly.

Amanda raked her teeth across the seductive softness of her lower lip. "In the visitor stand press box."

He shook his head, recalling full well the disappointment, knowing he never wanted to experience it again. "You broke my heart that night, Amanda Witherspoon." Worse, she had the ability to do it again, even more thoroughly, if this marriage of theirs did not play out the way he wanted.

"I broke mine, too." She cuddled closer, tightening her grip on his hands. "It took me years to get over what I had done." She leaned forward persuasively. "I still feel bad about it."

Riley could see that was true. "So make it up to me," he said with an offhand shrug, letting the last of his anger and resentment drift away.

Amanda blinked. "How?"

Riley grinned and rolled lithely to his feet. "Like this." Ignoring her soft "oh" of protest, he took her by the hand and led her back down the bleachers, the way they had come.

"Riley—"

Ignoring the low note of warning in her voice, the one that said she did not do anything she did not damn well want to do, Riley guided Amanda willy-nilly down the stairs, behind the tall metal stands. They were breathless as they reached his destination. "You owe me a make-out session behind the bleachers."

Amanda laughed and kept her gaze level with this. "If we get caught…" she warned, excitement gleaming in her eyes.

Riley caught her around the waist, and backed her up against a tall support post. He positioned his body possessively close to hers. "We're married," he told her huskily, ready to be as mischievous as their mutual reputations warranted. He tilted his head to one side. "Who's going to get us into trouble for doing what married people do?"

"That," said a low voice behind them, "would be me."

Chapter 10

Riley turned to see his brother Kevin standing there in his sheriff's deputy uniform. The shortest of the five McCabe brothers, at five foot eleven, he was also the scrappiest of the brood. He had been in countless fights in high school, while standing up for others who were unable to defend themselves, until he learned to channel that energy and redirect his gallantry. Now, he was as law-and-order a guy as they came. And Riley respected his youngest brother immensely.

Which didn't mean that he was always glad to see Kev.

Riley let out a frustrated sigh, aware this wasn't the first time Kevin had interrupted Riley's interaction with Amanda. Back in the days when they had all been kids, Kevin had seemed to have an instinctive sense of when to come crashing onto the scene...just in time to ruin everything. "Anyone ever tell you that your timing is the absolute worst?" he demanded grouchily.

"Everyone," Kevin agreed with a smug grin on his boyishly handsome face. He tipped back the brim of his hat, to get a better look at their faces. "Although you *might* thank me for showing up since the school grounds security guard is about to make rounds through here in five minutes."

Riley blinked. Tucking an arm about Amanda's waist, he brought her in close to his side. He loved the way she felt, cuddled against him in the cold, facing down "the law." "The high school has security now?"

Kevin nodded, sober as ever. "The sheriff's department patrols through here, just to make sure kids aren't up to any mischief."

Riley sighed, disappointed he was not going to be able to continue with his juvenile but oh-so-sexy plans for the evening. "All right. We're leaving," he stated reluctantly.

Kevin held up a palm. "Not so fast. I tracked you down here for a reason. I wanted to give you a progress report on the attempts to identify the kids. We've gotten return e-mails from every Texas child welfare agency."

Riley and Amanda tensed simultaneously.

"And?" she asked in a low, breathless voice.

"Nothing." Kevin frowned, his disappointment apparent. "No one has been able to help."

Not sure whether he was happy or sad about that, Riley asked, "What next?"

"We're sending out similar bulletins with the kids' photos to the social services agency in all fifty states. We're asking the head offices to forward the e-mails to every child welfare office in their jurisdiction, in hopes someone will see it, recognize the kids and lead us to their family, or at least tell us what happened to put them in this situation."

Sounded like a plan, Riley thought, admiring his brother's tenacity and willingness to help. "And if that doesn't work?" he asked.

Kevin shrugged. "We could put the kids on one of the morning shows on TV that is broadcast nationally and ask the viewers for help. But that tends to bring out all the nutcases, as well as people who genuinely want to help, and it would force the Texas Department of Children and Families to get involved and take custody of the children before Christmas. Right now, things are operating under Laramie County jurisdiction, and since we are a rural operation with limited funding, we have more leeway in what we do than they do at the state level."

"In letting them stay with us, for instance," Amanda said softly.

"Right." Kevin mulled over their options. "The state might do that, too, but there is also the possibility that they might not. There's no way to tell until it happens, and then it's too late. Decisions are made. The kids might be split up, at least for a while."

"That would devastate them," Riley said.

Amanda wrapped her arm around Riley's waist, demonstrating how much a team she and he had become. "And us," she said.

Kevin studied them. Admiration and respect shone in his eyes. "You two have really fallen in love with those kids, haven't you?"

Riley looked into Amanda's face. They nodded at each other, then turned back to Kevin. "Let's just continue to take it slow," Riley said. "Until we see what happens after Christmas, if someone comes back to claim them or not, and go from there."

Kevin tugged the brim of his hat low across his brow once again. "The sheriff's department is okay with that, if you are."

"We are," Amanda and Riley said in unison.

Kevin grinned, all brotherly mischief once again. "I'd tell you to get back to what you were, ah, doing, but..."

Riley censured his baby brother with a look. "Enough said."

Grinning, Kevin shook his head. "You married folk." He chuckled as he strode away.

Riley and Amanda were left alone once again. "So much for best-laid plans," Riley grumbled. "Not that interference or delay has ever stopped me." He tilted his head and slanted his lips over hers.

Amanda had figured Riley would want to pick up where they'd left off. She wasn't prepared for his kiss's impact on her. The depth of their combined passion rippled through her in long, shimmering waves, until she wanted to touch him everywhere, kiss him everywhere and never stop. She shuddered at the heat and pressure of him where he surged against her, hip to hip. She reveled in the comfort of his arms around her. And as he continued to kiss and hold her, something inside her melted and the barriers around her heart, everything that had been keeping them apart, disappeared. As all the feelings they had for each other manifested themselves in kiss after steamy kiss, Amanda realized she was tired of protecting herself, tired of shutting herself off from even the possibility of love. She wanted to make love to Riley more than anything, and if it hadn't been for the sweep of a flashlight catching them in its bright yellow arc—and the discreet cough behind them—who knew what might have happened, she thought ruefully as she and Riley broke apart.

"Looks like we've been busted." Riley flashed the stadium security guard an apologetic grin. He took Amanda's elbow. "Guess we better head home," he drawled.

Amanda waggled her eyebrows at him. "Not necessarily," she whispered as they strolled off.

"This has to be one of life's great mysteries," Riley mused half an hour later as he and Amanda sat on the floor of her tiny apartment, surrounded by the presents they had bought for the three kids.

"What?" Trying not to be affected by the husky timbre of his voice—they'd never get done here tonight and they needed to get this yuletide task accomplished—Amanda selected a roll of pretty red-and-green wrapping paper.

He sighed his impatience. "Why the manufacturers don't make paper to fit the sizes of the toy boxes for kids."

Amanda lounged on the carpeted floor, admiring the way he looked in her apartment. So at home, so big and sexy… and male. "Do you want me to try and wrap that one?" she offered sympathetically.

The testy tone returned to his voice. "No, no. I've got it."

Wasn't that just like a man to never admit defeat or an inability to do something. "Okay," Amanda allowed with a shrug. "But if you need help…"

He scoffed at her. "Oh, ye of little faith."

His expression more determined than ever, Riley cut a length of paper and flattened it on the floor in front of him. Amanda had only to look at it to see they had a problem. She cleared her throat. "Um, you know, Riley…"

Riley held up a silencing palm, cutting her off in midsentence. "I realize I've got to turn the box on its side." He set it down in the middle of the paper. Pulled the paper up around the box. It didn't begin to reach.

She started to speak.

He shot her a look.

She restrained herself from offering more advice but couldn't quite suppress an amused smile. Riley turned the box yet another way. And another, and another. Seeing he couldn't cover it all in any direction, he frowned.

Amanda finished wrapping another package and put it on the pile of already wrapped presents. "Care for some help?"

He shook his head, frowned again. "I'll just save this piece for another box," he said.

He cut another length of paper. This one was way too long, but still fell short of covering the entire girth of the box, no matter how he tried to position it. As his engineering efforts failed, one after another, his easygoing smile fell victim to a heartfelt glower. "All right, come and help me," he said finally, with a grim expression and beleaguered sigh.

"Since you asked..." Amanda murmured, a little amused that a man who was so talented in almost every other aspect could let such a small thing annoy him so much. But then, she thought, maybe that was the point. Riley didn't have to struggle to be wonderful at other things; he just was.

Heart racing at the proximity of their bodies, she knelt beside him and showed him how to position the box so the sides were covered.

"That still leaves the ends," Riley said, as she secured the paper with strips of tape.

Amanda's knee nudged the hard musculature of his thigh as she moved around. Another thrill swept through her, threatening her concentration even more. She ignored the tightening of her nipples beneath her sweater and forced herself not to think about how wonderful and right those same legs felt draped over hers. They weren't here to get distracted by their desire for each other and make love, they were here to wrap presents for the kids, while they had the opportunity to "play Santa," unobserved.

"I know." It took every ounce of willpower she possessed to concentrate on the task at hand. And that meant not noticing the telltale fluttering in her tummy or how good he smelled, like a wintry mix of pine and spice. Never mind how the blinking lights on her Christmas tree and the soft lamplight in her apartment brought out the gold streaks in his thick brown hair.

"We're going to have to cover the ends separately with additional squares of wrapping paper, cut to fit," she continued to explain. "And slide the 'patches' up underneath the existing wrapping paper, like this, so it's not so obvious it's a piecemeal job."

Less clumsy, now that they had a workable plan, Riley helped her secure the paper on one end, then the other. They set it upright, labeled it for Chloe, put a big red bow next to the tag and set it next to the roadster-tricycle they had purchased already put together.

"Maybe you should do all the big packages from now on," Riley said, his voice relaxing into a deeper baritone.

"Why don't we do them together?" Amanda asked. "It's easier."

"Okay." He smiled at her with lazy familiarity.

"Especially when we make such a good team," Amanda continued before she could censor herself.

The minute the words were out, a self-conscious blush moved from her neck to her cheeks. "Careful now," he teased her lightly, no doubt about what was on his mind, either. "Those are kissing words."

She grinned as he leaned over and lightly touched his lips to hers. "Work first," she commanded, although deep down she yearned to surrender everything to him.

Riley sighed and leaned back obediently. "Somehow I knew you were going to be quite the taskmaster this evening," he told her ruefully.

Amanda rolled her eyes, pretending she hadn't been thinking about making out with him ever since she'd read that note he'd left for her. Having to leave the stadium after indulging in only one very hot and steamy kiss had been torture. And yet she knew they needed to establish far more than sexual compatibility to make their relationship a real and lasting one. Friendship and emotional intimacy, an ability to work together on common goals, were important components of successful unions, too. Not that they would actually stay married to each other unless she thought Riley could love her, too. Swallowing around the sudden tightness of her throat, Amanda batted her lashes at him coquettishly and picked up the banter every bit as casually as he had left off. "And here you thought I only invited you back to my apartment for the…um…"

Devil-may-care lights flashed in his amber eyes as he picked up where she had flirtatiously left off. "Nooky?"

Amanda reveled in their spirited wordplay. She told herself there was nothing wrong with either kissing or flirting as long as they continued to build the rest of their relationship, too. She favored her husband with comically exaggerated reproof as she picked up another present and selected a roll of gift wrap they had yet to use. "Now, that's a word I haven't heard in a while."

Riley filled out a name tag for the present he had just wrapped. "Well, brace yourself, woman, because more oldies but goodies are coming up as soon as we get our Santa's Workshop chores done this evening."

They continued to wrap. The silence that fell was comfortable. Amanda realized they were having a good time, just being together, working on something for the kids.

"You know, you haven't told me what *you* want for Christmas," Riley said absently.

Easy, Amanda thought. She wanted their marriage to be real. She wanted the children to be theirs. She wanted the life they were playing at now to be theirs forever. But afraid to say that for fear of tempting fate and ruining everything, she avoided his searching gaze and answered only, "I don't know. I have everything I need. In terms of material stuff."

"Well, that's a big help," he muttered.

Amanda shrugged. She figured he was smart enough to come up with something on his own, if so moved. Not that she wouldn't like *anything* he gave her. Curious, she asked him, "What do you want for Christmas?"

He replied without hesitation. "I want the kids to be happy and safe and loved."

Good answer. "I want that, too," she said softly.

"And even though it's selfish of me, if their family can't be found or can't take care of them, I'd like you and me to be the ones doing the parenting of them." He met her eyes calmly, casually assessing her reaction to his words. "What do you think of that?"

Was he putting her through some sort of test here? If so, it was only fair, since, in her own way, she had been testing him all evening. She only knew if his protectiveness toward the kids was a character flaw, she shared it, too. "I don't think it's selfish," she said, her tone as guarded as his had been.

Riley shrugged stubbornly, not as willing to let either of them off the hook. "It sort of is," he stated, as they picked up bits of ribbon, paper and tape, and stuffed them in the garbage sack she had brought out. "Getting a ready-made family this way is almost cheating. It's as if all the hard work has been taken out of it, and the two of us just get to step in and enjoy."

Put that way it did sound a little self-serving, Amanda noted uncomfortably. She knew, even if he didn't, that their actions had been propelled by kindness. Sure, they were benefiting from the situation. The love they were giving the kids and getting back in return was making their Christmas season much happier and more emotionally fulfilled than it would have been otherwise. But that was just the way things were working out. They hadn't asked for any of it.

Aware Riley had never opened up to her this way before, and shown her the inner workings of his heart and soul, she guessed quietly, "Sort of the way you purchased your house, completely furnished and decorated, and ready to move in?"

"Right."

And because it had been so easy, he didn't quite trust it all to work out. Amanda knew exactly how that felt. Nothing wonderful had ever come all that easily to her, either.

Silence fell between them, and with it the understanding both had sought.

Riley kneaded the muscles in the back of his neck. "Although," he admitted in his soft Texas drawl, "not everything about getting the kids has been as easy as purchasing the house was."

Hearing the hint of Riley's generally humorous outlook back in his voice, Amanda smiled. "What hasn't been?" She tied the sack closed and took it to the front door, to take out as they left.

Riley stood, working out the kinks in his long limbs. He picked up the rolls of wrapping paper and stacked them neatly by the stairs. "Winning your heart and your trust," he told her with a rueful grin. He closed the distance between them, wrapped his arms around her waist. "I think I'm still working mighty hard on both of those."

Not so hard, Amanda thought, considering the fact she had already fallen head over heels in love with him. Even if she hadn't dared tell him yet.

"But seeing as Determination is my middle name," he teased, raining kisses down the side of her neck, then giving her a long thorough kiss meant, she was sure, to shatter any lingering resistance she might have.

So what if none of this was going to be easy, Amanda thought, as Riley swept a hand down her spine, urging her closer yet, so her breasts were crushed by the hardness of his chest, the depth of their need for each other no longer secret. The two of them could make this hasty marriage of theirs a real one if they wanted it badly enough. She already loved Riley. He was close to falling in love with her, too. She could see it, feel it, taste it. Now all she had to do was make him realize it, make him see that she was the only woman for him, the only woman who could give him what he needed and wanted. If she were as resolute as he, if she dared risk all, maybe they could make it happen.

"I plan to achieve those things, too," Riley continued, kissing her as if there was no tomorrow, until she had never felt sexier in her life.

"Maybe you don't have to work for any of that," Amanda said softly, caught up in the intensity of what she was feeling. Daring to put her feelings on the line, more than she ever thought she could, she whispered without an ounce of pride, "Maybe you already have everything you need from me to make our relationship work over the long haul." Riley lifted his head, grinning as if he had just won the million-dollar lottery. She swallowed hard. Bypassing any discussion of her heart, she continued swiftly, wanting him to know this much, "I know I've already gotten what I really want for Christmas."

His eyes darkened even more. A sensual smile tugged at his lips. "Which is…"

"This." Amanda went up on tiptoe, putting everything she had into the impromptu kiss. Fitting her lips to his, slanting her head to just the right angle as she stroked his tongue and lips, all the while caressing the hard musculature of his shoulders with slow, seductive strokes. "You."

His arms tightened around her, strong, insistent, cocooning her with warmth. And just like bcfore, he knew with damning accuracy just how to get to her. Her senses spun as he sucked at her bottom lip and touched the tip of her tongue with his own. Her excitement mounted, fueled by the rasp of their breath, the torridness of their kiss, the promise of the hours ahead. She arched against him, just as relentless in her pursuit of him.

Eventually, they had to come up for air. When they did, slowly, inevitably, he lifted his head. "Mrs. McCabe!" he chided playfully, as ready to be seduced as she was to entice. "Are you flat-out coming on to me?"

Wanting to make this an evening he would never forget, Amanda moved away from him. "Yes, I believe I am." Deciding if she was going to do this, she was going to do it all the way, Amanda went over to put on some music. Off went the more pedestrian Christmas carols. On came the sexy, sultry strains of "Santa Baby." "Got a problem with that, Doctor McCabe?" she asked, for the first time in her life feeling beautiful inside and out.

Riley couldn't hold back a smile as Amanda took off one

Western boot, then the other. Wiggled her way out of her jeans. "Not a one," Riley said hoarsely as her red chenille turtleneck came over her head. She sashayed toward him in a lacy see-through red bra, matching thong, and…the obligatory Christmas socks. He grinned, aware he was already hard as a rock. "I like your style."

"Good. I like yours. And I especially like you stripped down." She picked up the remote to her stereo, pressed play. The song they had been listening to started all over again. She lounged against the side of the sofa, arms crossed in front of her. "Your turn, Santa."

Trying hard not to notice how her posture plumped up her breasts and had them spilling out of the tops of her décolleté bra, lest he get ahead of where they both wanted him to be, Riley drawled right back, "I knew you had a wicked streak."

"So?" Amanda vamped. "Show me yours."

Never one to pass up an opportunity to clown around, Riley put some hip action into it as he unbuttoned. Opening the edges of his shirt wide, he showed off his chest and shimmied around in his best parody of a male dancer. Amanda was laughing softly as he slipped his shirt off, and swung it around, lasso style, over his head. It hit the banister. His T-shirt followed suit. His boots and socks came off, too.

Riley decided he liked the excited glitter in her eyes as she watched him unbuckle, unzip and peel down. He also liked the way her chest was rising and falling with each ragged intake of breath, the way she couldn't seem to take her eyes off the bulge behind the fly of his Christmas boxers, even as she tilted her head in a way that dared him to take this particular brand of love play any further.

So, of course, he did.

Her breath caught as she saw how very much he wanted her.

Had always wanted her.

"Got a problem with not making it all the way upstairs to my bed?" Amanda asked in a hoarse voice.

Riley noted the way her nipples were poking ardently through the lace. "You had somewhere else in mind?"

Amanda took the quilted lap rug off the back of the sofa and spread it out across the floor. She dropped down to her knees. "How about right here, next to the tree?" Her eyes darkened ardently. "I've always wanted to make love in the glow of the Christmas lights."

"I think that can be arranged," Riley promised, already turning off every other light in the room.

Wanting to remember every moment of this night, Riley let his glance sift slowly over her. Amanda was gorgeous no matter what she was or was not wearing. But she had never looked more radiant than she did at that moment, with color blushing her cheeks, her hair tumbling, straight and silky, over her shoulders.

He dropped down beside her, taking in her long slender legs and smooth thighs, the shadowy vee visible through the lace of her thong. "Tell Santa what you want, Mrs. Claus…." he encouraged, already divesting her of her lingerie.

She trembled as he bent and kissed her budding pink nipples one by one. She clasped his shoulders and sighed as his mouth moved urgently over her breasts. "Peppermint kisses…"

He slid down, kissing the hollow of her stomach, stroking the soft insides of her thighs. "Like this?" He traced her navel with his tongue, then dropped lower still, to deliver the most intimate of kisses, until she was overcome with pleasure, shuddering.

"Oh, yes…" she whispered.

"And this." He stretched out over her, fit his lips to hers, and let her lead him where she wanted to go.

"Definitely yes." Amanda groaned as their tongues twined

urgently and his body took up a primitive rhythm all its own, until there was no doubting how much he wanted her.

"How about this?" He eased her knees apart, lifted her up.

She gasped as he plunged into her, deliberate and slow.

Her eyes widened as she stretched to take him inside her. "That's nice, too."

He kissed her slowly, thoroughly. Sliding an arm beneath her he coaxed her to take all of him, again and again, until she was moaning, moving against him. What few boundaries existed between them, dissolved. She was his. He was hers. He pressed into her as deeply as he could go, and then they were lost, all coherent thought spinning away in ribbons of endless pleasure.

Afterward, they lay wrapped in each other's arms. His body still humming with the aftershocks of passion, Riley felt a fierce wave of possessiveness.

He still did not know what was going to happen with the three kids, but he knew this: he could no longer imagine his life without Amanda.

"Did Kevin find you?" Laurel asked, the moment Riley and Amanda walked in the door, shortly after midnight.

"Yes, he did," Amanda replied.

Riley helped Amanda with her coat, took off his own.

"Any word on the kids' identity?" Micki asked, looking equally concerned.

He shook his head, not bothering to mask his discouragement about that. "The sheriff's department is still looking but nothing yet."

"Well, maybe the person or persons responsible for this will contact you after Christmas is over, to talk or something," Laurel said hopefully. "You know, once the kids have had a merry holiday and all that."

Looking as though she were trying—and failing—to figure out a way to comfort them, Micki finally nodded her agreement. "Maybe you should just enjoy Christmas with the kids and not worry about it so much."

"That's kind of hard to do when we don't know if we're going to be able to keep them or not," Riley returned with a frown. He walked to the fireplace and warmed his hands on the flame. He glanced over at the TV. The weatherman for the late news was on the screen, predicting a white Christmas in Laramie County—something that happened only once every decade or so—to the skeptical guffaws of his news show colleagues.

"But if you could, you would adopt all three of them?" Micki said.

Riley and Amanda nodded in unison, very much in agreement about that. "We have no intention of splitting them up, or allowing anyone else to do so, either," Riley said firmly.

"That's good." Micki's shoulders sagged in relief. She looked at Riley and Amanda earnestly. "Because Laurel and I have both noticed the three of them are happiest when they are together. And I wouldn't want what happened to me and my sister when our parents died to happen to them."

Amanda stepped closer to the fire, too. "Did you and your sibling get split up?" she asked softly.

Micki nodded, sadness in her eyes. "Social services couldn't find a placement to take both of us for almost a year and we were put in different foster homes. Losing each other was almost worse than losing our parents. And if that's how my older sister and I felt, at eight and fourteen," Micki recollected sadly, "I can't imagine how Chloe, Amber and Cory would feel."

Riley wasn't surprised Micki and his sister were so protective of the three children—the two college girls had spent almost as much time with the children as he and Amanda had. Plus, they probably felt some responsibility because they had been the ones who had found the kids by the hospital's employee entrance. "You don't have to worry," Riley told them both firmly, taking Amanda's hand in his. "Amanda and I are going to do whatever it takes to protect the kids."

"Even if it means staying married?" Laurel asked curiously.

"Even then," Riley said.

"I'm not sure you should have promised them that," Amanda said after the girls had left. She stood before the fire, shivering, rubbing her hands together.

Although he was almost overly warm in the heat of the room, Riley moved to stand next to her. He, too, looked into the licking flames behind the safety glass. "Why not?"

"Well—" Amanda shrugged as she turned toward him "—we haven't been together all that long yet and…"

"And?" He reached out and touched her face.

"…and we don't know what's going to happen between you and me." Worry was back in her eyes.

Riley figured she was thinking about what had happened in her previous marriage. "I'm not going to fall in love with anyone else, or leave you for them," he told her, knowing on this subject she had her own demons to wrestle. That it might take her a while to believe.

A tremulous smile crossed her lips. She didn't quite meet his eyes. "You never know. Love is a funny thing," Amanda said softly, stepping closer, and resting her head against his shoulder.

"The emotion may be unpredictable," Riley agreed, doing his best to erase her insecurity as he wrapped a comforting arm about her waist. "I'm not." He lifted her chin and waited until she looked him in the eye before he continued persuasively, "You can count on me, Amanda. I promise you that." And to prove it, he took her to bed and made slow, thorough love to her all over again.

"Are you sure you don't mind watching the kids by yourself all day?" Riley asked Amanda over breakfast the following morning, marveling that she could look so pretty and pulled together after so little sleep. Fifteen minutes in the shower, another ten with her blow-dryer and makeup, and she looked good enough to grace the covers of a magazine.

"Laurel and Micki aren't going to be able to help," Riley continued, moving his gaze away from the shimmering softness of her hair. "They're slated to volunteer at the hospital today."

Amanda looked up from the pancakes she was cooking. She flashed him a confident smile. "I can handle it."

Riley quirked a brow, recalling how difficult the previous morning had been for him, when she had been gone. "All three of them at once?"

Amanda gave him an indulgent smile. "Sweetheart, you're talking to a woman who was handling a minimum of four of her siblings at a time, from age twelve on. Believe me, it will be a piece of cake."

"I wish I had some of your multitasking skill," Riley murmured admiringly. He could change diapers and prepare bottles, and ready-made toddler and preschool meals easily enough. He couldn't manage to do dishes or laundry or even get all three of them dressed in addition. The very basics, keeping everyone happy at once, was all he could manage. And that took every ounce of energy he had.

Amanda favored him with a sexy wink. "You have plenty of talent, in many areas." She paused to press a kiss on his brow before setting his plate in front of him. "As for the rest—" her hand trailed lightly across his shoulder "—the more experience you have, the easier it will get."

Riley dug into his expertly prepared breakfast. "I'll take your word on that, although if things work out the way we hope, and all our Christmas wishes come true," he continued, speaking in a code Amanda would understand and the children wouldn't. "And we both go back to work, we're going to need to get some household help or at the very least arrange for a sitter."

Amanda's eyes darkened seriously. "Don't forget the hospital has a childcare center for employees that is open twenty-four hours a day, seven days a week. It's nice, because you can use your breaks to go down and visit with your kids."

Riley paused, realizing again how much he had to learn. "I hadn't thought of that."

"It'll all work out." She held his eyes deliberately. "Promise."

Riley hoped so. He wasn't sure what he would do without Amanda and the three kids. And he wasn't so sure, after what she had said the evening before about love being unpredictable, that she would stay forever if the kids weren't there.

Amanda looked as if she were having the same disturbing thought. She cleared her throat, took a sip of coffee, changed the subject every bit as smoothly and politely as he had come to expect. "So what's on your schedule today, Dr. McCabe?" she asked pleasantly.

Riley rocked back in his chair. "It's a secret."

Amanda lifted a brow, her interest piqued, as she forked up a bite of pancake with blueberry syrup.

"I could tell you," Riley teased, reaching over to take her hand in his and give it a tender squeeze, "but then you wouldn't be surprised. And Santa wants you to be surprised."

At the mention of jolly old St. Nick, Chloe and Amber looked on with interest. Only Cory, who was seated in his bouncy chair, sleepily sucking on a pacifier, looked oblivious.

Amanda rolled her eyes. "Well then by all means, go ahead," she counseled dryly. "Just be sure and save some time for me, 'cause I've got some personal shopping to do before tomorrow, too."

By the time the breakfast dishes were done and Riley had showered and dressed, Amanda had Cory asleep in the bassinet in a corner of the kitchen. Chloe and Amber were wearing aprons, humming "Feliz Navidad" right along with her, and "helping" Amanda make cookie dough.

The scene was so cozy and familial—so reminiscent of the happiest days of his own childhood—he couldn't help but linger. "Now, I don't want to leave," he grumbled, wrapping his arms around her slender waist.

Amanda turned and splayed her hands across his chest, her touch as warm and inviting as the look in her pretty eyes. "You can help us when you come back," she said.

"Promise?" he said softly, affectionately tracing her face with his hand.

She rose on tiptoe to give him a sweet, exceptionally gentle kiss on the lips that brought an answering fullness to his heart. "It wouldn't be Christmas without you," she murmured.

Chapter 11

"You wanted to see me?" Laramie Community Hospital chief of staff, Jackson McCabe, asked.

Riley nodded as the two men shook hands. In his private life, Riley knew his uncle appreciated a good joke as much as anyone, but when it came to the hospital the talented general surgeon was all business. "First, I want to apologize for the ruckus earlier in the week," Riley said as they continued on into Jackson's private office and shut the door behind them. "And second, I want you to stop holding Amanda accountable for any part of it and reinstate her immediately."

Jackson quirked a dark brow now threaded with silver. "What's changed from the last time you two were in here?" he asked, as blunt and to the point as ever.

Everything, Riley thought, as he dropped down into a chair in front of Jackson's desk. "We're still married, for one thing."

Jackson cast a wary look at Riley's hand. "I don't see a

wedding ring on your finger. Nor did I see one on hers when I ran into her yesterday."

"That's being taken care of, as soon as I finish here today."

Jackson frowned at Riley. "In what sense?"

"In the sense that I'm getting her one for Christmas," Riley told his uncle seriously.

Jackson's features softened in relief. "Then you're planning to stay married?"

"Yes." Even if he hadn't yet gotten Amanda to agree to it.

The hard edge was back. "Why?"

Riley did his best to curtail his frustration. He wasn't used to being grilled about his private life by his superiors. But then, he wasn't used to being embarrassed at his workplace the way he had been the day the kids had been mysteriously delivered to him, either. "Isn't it obvious?"

Jackson shrugged. "Maybe I want to hear you say it."

"We've discovered we like being married."

Jackson gave Riley a stern look. "Being married or playing house?"

Riley recognized the tough love approach for what it was. It didn't mean he had to like it. "You're crossing the line," he warned.

Jackson shrugged his broad shoulders nonchalantly. "Then that makes two of us, doesn't it?"

Tension stiffened Riley's frame as the conversation veered into dangerous territory. "What do you want from me?" he demanded.

Jackson refused to relent. "Probably the same thing your wife wants."

"Which is—?" Riley returned evenly.

Jackson regarded Riley for a long moment. "Oh, for starters, a declaration of your undying love."

Riley hadn't felt like this since he'd been called in to the principal's office, for chastisement about one of the many practical jokes he had played on Amanda. Problem was, he was no longer a mischief-prone kid, Amanda no longer his teenage rival. "Amanda and I haven't…that's not our style."

Jackson shook his head in silent reproach. "So you don't love her," Jackson surmised with a scowl.

As a matter of fact, Riley did. But not about to tell his uncle that before he'd even had a chance to tell Amanda, he curtailed his resentment and returned mildly, "My feelings and hers are irrelevant to this discussion."

Jackson leaned forward and rested his forearms on the desk. "I don't think so." His penetrating gaze narrowed even more. "And I don't think Amanda would think so either if she were here."

"Look." Riley returned his uncle's unrelenting judgment with a warning gaze of his own. "All I want is for you to stop taking your disappointment in me out on her."

"What about the kids?" Jackson waited, letting his words sink in before he continued. "What happens to them if no one claims them?"

That at least was easy. "Then Amanda and I have agreed we're going to adopt them and bring them up ourselves."

Another lift of the brow. "That's quite a commitment."

"And one we would not undertake lightly," Riley underscored, just as firmly.

Jackson nodded. "I respect you for that." He sighed, shook his head. "Even though I think you're a fool for staying married to a woman you can't even say you love."

Riley was going to say it. But on his own time, in his own way, when the moment was right. Not when someone was thinking the usual worst of him and demanding he do so. Ignoring that part of the lecture, Riley pushed on for the answer he had come to get. "So will you let Amanda back on staff?"

Jackson pushed his chair away from the desk. "I'll let you both back on staff as soon as Christmas is over and we find out what is going to happen to Amber, Chloe and Cory."

"What do they have to do with this?" Riley asked. He got to his feet, too.

"Everything, apparently." Jackson walked him toward the door.

Riley stared at him in confusion. "I don't get it."

"The kids are obviously the glue holding you together. If the situation changes, if that is no longer the case, your relationship with Amanda could change," Jackson explained, not particularly happily.

Riley thought about the way Amanda had returned his kisses and caresses, the way she looked at him, the love he felt flowing through her, even though she hadn't come close to saying the words to him, either. "No, it won't," he returned stubbornly.

The skeptical look was back on Jackson's face. "Well, let's be sure." He frowned. "I want your marital situation resolved one way or another before either of you comes back to work."

Riley left his uncle's office. He wasn't sure how that meeting could have gone any worse. He was glad he hadn't mentioned it to Amanda, though. "Hey, Riley," director of nursing Meg Lockhart-Carrigan intercepted him in the hall. "Since you're not working, how about doing the pediatric floor a favor?"

"Sure," Riley said.

Meg steered Riley into the staff lounge. She picked up a bulging laundry bag, handed it over.

Riley was all for doing penance, if it got him what he wanted—a life with Amanda and the kids, and both their jobs back, but this was ridiculous. He looked askance at Amanda's boss. "You want me to do your wash?"

"No, silly," Meg whispered, leaning close, laughter in her eyes. "I want you to answer the letters to Santa so 'Mrs. Claus' can pass them out to the letter writers on Christmas Eve."

"Sure," Riley agreed readily. "I'll get Amanda to help me with that tonight. But in return you have to do a favor for me and get Amanda's ring size."

Meg's eyes twinkled with approval. "I already know it. It's a six. She tried on the ring Luke gave me for my birthday, last month. We're the same size."

"Thanks."

"No problem." Meg regarded Riley slyly. "You getting her a wedding ring?"

Riley just smiled. "Do not tell her I asked. Not even a hint," he warned.

"Okay, but just so you know, she likes diamonds."

"Don't you all," Riley tossed back, knowing a diamond was exactly what he was in the market for.

Whistling, he headed down the hall, stopped when he saw Micki standing at one of the playroom windows. She appeared to be wiping tears from beneath her eyes. Concerned, Riley went over to her. He rested a hand on her shoulder. "Hey. Everything okay?"

Micki started, then seeing it was him, relaxed slightly, even as she brushed fresh tears away. "Fine."

She didn't look fine, Riley thought. "Did something happen?" he asked her gently.

"No." Her freckles stood out against the paleness of her skin.

"Then why are you crying?" Riley persisted, aware in all the time he had known the young woman that he had never seen her tear up like this.

Micki shrugged, refusing to meet his eyes. She ran a hand through her red hair and didn't answer.

Riley wanted to respect her privacy as much as he wanted to be her mentor. He sensed right now she just needed a friend. "Are you homesick?" he guessed at the reason behind her unhappiness. "I know you're not going home to Colorado for Christmas this year…." Riley paused, unsure how much to push, knowing he had to offer something. "It's probably not too late to change your mind, you know," he told her helpfully. "You could still get a flight."

"No. I'll be okay." Micki shook off her tears determinedly. "I'm just...I don't know." She smiled at him bravely. "Feeling overly sentimental or something. I'm okay. *Really.*"

Then why, Riley wondered, didn't he believe it?

Riley drove up just as the Overnight Delivery truck was pulling away from the curb. He waved a cheerful hello at the driver, parked his car, grabbed his gift-wrapped packages and walked inside. Pausing only long enough to tuck his Christmas presents for Amanda in the bottom of her stocking, he headed for the rear of the house.

Chloe, Amber and Cory were all napping in the family room. Amanda was standing at the kitchen window, talking on the phone. An opened blue-and-white cardboard envelope was on the kitchen table. She appeared to be holding an airline ticket in her hand.

"I know it is nonrefundable, Mom. And I appreciate it. But you and Dad should have talked to me before you purchased it." She sighed loudly. "I can't." Exasperation crept into her low voice. "Okay, then, I won't. No." Panic edged her tone. "Now, don't do that, either. Priscilla should enjoy the holidays with all of you." Amanda rubbed her temples. "Mom, I mean it," she warned. "Don't. Do. This."

Amanda pulled the receiver away from her face and stared at it. She sighed again and clicked the End Call button.

Fairly sure it was safe to enter her domain, Riley slowly closed the distance between them. As he neared her, he saw tears glistening in her eyes. He didn't even have to think about what to do next. Wanting her to feel as cared for and loved as she made him feel, he put his arms around her, held her close and stroked her hair.

Amanda's voice was muffled against his shirt. "You're

not going to believe what my family is doing now," she told him in a low, miserable voice.

Riley looked at the airline ticket she still clutched in one hand. He took a wild guess. "Trying to get you home for the holidays?"

"They're just doing this to try to break us up," Amanda sniffed, indignant.

Riley shrugged, not so surprised about that after Priscilla's visit. Nor could he really blame the Witherspoon clan, given all they didn't know. "Well, it won't work, even if you do go home to California for the holiday," he soothed.

Amanda lifted her head from his chest. She looked deep into his eyes. "You'd really be okay with that?"

Riley nodded, almost as surprised by his unselfishness as she was. "If it was what you wanted and needed to do? Sure. Which isn't to say I wouldn't miss you like hell. I would," he told her wryly. He wrapped his arms more tightly around her. "But I'll always be supportive of you, Amanda. That's what husbands do for their wives." And McCabe men had a long tradition of treating their women with the respect and consideration they deserved.

Amanda sighed and dropped her head back down to rest on his chest. She let him protect her the way Riley had always wanted to protect her. "I wish my family could see and hear this."

He stroked a hand through her hair, loving the silky softness of the honey-colored strands. "You could invite them all here."

Her answering laugh had a hollow sound. "Be careful what you wish for," Amanda told Riley sadly. "Besides, there is no way they could afford that, any more than they could afford the nonrefundable ticket they just bought for me."

Riley refused to let her take responsibility for a situation not of her making. "It's not as if the ticket has to go to waste. You can always change it for a later visit if you pay the change fee."

Amanda wrapped both her arms around his waist. "That's not the point."

"I know." Riley enjoyed the feel of her soft slender body cuddled close against him. He tucked a hand beneath her chin and lifted her face to his. "But it's the reality of the situation. They gave you a wonderful gift. It's up to you to decide how to use it without allowing them to make you feel guilty."

Her lips took on a rueful curve. "You sound like you know something about that."

Riley acknowledged this was so with a dip of his head. "It's true. I've fought my own battles on that score."

"When?" Amanda asked, wanting to understand him the way she never had in the past.

"After my mom died," Riley said quietly. He looked deep into Amanda's eyes. He had never talked about this to anyone. Now he found himself wanting to lay bare his soul. The gentleness and understanding in Amanda's expression encouraged him to go on. "My mom had been ill for a long time, but it was still a shock when she finally lost her battle against breast cancer. We were all so devastated. I can't even put it into words. She was more than just a mom, she was the heart and soul of our family. And when we lost her…" Riley's voice caught. For a moment he was so choked up, he couldn't go on. "Anyway, my dad was a wreck." Riley let go of Amanda and moved about the kitchen restlessly as he continued to recollect, "It seemed the only way he could cope was by burying himself in work, which left the rest of us to fend for ourselves."

Amanda's heart went out to Riley. She hadn't expected Riley to confide in her this way, but she was glad he was. It made her feel closer to him. It made her feel as if he was at long last letting her in. "That's when you had that whole series of housekeepers, right?" she prompted, recalling.

Riley nodded, his expression sad but accepting. "Yep. Anyway, to say we kids were resentful is the understatement of the century. We gave every one of those housekeepers pure hell. And Kate, too. Our acting out was the only way we could cope with the loss. For Brad, that meant dating every girl in sight. Will began sneaking drinks. Kevin stopped communicating and kept trying to climb out on the roof, even after he fell off and broke his arm. And Lewis was sensitive to a fault."

Amanda recalled hearing all about the McCabe family shenanigans—back then, Sam's motherless brood had been the talk of the town. "What about you? What did you do?" Anything she didn't already know?

"Got myself into more mischief than any kid had a right to pursue." He paused, shook his head. "Luckily, most of it was harmless. But I know that my constant joking around really bothered the rest of my family. You could see they were all grieving in one way or another. It looked like I didn't care at all. Or feel any loss. And of course I did. I just couldn't admit how miserable I was. Knowing what people thought about my pranks made me feel guilty. The more guilt I felt, the more I acted out."

"A vicious circle," Amanda summed up, commiserating with him.

"Yep."

Amanda angled a thumb at her chest. "And here I thought I was the inspiration for all your jokes."

"Are you kidding?" Riley flashed her a sudden grin, which she promptly returned. "You were my saving grace. Had I not focused on you and tried so hard to keep your undivided attention all through high school, who knows what kind of pranks I might have cooked up to distract myself from my loss."

"When did the guilt stop?" Amanda asked softly, closing the distance between them once again.

"That's the hell of it." Riley inclined his head. "With families it never really does. At least not in my experience. 'Cause you always know when you have disappointed your loved ones, just as you know what you have to do to redeem yourself in their eyes."

"Like going home for Christmas," Amanda said.

"Or taking marriage seriously," Riley replied. "Which is what both our families seem to want for us. They're only irritated with us because they think we still see our situation as a joke. Once they realize that has changed," he told Amanda confidently, "they will all not only forgive us, they'll approve of what we've done here. You'll see. In the meantime...how long have the kids been asleep?"

"Thirty minutes, tops."

"How long do you expect them to nap?"

"Another hour, minimum. Why?"

"Let's turn the baby monitor on down here and head upstairs."

Before Amanda could do more than gasp, Riley had swept her up into his arms and was heading for the stairs. Her heart pounded in her chest. "I can't believe we're actually going to do this in the middle of the day," she said breathlessly.

A mischievous grin tugged at the corners of his lips as he headed to the master bedroom. "Why not?" Riley whispered playfully as he carried her sideways through the door. "It is nap time, after all." He flashed another smile as he deposited her ever so gently on the bed. "And I did ask you to open your heart and mind to the possibility of us making our relationship a real and loving one in every way. It seems to me lovemaking is very much a part of a real and viable marriage."

Amanda hitched in a breath as she raised herself off the pillows as far as her elbows would allow. Detecting a change in his attitude, she demanded huskily, "What are you saying?" She stared at him, aware he was already yanking off his sweater vest, pulling it over his head, dropping it on the chaise in the corner. The devil-may-care look she recalled so very well from their youth was etched on his handsome face, along with a seriousness that spoke to her soul.

"I'm telling you I am tired of playing house," he said, ever so softly. Dropping down to sit beside her, on the edge of the bed. "I'm telling you I want us to be for real. And that telling each other everything that's in our hearts and making love is the best way I know of to get where we both want to be. So unless you tell me to scram..."

But he didn't want to, Amanda noticed, as he sat there, waiting for her decision. And neither, if she were being truthful, did she. "Oh, Riley." She let herself fall back against the pillows and draped her forearm across her brow. "You really are so very bad for me," she whispered tremulously.

"In that case," Riley leaned forward as the staticky silence of the baby monitor filled the room. Planting a hand on either side of her, he caged her with his arms. "Let me attempt to live up to my very wicked reputation."

Amanda wrapped her arms around his neck. "And me, mine," she whispered right back.

His head lowered. She shut her eyes, ignoring the fact that he had yet to say the words she most wanted to hear. Surely one day Riley would tell her that he loved her as much as she loved him. And until then, it was Christmastime, after all. And being with Riley was her most fervent wish. She hadn't wanted to fall in love with him, hadn't wanted herself to be that vulnerable. But she already knew in her heart it was too late. She did love him heart and soul and always would. Even if the worst happened, in the end, and their marriage didn't last, and the cautious side of her kept telling her it most surely would not, she would have these precious moments to remember from this day forward. Short of having a family and husband of her very own, the kind that would be hers forevermore, making love with Riley was the very best thing.

The last of her doubts slid away as his lips met hers in a

scorching kiss that brought with it the fulfillment of every sexual fantasy she had ever had. Her hands moved from his neck to his chest, where she busied herself opening up each one of the buttons, one by one, laying bare the inviting hardness of his chest, the satiny smoothness of his skin and the springy tufts of masculine hair. Without breaking off the kiss, she helped him out of it, let it fall to the side of the bed.

Riley's lips left her mouth, forged a burning trail across her cheek. "Are you undressing me, Nurse McCabe?" he whispered in her ear.

"Why yes, Doctor McCabe," she whispered right back, lowering her hands to his belt. She batted her eyelids at him coquettishly, then indulged in a kiss that was deeply passionate. "I believe I am."

"Did I give you my permission?" he asked, slanting his mouth across hers, devouring her with a boldness that was as heady and new as her own.

Noting he had already taken off his shoes, Amanda worked his trousers, and boxers, down his legs. She paused to kiss the insides of his knees, his calves, as she knelt before him and removed his socks. There was something so wonderfully wanton, being fully dressed, while he was splendidly naked and handsome as could be. Something so unlike her...and yet so right, nevertheless. She had always wanted to be free in the bedroom. Riley made her feel as though she could do and say and want anything and it would be okay. More than okay.

"Because," he continued teasing her playfully, looking his fill of her, too, "I don't *recall* giving it."

Running her palms along the gloriously muscled insides of his thighs, Amanda trailed kisses over his knees, higher still, as she murmured, as innocently as she could, "It was implied."

"Oh...really?" Riley tangled his fingers in her hair.

Already so needy and hot she ached, Amanda nodded, "In that kiss."

"Mmm." Riley caressed her shoulders, the slope of her neck. "What else was implied?"

"Maybe a little of this," Amanda whispered, daring more than she had ever dared in her life.

Riley sucked in his breath.

Smiling at the pleasure she was giving, Amanda murmured lovingly, "And this." She explored the muscular perfection of his body, the throbbing desire, the need. "And this," she whispered, even more tenderly.

"Amanda," Riley moaned, letting her command his surrender, in the same way he had first commanded hers. He let her have her way with him until it was suddenly all or nothing and he could stand it no more, and then Amanda found she was lying back against the pillows once again.

"My turn," he whispered, easing the zipper down on her skirt.

Amanda lifted her hips off the bed as he relieved her of her skirt, cardigan and turtleneck. Reclining in nothing but her bra, opaque black tights, and panties, she managed, "I don't think I can wait much longer."

Riley stopped her from removing her bra just then. He draped his naked body alongside hers, in no hurry to rush the pleasure along. He turned slightly to face her, the hardness of his thigh pressing up against hers. "Sure you can."

Amanda trembled as he ran his lips across the tops of her breasts and the U of her collarbone, the side of her neck, the inside of her ear. She trembled as he found her mouth again, delved deep, luxuriating in the feel of his warm, callused hands caressing her skin. "Says who?"

His arousal pressed against her, creating an ocean of warmth inside her. "Your very own St. Nick." He shifted her closer, his tongue parting her lips, touching the edges of her teeth, and then returning in a series of deep, mesmerizing kisses that robbed her of the ability to think past that moment, and the inevitable continuing consummation of their marriage.

"Christmas after all," he said, continuing on his sensual quest, finally taking off her bra and teaching her pleasure in ways she had never imagined, "is something that should be enjoyed to the absolute limit." Hands hooked beneath the elastic of her panties and tights, he pushed those down, too.

Amanda drew in a shaky breath as he settled between her thighs and sought out the most feminine part of her. "I think you're doing that, all right," she moaned, as he pushed her to the absolute limit, until at last there was no more waiting, no more denying the passion that had taken hold of them both, and they were both gasping. She wanted him deep inside her, and he gave her that, and so much more, drawing her into a realm of sensation that had them both reaching the outer limits of their control. Holding tight, they soared into soft, sizzling love and shuddering pleasure.

They stayed like that, for long moments after. Feeling exhausted and replete, Amanda turned blindly into Riley's arms and buried her face in the hair on his chest. Heart brimming with tenderness, loving the gentle way he held her close, she snuggled closer. "Riley?"

He stroked a hand through her hair. "Hmm?"

I love you. So much. But as much as she tried to form the words, they would not be said. Not now. Not yet.

He waited. When she still didn't say anything, he unwrapped his arms. Releasing her reluctantly, he shifted onto his side, bent his elbow and propped his head on his hand. An awkward silence fell between them as he searched her face and asked quietly, "What did you want to tell me?"

Needing to reassure herself by touching him, she stroked a hand across his chest. Knowing it was too soon, that she could ruin everything if she declared her feelings for him this quickly, she pushed away the impulse to share everything with him, and said only, "I just wanted you to know that—"

she paused to take a bolstering breath "—this was the best Christmas present I've ever had."

He looked deep into her eyes. A slow sexy smile crossed his face as he took her hand and lifted it to his lips. The tension in his shoulders eased. "For me, too." He winked. "Not that we're through yet…"

Amanda had only to look down to see the proof of his desire, feel her own body quicken in response and know that her longest-held wish—to be cherished, body and soul—was finally coming true. "Again?"

"This is the season for giving, you know." Riley clamped an arm about her waist and drew her closer, looking at her in a way that made her feel beautiful and wanted in a way she had never been. His voice dropped a husky notch. "And I want to give you so much joy, so much pleasure…."

Her head swam with the scent and feel of him. "You are one very hard man to resist," she murmured as he laid claim to her mouth with fierce possessiveness.

Riley smiled. Rolling onto his back, he pulled her on top of him and wrapped his arms around her. "Keep thinking that way, Mrs. McCabe, and we will have a very merry Christmas indeed."

"The cuff links are certainly very nice," the salesclerk told Amanda.

One hundred stores in the mall, and where had she ended up? The jewelers. "I don't know." Amanda hesitated, feeling more foolish and uncertain than she could recall in a very long time. "It seems sort of…"

"Impersonal?" the expensively dressed brunette asked.

"Yes."

The clerk slid the velvet-lined tray back in the glass case. "How long have you and your man been dating?"

A self-conscious flush warmed Amanda's cheeks. "We're not really dating."

"Of course," the clerk agreed readily. "A passé tradition for women our age."

At what age, Amanda wondered, was dating no longer acceptable? The clerk had to be at least ten years older than she was. And she wasn't wearing a wedding ring, either. But then, she probably wasn't married to anyone, technically or otherwise.

"I just meant we're not in high school anymore," the clerk amended hastily, seeming to think she had offended Amanda on some level.

Amanda realized it wasn't really the clerk bugging her—it was the situation, and the uncertainty that went along with it. And the wariness her mother had engendered in one long-distance phone call. Amanda was thirty-two now. A grown woman who had been married and divorced. She was a registered nurse. And yet, the last few days around Riley had made Amanda feel as if she was an emotion-driven, lust-filled, mixed-up, crazy-in-love teenager!

She wasn't used to that.

Wasn't sure she wanted to get used to that!

Without Riley her life had been dull and, with the exception of the work she enjoyed, absolutely passionless. Now she had passion, but along with that came worry and uncertainty, two things Amanda felt she could happily do without.

"So is this a long-term relationship?" the clerk asked delicately, bringing out a tray of elegant diamond and gold rings.

Amanda couldn't see Riley wearing one of those, either. They were simply too fussy and flashy. She shook her head, even as she answered the clerk's question with a mumbled, "It's supposed to be."

The clerk's elegant brow arched. "You don't sound sure."

"A lot is involved," Amanda said stiffly.

"Of course." With an indulgent look, the clerk brought out a tray of gold chains, suitable for a man.

Again, no.

"We have these children," Amanda explained, as the clerk slid yet another tray back into the case.

"Oh!" A wealth of understanding in a single word.

"They're not ours. Not yet anyway," Amanda amended hastily.

"Oh." More subdued.

"If we continue stewardship of them, then I believe we will stay together," Amanda explained. If only because Riley couldn't handle all three of them alone, and—having lost his own mom at the tender age of thirteen—firmly believed all kids needed a mother and a father.

The clerk's brows knit together. "So it's not really a romantic involvement, then, between you and this gentleman you wish to purchase a gift for?"

Actually, Amanda thought wistfully, their love affair was highly romantic, which of course made the cautious side of her mistrust the longevity of her impetuous but passionate romance with Riley all the more. If only he'd said he loved her, maybe then she'd feel secure. But he hadn't and neither had she, so all she knew was that he was crazy in lust with her and that he wanted to make their marriage a real one in every way, and so did she.

"Or is it a romance?" the clerk inquired, abruptly looking as flummoxed as Amanda felt.

Not sure how to answer that, but certain she didn't want to try and put it in words, Amanda merely shrugged off the question.

"The thing is," she said finally, swallowing hard and turning her attention firmly back to the task at hand. "I've never really seen Riley wear a shirt that required cuff links, or any other kind of decorative jewelry, either. He's more of a button-up and button-down kind of guy, if you know what I mean."

"Are you absolutely certain he wouldn't like a ring?" the clerk asked, determined, it seemed, to get her sale and commission. "We have some that are very understated."

The only ring Amanda wanted to see on Riley's large, capable hands was a wedding band. Again, she shook her head. "Riley's not really a ring kind of guy, either."

"How about a watch, then?" the clerk suggested brightly. "We have wrist or pocket. Both styles are excellent, elegant gifts as well as practical timepieces."

Time, Amanda thought, as the clerk brought out yet another velvet-lined tray, was the one thing running out. In two days, Christmas would be over. Whoever had left the children might very well show up to claim them. Or the police might track them down. When that happened, Amanda and Riley would meet the person or persons responsible for the abandonment face-to-face and they would know whether or not the children were being put up for guardianship and/or adoption. And that, more than anything, would determine the future between them.

"Bad shopping trip?" Riley asked when Amanda strolled in the door, close to dinner time. She brought with her two pizzas and a garden salad.

"Why would you say that?" Amanda asked brightly.

He looked at her, his expression vaguely suspicious, his lips set in a thoughtful line. "The glum look on your face before you adjusted it." He took the cardboard boxes and takeout sack from her hand, then sauntered closer still.

"Don't mind me." Amanda wrinkled her nose in aggravation. *I've just been busy wishing for the best and expecting the worst.*

Still studying her, he braced a hip against the kitchen counter and crossed his arms. The pleasure he felt at seeing her again was in his amber eyes. "Stores crowded?" he asked her coyly.

Aware there was very little space between them now, she matched his provoking grin. "Oh, yes."

His eyes lit up with a teasing glow. He hooked an arm

about her waist and brought her all the way against him. The warmth of his body, where it pressed up against hers, gave new heat to hers. Amanda caught her breath as he rubbed his thumb across her lower lip, tracing its sensual shape. "Buy me something wonderful?" he murmured in her ear.

Amanda trembled in a way that let him know just how sensitive she was to his touch. "I never shop and tell."

He peered at her argumentatively. "How about kiss and tell then?"

"Not that, either."

"Hmm." He acknowledged her confession with a wry smile, then leaned over to kiss her cheek. "Guess I'll have to wait then."

That was the problem, Amanda thought, she didn't want to wait for anything. "I guess you will," she flirted back. Their eyes locked. The familiarity and ease between them deepened. Another silence fell between them, happier this time, and fraught with tension.

Chloe and Amber burst into the room. Amanda knelt, giving both little girls the perfect proximity to hug her fiercely. "I missed you," she said, kissing them both.

Amber drew back. She touched Amanda's face with the flat of her hand. "Pretty," she said, repeating the one and only word she could pronounce intelligibly.

"I think so, too," Riley winked.

Amanda flushed self-consciously. "Thank you," she told Amber. "I think you're pretty, too, sweetheart."

Meanwhile, Chloe held on tight, her little face buried in Amanda's neck. Realizing some extraspecial attention was needed for the oldest child, Riley swooped seventeen-month-old Amber up into his arms. Chloe kept right on hugging Amanda. "Everything okay this afternoon?" Amanda asked Riley.

He nodded. "We've been singing Christmas carols. Or

rather, I have. I keep hoping someone will join in, but so far…"

His voice trailed off as Chloe finally drew back. She looked into Amanda's eyes. For a second, Chloe's mouth worked, her eyes grew intense, and Amanda thought she was at long last going to speak. She knew for certain the little girl wanted to communicate something to her, but…the moment passed, and Chloe's face relaxed, and she withdrew into herself again.

Amanda kissed Chloe's cheek, hugged her tight, then swooped the four-year-old up into her arms and carried her into the kitchen, where Cory was sleeping in his bassinet. "I was telling the kids that we're going to bake those Christmas cookies after dinner tonight," Riley said. "Is that okay with you?"

Enjoying the sweet sense of family, Amanda smiled. "As a matter of fact, that is exactly what I had planned."

"Maybe doing the familiar," Riley continued as he helped both girls into their seats, "will spark something verbal from someone, if you know what I mean."

Amanda nodded, easily understanding Riley's coded message. "If not right away, then soon," she said.

"Because Christmas is all about wishes coming true."

The question was, Amanda thought, what exactly were Riley's? The same as hers? Was he searching for a forever kind of love, too? Or something a lot more casual?

Chapter 12

"What's so funny?" Amanda asked, catching her husband's amused smile, as they surveyed the damage done during an hour of gleeful cookie baking and decorating with the kids. All of whom had since been put to bed.

"You." Riley tapped Amanda playfully on the nose. "You've got red sprinkles on your eyebrow, green frosting on your cheek and flour in your hair."

Amanda studied him as a kaleidoscope of emotions twisted through her. "Ha! You're one to talk. You've got confectioner's sugar on your temple, and pizza sauce on the back of your neck."

He raised a quizzical brow.

"From dinner." Amanda got a clean cloth out of the drawer and dampened it beneath the faucet. "Those kisses and hugs the kids gave you left their mark, too."

Riley stood still while she dabbed at the offending marks on his skin, then took the cloth, cupped her chin in his hand and did the same. "That makes us two of a kind, then."

Amanda melted under the gentle ministrations of his hands. The next thing she knew, his head was dropping. His lips were on hers in a sweet, sensual kiss that stole her breath away. "You taste like cookie," she murmured.

"So do you." He steered her beneath the mistletoe hanging from the entranceway to the kitchen and delivered another kiss. She melted into it, thinking all the while this was her merriest holiday ever.

"Want to…?"

"Yes," she said softly, looking deep into his eyes. "But we can't. Not yet anyway. We have to answer those Dear Santa letters for the kids in pediatrics, remember?"

Riley nodded, a faint smile curving his lips. "I've been putting it off."

"Hard to know what to say," Amanda agreed.

He retrieved the wicker basket at the end of the counter. "Meg gave me a list of possible replies, as well as Christmas cards and envelopes to write on, so if you'll help…we can get it done and get to the good stuff."

"You're incorrigible."

Riley winked. "Never more so than when I'm around you."

They cleared the table of just-frosted cookies and wiped it down. Riley began opening envelopes while Amanda loaded the dishwasher and turned it on. She wiped her hands on a towel and sat down to join him, just in time to see him slipping an envelope into his sweater vest. "Ah ah ah!" Knowing full well by the sly expression on his handsome face that he was up to no good, she made a grab for the pilfered letter. "What's this?"

"Nothing you need to see," he declared.

She wrested it from him anyway, noticed his handwriting on the front. "That's your letter to Santa! Which must mean mine is in here, too."

"Yep." Riley pointed to another envelope right in front of him. "All the other staff letters seem to have been removed."

"They were probably forwarded to the appropriate spouses and significant others," Amanda murmured, taking charge of her letter. "What did you ask for in yours?"

Riley held his just out of reach. "I'm not telling—until you let me in on what you asked for," he teased.

Did she want him to know what she had wished for?

"I'll show you mine if you show me yours," he persisted.

Amanda had the feeling that despite his outward bravura that Riley was a little embarrassed about what he had written, too. "Mmm. I need to think about it," she allowed finally.

Mischief tugged at the corners of his lips. "Your request was that racy, hmm?"

"You never know," Amanda fibbed, feeling a self-conscious flush warm her cheeks.

He rubbed the inside of her wrist. "You do constantly surprise me."

Ribbons of sensation flowed through her. She looked deep into his eyes. "I gather your request was rather tame?"

"Maybe." He favored her with a smile that was rife with sensual promise. "And maybe it was as wild as can be. There's only one way to find out, and that's to open them both on Christmas Eve."

An hour later, they were at the end of the letters. Most had been easy enough to answer. A few were not. Figuring they needed to warm up to those, Amanda and Riley saved the most difficult ones for last.

Amanda reported, "Shelby Huff wants a kitten for Christmas."

Riley frowned. "She's in the hospital because she had a severe asthma attack."

"Right. Which makes a cat impossible for her." Amanda paused thoughtfully. She rested her chin on her upraised hand. She liked the cozy feel of doing a yuletide task with him.

"Should Santa offer Shelby a stuffed kitty cat or a book or DVD about felines?"

"Probably," Riley allowed, already pushing back his chair and headed for the phone, "but let's call her folks and see what they want to do first. They may have a better idea."

Mr. and Mrs. Huff were in favor of a stuffed toy kitten and a movie about a kitten that runs away from home with several dogs. Both presents had already been purchased. So Riley and Amanda wrote a letter that said,

> Dear Shelby, I know you can't be around cats because of your asthma so I am sending you two very special presents that will let you love kittens without getting sick again. Love, Santa.

"That ought to do it," Amanda said as she addressed and sealed the envelope that had already been stamped with a return address of Santa's Workshop, The North Pole.

Riley continued sorting through the letters that were left. "Here's one from Laurel."

Curious, Amanda put down her pen. "What does it say?"

Riley opened it up. He read out loud,

> Dear Santa, Please give my friend everything my friend needs for a very Merry Christmas. Love, Laurel.

The mystery remained. "Still no boyfriend's name?"

Riley drummed his pen on the tabletop. "She was probably worried Mom or Dad would get handed this note, or somehow learn of its contents."

"And yet she wasn't worried enough not to write it."

"I guess there's a little belief in Santa's miracles in all of us."

Amanda knew that was certainly true of herself, given what she had written in her letter to St. Nick.

Riley sighed. "If Laurel has a flaw, it's identifying too much with other people's problems. Of course, that's not surprising since one of her parents is a psychologist and grief counselor who devotes herself to helping others."

"You'd think your parents would be more understanding of her," Amanda said.

"Well, you know parents." Riley shrugged in obvious regret. "They want to protect their children first, and worry about everyone else later. No good parent puts their own child at risk so they can help someone else, especially when the action required is to their own child's detriment. Unfortunately, Laurel seems unable to protect her own interests the way our folks would wish."

Amanda got up to pour them both a glass of milk. "What do you mean?"

Riley's gaze followed her as she moved about the kitchen, preparing them a bedtime snack. "When Laurel was eight, she sold her brand-new bicycle for five dollars because her best buddy had lost his lunch money and was too embarrassed to tell his parents or the teacher and she didn't want him to go hungry." He helped himself to one of the sugar cookies when Amanda brought a plate of them back to the table.

"She got put on academic probation in high school when she tried to help a football player who was really struggling academically to write an essay, and he took her sample draft, slapped his name on it and turned it in."

Amanda sat down and took a cookie, too.

"Her apartment at UT has been a revolving door for friends who need a place to stay but never contribute financially," Riley continued grimly, shaking his head, "so Laurel's always running out of money for food, rent, gas and utilities, and that was never truer than this past fall." He paused to take a drink of milk to wash down the cookie he had just eaten. "Mom and Dad don't mind her helping people. In fact they applaud it. They just wish Laurel would watch out for herself in the process. And not let others constantly take advantage of her."

Amanda bit into a delicate spritz cookie, with green sprinkles. "Helping out others is a good thing, though," Amanda argued, thinking Riley was being a little hard on his only sister. "Laurel's certainly been a good friend to Micki. Inviting her for Christmas."

Riley leaned back in his chair, stretching his long legs out in front of him. They brushed hers under the kitchen table. "That's something else that bothers me," he remarked, snapping the head off a butter-cookie reindeer.

Amanda sipped her ice-cold milk and waited.

"I've known Micki for four years," Riley said. "Granted, our relationship was totally geared around Micki's desire to go to medical school, but she always spent her holidays with her sister and her family in Boulder, Colorado. She never would have missed a Christmas with them."

Amanda shrugged, and still thirsty, got up to retrieve the bottle of milk from the fridge. "Maybe Micki's sister went on holiday elsewhere this year."

"Maybe. But wouldn't she at least have invited Micki to go with them, given the fact Micki has no other family?"

"Maybe she did. Maybe Micki didn't want to intrude," Amanda speculated. She'd been a fifth wheel enough times in her own siblings' lives to know how that felt.

"And maybe Micki and her sister had a fight," Riley speculated boldly, "and Micki refused to go home for the holidays or something like that."

Amanda paused. "You think that's why Micki was crying in the hospital earlier today?"

"Maybe, and maybe something else is wrong. Something her sister should know about."

"Like what?" Amanda asked, wondering where Riley was going with this.

"Well…what if Micki were pregnant or sick or just plain broke or something? Isn't it possible that Micki's family sent her money for a plane ticket home and Micki spent it on Laurel's latest charity case instead? And now is afraid to say so, lest her sister and her sister's husband react the same way my mom and dad have to Laurel's recent activities? You know how close the two girls are, how much they want to help people."

Yes, Amanda did. She knew Riley had a point. It was good to help others, but every person also had a responsibility to see to their own needs, too. She lifted a brow. "You thinking about interfering?"

Riley rubbed his fingertips up and down the outside of his empty glass. "I've been wrestling with my conscience all day." He paused to look Amanda in the eye. "Part of me knows that Micki is a grown-up and capable of making her own decisions, and certainly, at age twenty-one, entitled to her private life. The other part says if it were Laurel in this situation, upset and possibly hiding something and not coming home for the holiday, and someone else were in a position to help reunite Laurel with the family that loves her, I'd want that person to intervene."

"Do you have Micki's sister's number?"

"No," Riley allowed, with another frown, "but I know her sister's name is Adelaide Rowan, and her husband's name is Wiley."

"So, look them up, call to wish them a merry Christmas and tell Micki's sister how happy you are that Micki was accepted to UT-Galveston med school. Scope things out that way."

Riley paused. "You think it'd be okay?"

Amanda shrugged, no more sure than her husband was. On

the other hand, Riley's instincts in situations like this were usually good. "If you're right, it might be just what Micki needs to reunite her with her family in time for Christmas."

With a decisive nod, Riley went to his computer and looked up the phone number. Using the speakerphone function so she could hear, too, he dialed it and got the automated message, "This number has been disconnected." No new number was listed.

Scowling, Riley called the phone company, to see if they had an updated listing. They did not. Further searches on the Internet also proved futile. "Well, what now?" Amanda asked. "Are you going to ask Micki?"

"Eventually," Riley said. "But first, I'm going to see if Kevin can help us."

Still using the speakerphone, Riley telephoned Kevin. He was pulling a double shift in order to be off the next evening for the McCabe Open House at Sam and Kate's home. "Sure I can look into it," Kevin said, while Amanda and Riley both listened. "Got a couple things going right now, though. Is tomorrow soon enough?"

"Sure," Riley said. "Thanks." He hung up the phone and took Amanda into his arms.

He felt so warm and strong. "Feeling better?" she said.

Riley nodded. "You know what would make me feel even better, though?" he whispered, as he tunneled both hands through her hair.

Amanda grinned, guessing lightly, "The same thing that would help me?"

Riley swung her up into his arms. "Time's a wastin' then." He carried her up the stairs, down the hall.

"This is becoming a habit," Amanda teased, already trembling with need, as he deposited her on the bed.

"Gotta work off those cookies and milk somehow," he joked right back, in a voice that melted her reserve and appealed to her heart all the more. The next thing Amanda knew, Riley was stretched out beside her, one leg draped over hers. She lost her breath as his gaze lovingly roved her face and his lips covered hers once again.

They might not have everything worked out just yet, she thought dizzily, as she kissed him back as deeply and tenderly as he was kissing her, but right now, she didn't care. All that mattered to her was the chance to be with Riley like this. She knew he was the love of her life and if she didn't take advantage of this opportunity to be with him she would regret it forever, and she didn't want regrets where the two of them were concerned, only sweet, wonderful, blossoming love. The future, she was sure, would take care of itself. All she had to worry about now was the holiday ahead, and the hot, sizzling pressure of his mouth moving over hers. She moaned low in her throat, feeling everything around her go soft and fuzzy as he caught her lower lip in a tantalizing caress.

His expression fierce with longing and the primal need to possess, Riley stopped long enough to undress them both. Sensations ran riot through her, thrilling, enticing. Trembling, they climbed between the sheets and Riley took her in his arms again. He cupped her face, whispering her name, angling her head so he could deepen the kiss even more. Another shiver of excitement went through her. Heart pounding, the yearning in her a sweet incessant ache, she arched against him. Moving restlessly. Feeling the fullness of him straining against her thigh as he bent his head, his lips tracing an erotic path across her rosy-tipped breasts.

The hot slow strokes of his tongue across her nipples, the gentle suckling, was unbearably tender, intimate, seductive. Helpless to resist, Amanda closed her eyes. Pleasure drifted through every inch of her. Lower still, she felt a melting sensation, a weakening of her limbs. Her back arched, her thighs parted. They had barely started, and already she was on the edge of blissful oblivion. Loving the fragrance of his aftershave, so brisk and wintry, the sandpapery feel of his evening beard as it sensually abraded her skin.

"I want you," she murmured, as his hands and lips and teeth and tongue, found her there and there and there. "So much," she said as he shifted upward, fitting his mouth over hers once again.

He shifted onto his back, pulling her over him.

"I want you, too," he murmured, filling his hands with her breasts.

Eager to please him as he was pleasing her, Amanda caressed the smoothly muscled skin of his chest and shoulders, loving the way his flat male nipples pebbled beneath her questing palms. Lower still, the unmistakable evidence of his arousal nudged the softness between her thighs. Determined to give as much as she got, she worshipped him with her lips and tongue. She worked her way downward, past the silken hair and flat muscular abdomen to his abundant sex, even as she trembled with a fierce unquenchable ache. Wanting him to want her as fervently as she wanted him, she cupped the fertile part of him with one hand and stroked the length of him with the other, until he was quivering with need, repeatedly saying her name.

She slid upward once again, straddling his thighs. And then he was lifting her, positioning her just so. Amanda opened her legs and took him inside her, pulsing, aching, searching for pleasure and release. She had never felt as close to anyone as she did to Riley at that moment. She surrendered to him completely as their lips met in another searing, endless kiss. Trembling, they moved together, loving each other with every fiber of their beings, connecting as one heart, one soul, in a way that felt as real and indisputable and enduring as any marriage vow. And when they lay quietly, when they were still snuggled close, wrapped in each other's arms, Riley looked at the clock, and saw—as did Amanda—that it was just past midnight. And no longer December 23.

"It's Christmas Eve," he said, looking happier—more content—than she had ever seen him.

Amanda grinned, knowing this was her best holiday ever, too. "Well, then, Merry Christmas," Amanda responded right back, able now to envision many more blissful yuletides with Riley and the kids.

Riley planted a kiss on her brow and held her all the tighter. Tenderness radiated in his voice. "Merry Christmas indeed."

Riley and Amanda were finishing the breakfast dishes the next morning when they heard a soft, musical sound. Both abruptly stopped what they were doing and looked in the direction of the adjacent family room where the two older children were sitting on the floor, playing with their toys.

"Is that…'Feliz Navidad'?" Riley asked, his eyes lighting up with amazement.

"It certainly is!" Amanda smiled. Edging surreptitiously closer, they strained to listen. Chloe was indeed humming her version of the popular Christmas song. "This is a good sign," Amanda whispered happily.

Riley nodded and leaned down so his face was next to hers, his lips close enough to kiss. "Maybe Christmas will be what it takes to have our little angel talking again," he murmured softly, shooting an affectionate look at Chloe and her siblings.

"We can hope," Amanda said, her mood as festive as the song.

He steered her beneath another sprig of mistletoe, and they kissed, sweetly and tenderly. "You sure you're up for playing jolly old Mrs.-You-Know-Who for the kids at the hospital and the kids at the McCabe family's annual Christmas Eve Open House?" Riley teased.

Amanda nodded, warming at the intimacy in his voice and eyes. "Absolutely positively." She winked.

He waggled his eyebrows at her playfully. "If you want some help getting into the costume..."

Amanda splayed her hands across his chest, as eager as Riley to make wild, wonderful love again, and further the emotional bonds between them. "You just worry about watching the kids and helping Kate and your dad get ready for the party this evening," she instructed.

"You sure?" His heartbeat picked up beneath her palm. He bragged with macho self-assurance, "I'm very good with buttons and zippers."

"You can show me later," Amanda promised. She massaged the brawny width of his shoulders, let her hands ghost all the way down his muscular arms to his wrists. "Much later, when it's time to put on our kerchiefs and nightclothes and climb into bed and await the sounds of the sleigh bells on the roof."

Riley looked out the window. He looked handsome and relaxed in a burgundy pullover sweater that brought out the amber lights of his eyes. "You know the weatherman keeps insisting there's a chance of snow."

Amanda couldn't help but admire the way he filled out his gray gabardine dress slacks. The man had one nice backside. "They say that every year," she acknowledged as she moved closer yet. "It only happens once a decade or so."

"Well, maybe this year is the year," Riley hoped out loud.

"It certainly is the year for a lot of things," Amanda agreed, aware she had never felt happier.

Riley helped her into her coat. She went in to say goodbye to the kids, promising to meet up with them later at Kate and Sam's. Amber gave her an enthusiastic hug. The drowsy Cory cooed up at her from his bassinet. Chloe stopped humming to herself when she saw Amanda had her coat on and was getting ready to leave. As Amanda knelt to embrace her, the little girl held tight to Amanda's neck, drew back to look into Amanda's eyes. The old anxiousness was back, Amanda noted sorrowfully. "I promise. I'll see you later," Amanda reassured Chloe firmly. "We're all going to be together for Christmas, I promise."

For a second, Amanda thought Chloe was going to say something in return. But the moment passed, and the four-year-old merely offered a faint smile and hugged Amanda fiercely again.

Riley thought about Chloe's reaction to Amanda's leave-taking the rest of the morning, into the afternoon. Sadly, he knew exactly how the little girl felt. There was so much he wanted to say, too, so much he feared, too. What he had found with Amanda was a once-in-a-lifetime love and happiness. He could only hope Amanda felt it, too. One way or another, he would find out on Christmas Day.

In the meantime, he had three children to get ready and transport to the McCabe family gathering. And this time he would be doing it without Amanda's help. Fortunately before she left, she had helped lay out the clothes each child was to wear, readied the bottles of formula and packed the diaper bag with essentials to take along. So Riley's exit from the house went much smoother than it would have had he been left to his own devices. Eager to see his brother and find out if there was any new information on the children's identity, Riley sought out Kevin as soon as he arrived. "Got a minute?"

"I want to talk to you, too," Kevin told Riley. Kevin glanced at Micki and Laurel, who were seated on the floor, playing with Chloe and Amber. "But we should do it privately. Let's bring some more wood in for the fire," Kevin said.

Riley handed baby Cory to his brother Will. "Watch him, for a minute, would you?"

Will—the oldest of Riley's brothers and the most determinedly unmarried—looked as if he had been handed twelve pounds of dangerous material, instead of a baby. But he concurred nevertheless.

Riley and Kevin donned jackets and walked out back to the woodpile. The sky was a wintry gray overhead. The air felt damp and cold, ready for snow. Riley's hopes for a magically white Christmas intensified. "So what's up? Did you track down Micki's sister and brother-in-law for me?"

"No," Kevin frowned. "And I have to tell you why…."

Riley was still numb from what he had just learned when he and Kevin walked back inside. He knew what he had to do as he walked over to where Micki was playing with the kids. "Micki, could you help me with something?" Riley said.

Micki looked up. Once again, Riley was fairly certain, from the residual puffiness of her eyes, that Micki had been crying. Now, sadly, he finally understood why.

Micki looked surprised, but as willing to help out as ever. "Sure."

Kevin winked at Micki as he sat down next to Amber, Chloe and Laurel. "I'll keep your place," he teased the youthful group around him lightheartedly. "I'm more fun anyway!"

"Ha!" Laurel said, in response to her brother's teasing, as Riley and Micki walked toward the front of the big Victorian.

"Let's step into my dad's study," Riley said. It was the one place he knew they wouldn't be disturbed.

Micki began to look alarmed as Riley shut the double doors behind them. "Is something wrong?" she said.

Riley rested a hip against his dad's massive desk. "I thought maybe you could tell me."

Silence fell. Micki's lower lip began to tremble.

So much made sense to Riley now. "You're the one who left those kids for me," he said slowly. "Aren't you?"

Tears flooded Micki's eyes. "Please don't be mad at me," she begged. "I just didn't see any other way."

"Why don't we start at the beginning?" Riley suggested kindly.

Micki swallowed hard. "My sister and her husband were killed in a car accident last September. I was named guardian of Chloe, Amber and Cory. So I brought all three kids back to Austin with me and they moved in with me and Laurel."

Which explained a lot, Riley thought. Laurel's disastrous grades, her defiant proclamation she'd do it all again, the nonstop requests for more money from Kate and his dad.

"I tried—I really did—but even with Laurel's help I couldn't be both mother and father to them." Micki's chin quivered. Tears dripped down her face. She scrubbed them away with her fingers. "I knew I was going to have to find someone else to take them, someone who loved kids, somebody who wanted a family of their own but didn't have one yet."

"Why didn't you just ask me then?" Riley said gently, struggling to understand why the two young women had felt such an elaborate ruse was necessary to get him involved in the situation. Hadn't he gone all out to help Micki secure a position as a premed summer intern and written her a stellar recommendation to medical school?

"Because Laurel and I both figured you'd say no if we did, because you weren't married yet and you were starting a new job and you didn't yet have any experience being a daddy. On the other hand—" Micki paused and shrugged "—we decided if we left you the kids as kind of a Christmas gift and asked you to give them the holiday they deserved, and we stuck around to see you got a lot of help taking care of them, that everything would be okay. You would get to know them, and once that happened, we figured you'd love them, too, as much as we do, and want to keep them. We never imagined you'd think Amanda dropped off the kids as a joke on you or demand she marry you as a result!"

Riley ran a hand across his jaw, smiled ruefully. "That was a little dramatic, wasn't it?"

"No kidding!" Micki enthused. "People at the hospital are still talking about it. But even that seems to be working out all right." Micki paused to search his face. "Because you do love her, don't you, Riley," Micki noted with an emotional satisfaction that matched Riley's own. "You love both Amanda and the kids."

Amanda couldn't say why, but she just knew something important had happened between the time she had left the house and arrived at the McCabe family gathering. Micki looked different. So did Riley. But she had no chance to speak to either of them privately as she walked in, a big basket of presents over her arm. Speaking in a jolly bass tone, Amanda Ho-Ho-Hoed her way through the throngs of family and friends, passing out envelopes from Santa to those who had written him and dropped their letters off at the hospital pediatric wing mailbox, and distributed gifts provided by Kate and Sam McCabe to all of the children.

"Want to sit on Mrs. Claus's lap?" Riley asked Amber when Amanda took the chair of honor before the fireplace.

Amber gleefully complied. Struggling to stand up, she patted Amanda's face with both her tiny palms, running her fingers through the strands of curly white hair framing her face, examining the gold-rimmed glasses perched on the edge of her nose, and the velvety fabric of her costume. Finally, Amber patted Amanda's rouged cheeks and pronounced her, "Pretty!"

Everyone roared with laughter.

Riley winked. "I agree."

Next up were Brad and Laney's two preschoolers. Their older brother, Petey, also played along.

Several more cousins took their turns.

Then baby Cory.

Finally, it was Chloe's turn. Expression serious, she climbed onto Amanda's lap, looking soberly into her eyes.

Amanda adjusted her gold-rimmed Santa glasses. "And what would you like for Christmas, little girl?" Amanda prodded in the most compelling Mrs. Claus-voice she could manage.

Chloe looked at Amanda.

Then Riley.

Back at Amanda again.

There was no clue as to whether Chloe recognized Amanda or not. And to Amanda's disappointment, Chloe still didn't speak.

"It's just going to take time for the communication with you-know-who to be ongoing again," Riley said, hours later, as he and Amanda drove the short distance back to his house. "It will happen."

Amanda certainly hoped so. She couldn't help but feel a little like a failure. She had been so certain that Chloe's Christmas gift to them was going to be to start talking again. Or at least communicating more openly in some way. Instead, the self-protective wall remained up, strong as ever.

Although no one would ever know it from Riley's behavior. He hadn't been able to stop smiling whenever he looked at her or the kids all evening. Micki and Laurel had seemed to be extraordinarily relaxed and joyful, too. For the first time, Micki's face had lost that pinched, way-too-serious expression she wore whenever she thought no one was looking her way.

"Let's get the kids in their pajamas and tuck them in, and then we'll…talk," Riley said.

Amanda lifted a brow.

Riley flashed her a sexy things-are-so-good-you-just-don't-know smile again. It was the kind of grin someone had when they just knew they had gotten you the perfect Christmas present and couldn't wait to give it to you, Amanda thought. Which in turn made her wonder what Riley was going to think of the rather lame—but nice—wristwatch she had selected for him. At the time, she had felt it appropriate.

Now, it didn't begin to relay all she felt in her heart for him. She could only hope he would understand that so much had changed between then and now. And would continue to do so.

By the time they had the kids ready for bed, another half hour had passed and baby Cory was already sleeping soundly. Riley deposited him in his bassinet then joined Amanda, Chloe and Amber on Chloe's bed. Chloe was clutching a copy of *'Twas The Night Before Christmas* in her hand. She thrust it at Amanda. "You want me to read this?" Amanda asked. And thought, but couldn't be sure it wasn't her imagination, that Chloe nodded ever so slightly in response.

"Pretty!" Amber said as she scooted over onto the right side of Amanda's lap.

Chloe took up residence on Amanda's left side.

Riley sat against the headboard and stretched his legs out in front of him. "Sounds good to me," he said.

Achingly aware of how much a family they felt at this moment, Amanda opened the book and began to read. Amber was nearly asleep when she finished; Chloe, spellbound. Amanda closed the book. "You know Santa is going to come here tonight and leave you a present under the tree. And one for Amber and baby Cory too, but he can't come until you're asleep."

Chloe's eyes sparkled with excitement.

"We're pretty sure you're going to be happy with the presents Amanda and I have for you this year, too," Riley said.

Chloe's smile broadened slightly.

"Ready to go to sleep?" Amanda asked, gently ruffling the little girl's curls.

And this time Chloe did nod. Quickly, she scrambled to her feet, wrapped her arms around Riley's neck and hugged him hard. Kissed his cheek. Then hugged and kissed Amanda just as enthusiastically. Amanda and Riley kissed and hugged her right back. Amber joined in. And there was so much excitement it was another fifteen minutes before they had them settled into their beds. "Meet you downstairs in five?" Riley whispered at the bedroom door.

Amanda nodded.

She stayed nearby, until she was sure all three children were sleeping soundly and went back downstairs, her present to Riley tucked into the pocket of her red velvet jumper.

He had the Christmas tree lights on, and the rest of the living room lights off. A cozy fire burned in the fireplace. A bottle of wine sat open on the coffee table, along with two long-stemmed glasses. Amanda's heart took a little leap as she joined him on the sofa. "Looks like we're celebrating," she said lightly.

His eyes darkened. "You have no idea," he said dryly, taking both her hands in his, squeezing them affectionately. "I have so much to tell you I don't know where to begin."

Amanda'd heard an opening statement like this once before, the night Fraser had told her he wanted to reconcile with his wife, so he was divorcing her and taking his kids with him. But this couldn't be the same, she told herself sternly. For one thing, Riley looked happy with whatever it was. "So what happened today?" she asked, unbearably curious. "What haven't you told me?"

"I found out who the kids are, Amanda," Riley announced proudly. "I know who left them with me."

Chapter 13

"How? When?" Amanda asked, looking every bit as shocked and wary as Riley had felt hours earlier.

Riley took both of her hands in his. Briefly, he explained what Kevin had found out about Micki's sister and her husband. "They were killed in a car accident in September," Riley related sadly, his heart going out to his young protégée and her two nieces and nephew. "Apparently, Micki was given custody of her sister's children and she took Amber, Chloe and Cory back to Austin with her. They moved in with her and Laurel and, with Laurel helping her every step of the way, Micki made every effort to be a good guardian to them."

Amanda sat back against the cushions of the sofa, still struggling to take it all in. "Which explains why Laurel's grades went down," she theorized, slowly extricating her hands from his.

Riley nodded. "Apparently, Laurel figured it wouldn't matter what GPA she graduated with, but they knew Micki's grades had to be excellent if she wanted to get into medical school, and she did."

Amanda laid a hand across her heart. "And no one knew?"

Riley shrugged. "Micki didn't want anyone finding out, for fear that her custody of the three kids would somehow keep her from achieving her long-held dream of becoming a doctor. She especially didn't want me to know, since she had already asked me to write a recommendation for her, which I had done."

Amanda rose from the sofa and began to pace the room restlessly, her mood remote and tense. "So the two girls kept it a secret."

"Until they realized they were in over their heads. Micki wanted to come to me then and ask me to adopt the kids, but Laurel wasn't sure I would take it on alone, if they simply asked me."

Amanda paused in front of the fireplace. She ran both her hands through her silky hair. "So instead they hatched the plan to pretend the kids had mysteriously been left at the hospital for you."

"Right. Knowing all the while the two of them would be there to lend a hand and see the kids were all right. They didn't figure on you being made mother." Restless now, too, Riley stood and crossed to Amanda's side. He lounged opposite her, thrusting his hands in his pockets, leaning one shoulder against the mantel. "But they couldn't be happier about the way things have turned out."

Amanda tipped her head up to his. Some of the light left her blue-green eyes. "What do you mean?"

Riley smiled at Amanda determinedly. He looked deep into her eyes and cupped her shoulders warmly. "I told them both that I'm going to stay married to you and we're going to raise the kids together." He paused, aware the words weren't having the effect he had hoped, given the passionate and romantic turn their relationship had taken the last few days.

Her unexpected reserve confused and frustrated him. He had been certain from the way Amanda had been behaving toward him, that this was what they both had been hoping would happen—that the kids would be theirs, and the way would be clear for them all to be together in the traditional family way. Yet Amanda was behaving as if he were backing her into a corner against her will.

Out of nerves or simply the traditional premarriage doubts and fears?

Figuring if ever there was a time to be presumptuous, this was it, he continued with a bolstering smile. "Micki and Laurel couldn't be happier."

To Riley's consternation, Amanda looked even more nervous and on edge. She backed away from him once again. "So everyone at the party—your whole family—knows this?" she questioned him, incredulously.

"No." Riley paused, searching her face. He knew everything was happening very quickly. It had been a shock to him, too. "Just me, and Laurel and Micki, and Kevin and now you. Micki was adamant we not sadden everyone's Christmas with the news of her tragedy." Riley closed the distance between them once again.

"Micki is ready to move forward on the adoption immediately," he told Amanda seriously.

Twin spots of color appeared in her cheek. "I see," she returned in a brisk, emotional voice.

"Assuming," Riley continued gruffly, "you still want to be a mother to the kids and stay married to me." Right now, he noted, as dread filled his soul, she did not look as if that were the case.

Amanda tossed her head. "You think there's a reason why I shouldn't?" she asked, testy.

Riley sighed. Still eyeing her determinedly, he released a short, impatient breath. "I think that you think there's a reason why we shouldn't." And he didn't like that at all.

* * *

It was the moment of truth, Amanda knew. Riley was offering her all she had ever wanted. Yet something about his matter-of-fact recitation rang hollow with her. And the emptiness of his words echoed the void deep inside her. "You know that I love the kids with all my heart," she started thickly, achingly aware of all he hadn't said. That he loved her, that she was the only woman for him and always would be. That the two of them had what it took to build a lasting marriage that would serve as the solid family foundation needed to adopt the three children and see them through to adulthood and beyond. This was a lifetime commitment they were about to make, yet it didn't seem as if Riley were thinking much past the immediate future. And while Amanda appreciated his gallantry, she knew they couldn't pretend that passion, friendship and mutual concern about the children was enough to hold a marriage together. Bitter experience had shown her that was not the case, that without a deep and abiding romantic love between husband and wife a family could not survive over the long haul.

"And yet...despite this love...?" Riley prompted, sauntering closer.

Amanda swallowed as he advanced on her slowly, his eyes holding hers. She had to make him see the truth of their situation. Trembling at his nearness, Amanda held up her hands. Heart breaking, she paced away from him once again. "What did your letter to Santa say, Riley?"

Riley blinked and regarded her cautiously. "What does that have to do with this?" he demanded.

"Bear with me," Amanda replied in the same short tone. She retrieved both letters from the antique writing desk by the window and handed the one she had written to him. Struggling with all her might to hold back her tears, she commanded, "Open it."

Riley shot a curious look at her, tore the seal.

"Read it," Amanda ordered.

With a frown, Riley complied, reading the first five words that were there for everyone participating in the letter writing activity and then the ones that were handwritten on the blank line provided.

Dear Santa, Please give me the loving husband and children I have always wanted. This time, for keeps.

Riley looked up, as if not sure what her point was. "So we're on the same page," he said with an indifferent shrug. "So what?"

But Amanda knew, and she didn't much like the unwelcome truth that was staring them both in the face. She regarded him politely. "Now may I read your letter to Santa?"

He stood, legs braced apart, arms folded in front of him. Looking increasingly disillusioned, he ordered tersely, "Go ahead."

Amanda carefully slid a delicate finger beneath the seal, loosened it, and withdrew the letter without ripping the envelope. She read the scripted words out loud. And then the ones he had written in his commanding scrawl,

Dear Santa, Please give me a family. And Chloe, Amber and Cory one that loves and cares for them, too.

Riley started toward her impatiently. "Now that we know we both ultimately want the same thing…" he said, handing over the offending paper.

"Don't you see?" Amanda waved the letter in front of him, like the red flag it was. Emotion choked her voice so she could hardly speak. "We both want this to work out so badly we're willing to convince ourselves of darn near anything."

Riley stared at her, his jaw hardening to the consistency of granite.

Knowing it sounded like the cruelest kiss-off possible, Amanda forced herself to forget her own selfish ambitions and do what was right nevertheless. "Our shared affection for the children is not enough to build a family on, at least not one that will last," she said as a heartrending silence fell between them.

She shook her head, feeling unbearably weary. Resigned. "Divorce is really hard on kids, Riley," she told him emotionally. She couldn't bear to knowingly hurt the three children they already loved so much. "Chloe, Amber and baby Cory have already been through so much, losing their folks, living with Micki and Laurel, being dropped off with us." Amanda's voice broke. She shoved both her hands through her hair. "It wouldn't be fair to let them think we were in a situation that would last forever if it isn't going to last forever."

Hurt and anger faded, to be replaced by an icy resolve that chilled Amanda to her soul. A stoic look in his amber eyes, he asked her calmly but brusquely, "Are you telling me you don't want to be married to me?"

Under these conditions? "This is exactly what I'm telling you," Amanda told him firmly but sadly. As difficult as it was for both of them, she knew she was doing the right thing.

Riley knew he was supposed to bow out like a gentleman and let her go. Trouble was, he had never felt less gallant in his life. "I don't get it," he told Amanda angrily.

Shaking her head in futility, she brushed past him and headed for the rear of the house. "I know that you've wanted a family for quite a while. So have I. And I know how you like to fast forward your way through all things domestic."

He followed her out the door into the garage. "Speak your mind, why don't you?"

She paused next to the trunk of her car. There was no missing the mounting disappointment and resentment in her eyes. "Listen to me, Riley. You bought this house because it was already furnished right down to the dishes and you didn't have to do a thing but move in. Granted, you didn't plan or even ask for any of this, but the end result was that you got three kids and a wife practically the same way. Boom. One minute you're a single guy. The next you're both a husband and a daddy to three gorgeous kids."

Riley watched as she unlocked the trunk, then pushed it open for her. "I didn't hear you objecting all that much at the time," he said, staring down at the presents heaped inside.

"Because, as these letters just demonstrated, it was my fantasy, too." Amanda brought out several gaily wrapped packages. Riley followed suit. "But we have to be realistic," she continued stalwartly. "If these three kids hadn't been dropped into our laps, we would most definitely not be married today."

He followed her inside. "You don't know that."

"I know this." Amanda set the packages down underneath the tree, then whirled to face him. She tapped a finger against his sternum. "Sex, fun, domestic compatibility and a shared love of practical jokes is not enough of a foundation for a marriage."

He followed her back to the garage to get more presents, his actions as deliberate as hers. "I thought we were doing pretty good."

She stalked across the cement floor of the garage, the long feminine skirt of her red velvet dress swirling around her shapely calves. "Really."

"Yes."

She whirled to face him. "Riley, we've been playing house."

He ignored her withering glance. "I haven't been *playing* anything."

"You're right," Amanda returned bitterly. "You've been honest. You never pretended to be doing this for anything other than your desire to give the kids security."

Riley's heart slammed against his ribs. "I told you how I

felt about you," he reminded. It had been in every look, every action, every kiss, every time he made love to her.

Amanda pressed her lips together grimly. "Sex is not love, Riley."

What they had experienced could not be faked. "Says who?" Riley volleyed right back.

"Says me!" Amanda cried emotionally. "And every other adult who has fallen into the trap of making love for all the wrong reasons, the way we have been, and then gone on to regret it." Her turquoise eyes glimmering moistly, she turned away from him.

"Like you are now," Riley guessed, watching her rummage blindly through the presents still in the trunk.

"Yes." She finally picked up two of the lighter ones.

"Why?" Riley grabbed the heaviest packages.

Amanda drew a stabilizing breath. Spine stiff, she headed back into the house again. "Because the fact that we are very good together in the sack muddles things terribly," she whispered.

Riley waited until they had set their presents down in front of the tree. He took her by the shoulders. "You're wrong, Amanda. The fact we are good together clarifies everything."

She wrested free, stepped back with dignity and grace. "It certainly shows just how vulnerable we both have been," she observed quietly.

"So you're saying you bedded me because you were lonely?" Riley snapped, folding his arms and assuming a militant stance.

"And because it's Christmas," she retorted, just as fiercely. "And because we've been caught up in the spirit of the season. And we wanted to be able to stay together for the kids," she concluded miserably.

He stared at her in frustration. "We still can."

Cupping a hand around the back of her neck, he tried to make her look at him, but she wouldn't and she wasn't listening, either. "Riley, I can't be married to you without also knowing we have the kind of love that lasts a lifetime." She speared him with a censuring gaze.

"And you don't think we do." For him, her actions were a bitter replay of the past. Evangeline had turned down his marriage proposal because she didn't want marriage, love or kids. Amanda was turning him down because she did. She just didn't trust him to be able to give them to her, not in any lasting fashion anyway.

"Sadly, no," Amanda stated carefully. "I don't."

"So what was the last week about, then?" Riley asked angrily. "The ultimate in practical jokes? An extension of the one you last tried to play on me?" Had all of this, the lovemaking, the sweet words, the confidences, been nothing more than payback for past jokes? he wondered.

Amanda tried to go around him. "This is nothing like our meeting in the high school stadium that night."

He moved to block her way to the garage. He knew they still had more presents to bring in, but that could wait—this truth-telling session couldn't. "Don't you mean the meeting that didn't happen?" he asked her silkily, ignoring the killer look she aimed his way. "Will your friends be laughing with you over this one, too, Amanda?" he continued cynically, feeling like the biggest chump there ever was. "'Cause I know it's something everyone in Laramie won't soon forget."

Amanda stood as still and lifeless as a statue. "It doesn't matter what other people think."

"Maybe it didn't before," Riley differed curtly, "when we both left Laramie and headed off to college. Now things are different." He struggled to regain control of his emotions. "Now we are both going to stay." And he would forever be labeled as Amanda Witherspoon's fool.

The phone rang. Almost grateful for the interruption—anything had to be better than this misery—Riley stalked over, picked up the receiver and barked into it. "McCabe here."

"Riley, Jackson."

Riley quickly noted his uncle was using his chief-of-staff tone.

"Someone put tainted eggs into the nog at First Baptist's Christmas Festival this afternoon. We've got a hundred people here at the E.R., all sicker than dogs, and more arriving by the moment. Can you come in and help us out?"

As ready to roll in an emergency as ever, Riley said, "I'll be right there." He hung up the phone, turned back to Amanda. "I've got to go to the hospital."

She looked at him, composed, matter-of-fact once again. "What are we going to do about tomorrow, the kids, Christmas?"

Riley shrugged and didn't reply. Too hurt to even think about it, too choked up to get a single word out, he went to grab his coat.

"I'll stay with the kids," she offered.

But not with me, Riley thought, heartbroken. He swallowed hard around the gathering lump in his throat. Reminding himself that the kids' needs still required attention, Riley tabled his own anger and hurt and made his tone as cool as hers. "Thanks." With a growing sense of helplessness, he was out the door.

Over at the hospital, things were even worse than what Jackson had described on the phone. People of all ages were reaching for basins, or running for the bathrooms. The children and the elderly were particularly hard hit. It was nearly midnight before they had everyone treated and either released or admitted to one of the rooms upstairs.

Riley had never been partial to nog, but he knew he would never be drinking it again. Nor would anyone he cared about, unless he was certain it had been made with pasteurized egg product instead of raw eggs.

"Can I talk to you for a minute?" Jackson asked as he and Riley headed out to their cars in the physician's parking lot.

"Sure." The cold air felt good. Riley looked up. He still didn't see any snow. But the air was so damp it almost stung against his face.

"Thanks for helping out tonight," Jackson said, their low voices and footfalls the only sound in the otherwise silent night. "I'm aware you didn't have to give up your holiday to come in, under the circumstances."

Riley shrugged. He watched their breaths turn frosty in the winter air. "I wanted to help. I'm a doctor. This is what I do."

"I know that." Jackson paused as they leaned against Riley's SUV. He looked Riley straight in the eye. "I think I misjudged you, earlier in the week. When those kids were delivered to the hospital—"

Riley held up a hand. "I reacted badly, I know."

Jackson shook his head, disagreeing. "You reacted admirably under the circumstances," he corrected. "After your initial shock, anyway. Taking charge, making sure the kids had a good holiday. Even your relationship with Amanda was a lot more complex than I first thought."

"And maybe not," Riley sighed. He thrust his hands in the pockets of his coat.

Jackson's glance narrowed. "What do you mean?"

Riley knew he had to confide in someone. "I asked her to stay married to me tonight." He sighed his frustration and regret. "She said no."

Jackson blinked. "Why?"

Riley shrugged and ran the toe of his boot across the blacktop. "Beats the heck out of me. None of her reasons made a whit of sense."

"Doesn't she love you?"

"I thought she did," Riley replied shortly.

Jackson paused. "She knows how much you love her, doesn't she?"

Riley frowned. "She certainly should. I've shown her in every way I could think."

"And of course," Jackson returned with a dry look, "you've said the words out loud, too."

It was Riley's turn to pause.

"Oh, man. Tell me you didn't neglect to do that!" Jackson shook his head.

Riley threw up his hands and defended himself hotly. "I was working up to it."

"Well, I wouldn't stay married to you either under those circumstances!" Jackson retorted.

"Thanks ever so much for the support." Riley turned away.

Jackson slapped a familial hand on Riley's shoulder, turned him back. "I know your pride is hurt by the rejection, Riley. And victory in this competition or whatever it is between you and Amanda has meant everything to you, up to this point. But maybe it's time that changed."

Amanda had just corked the wine and was putting away the unused glasses when the phone rang again. It was her sister, Priscilla. "You have to know we were all very disappointed you didn't get on that flight this evening and come back to California, Amanda."

Amanda released a long, slow breath and said calmly, "I told you I wasn't going to do it." Her days of dancing to her family's tune were over.

"For a change fee, you could still come home early tomorrow and be here for Christmas Day. I checked. There is space available on the 7:00 a.m. flight out of Dallas."

Amanda frowned. Had it only been a few hours since Riley had left to go to the hospital? It felt like a lifetime. "Priscilla, I appreciate all you and everyone else including Mom and Dad have done for me over the years. I'm happy you want me in California for the holidays. But my home is here in Laramie now and so is my family," she finished, before she could stop herself or think about the enormity of what she was saying.

Priscilla gasped. "You can't possibly be thinking of staying married to that troublemaker Riley McCabe!"

Was she? Amanda had gone into this relationship with him more on a lark or a dare than anything else. But all that had changed in the time they had spent together. She had never dreamed she could have it all with him. But Riley had stormed through the walls around her heart and shown her that she had never lost the potential to love or be loved in return. He just hadn't loved her. At least not in any conventional way. And yet what they had shared had been so much better and more fulfilling than anything she had ever had, because she had paid less attention to what other people thought she should do and had instead done what felt right to her in her heart. And that had been to love Riley with every fiber of her being, without worrying what he might or might not give her in return. And they had done the same for the children. To Amanda's surprise, giving of herself so freely and unconditionally still did not feel like a mistake. What was it people said about love? That it was the gift that kept on giving?

Aware her sister was waiting for her response, Amanda said firmly, "Whether I stay hitched or not is my business and my decision and no one else's. Please send everyone my love and tell them Merry Christmas for me." Amanda hung up the phone. Her heart felt lighter than it had in years. And at the same time, heavier.

Hearing baby Cory begin to stir upstairs, Amanda put a bottle in the warmer, and went up to get him. She eased him out of the bassinet, paused long enough to check on Chloe and Amber—both were still sleeping soundly—and, clean diaper in hand, carried Cory back downstairs. As she walked through the foyer, she heard a car door outside.

Riley! Amanda thought hopefully. Her heart sank as she saw Micki stepping out of the car. Amanda had the front door open by the time Micki reached the stoop. She ushered her inside.

"I'm glad you're still up," Micki said.

Amanda noted it looked as if Micki might have been crying again. "I had a chance to talk with Riley," Micki rushed on, slipping out of her coat. "But I didn't get to speak to you. And there's so much I want to say."

"I've been wanting to talk to you, too," Amanda told the young girl gently. "You've really had a rough time." Amanda laced her free arm around Micki's shoulders. Together they walked into the kitchen.

"You don't know the half of it." Micki wiped fresh tears away.

Amanda plucked the bottle from the warmer. Still cradling Cory in one arm, she tested it on her wrist, while Micki talked about the accident that claimed her sister and brother-in-law's life, explaining about the will that left all three children to her.

"I had doubts all along about whether I could do it or not," Micki confessed, "especially when Chloe shut down and just stopped talking and withdrew into herself, but I knew I had to try. So I took the kids back to Austin with me, and Laurel was great about letting them all move in with us and helping me take care of them, to the detriment of her own grades."

"I understand Laurel helping you," Amanda said. "Why didn't she tell her folks?"

"Because I asked her not to." Looking more stressed out than ever, Micki rubbed at the tense muscles in the back of her neck. "I was still trying to get into medical school under early admission, and I had asked Riley to write a recommendation for me." Micki paused, bit her lip. "I was afraid if he knew I had custody of three children that he would feel I had too much on my plate to undertake physician education and training in addition to parenting. I know it's selfish, but I didn't want to be refused my dream for that reason."

Amanda looked at Micki with understanding. "When did you decide you wanted Riley to have the kids?"

Micki rested her chin on her upturned hand. "I knew I had to find a family for them by early November, but I didn't want them to go to just anyone and I knew from my sister's and my own experiences that once you become a ward of social services that things happen under their rules and guidelines. The person giving the children away doesn't get to say who they end up with. I had heard from Laurel how much Riley wanted a family of his own, how impatient he was for that to happen. I figured if I brought them here, and Riley adopted them, that he'd have his whole family—all the McCabes—to help him. I never figured on you and Riley falling in love, but I have to tell you," Micki confided earnestly, "that made my giving the kids to him all that much easier."

Amanda shifted Cory to her shoulder for a burp. "Why didn't you just tell him outright what you wanted him to do?"

"Laurel thought Riley would refuse, without really even considering it, because he was going to start a new job and he hadn't had any experience being a daddy. We also both knew what a softie he is, deep down, and we sensed that if he was around them that he would love the kids as much as we did."

"Well, convoluted as your plan was," Amanda said kindly, "it did work. Riley and I both love the kids dearly." To the point Amanda did not want to give them up, any more than she wanted to give up Riley—and their marriage.

"And they love you, too. I can tell. In fact, I think Chloe's about ready to start talking again. She was on the verge of blurting something out several times today."

Amanda smiled, agreeing. "I've had that feeling, too."

Micki watched as Amanda continued giving Cory his bottle. "It's because you and Riley make her feel safe in the same way her parents did, the way I just can't, no matter how hard I try." She shook her head in obvious frustration, then went on frankly, "I mean, I know all three kids love me and like spending time with me, but it's as an aunt, not a mommy." Micki paused, looking relieved she had gotten that off her chest. "Riley said if you adopt the kids I can still see them a lot and be an aunt to them. Do you feel the same way?"

Amanda nodded emphatically. "I think you should be in their lives, Micki. I think they'd miss you terribly if you weren't. And the same goes for me."

Fresh tears appeared in Micki's eyes. She got up and came over to give Amanda a hug. "You're the best," she said thickly, wiping her eyes. "Riley and the kids are so lucky to have you in their lives. Riley knows it, too. Everyone was talking about it at the party after you guys left. They said they'd never seen Riley look at anyone the way he looked at you tonight."

Hope rose in Amanda. She knew she had never looked at anyone the way she looked at Riley. Was it possible…?

"No one thought your marriage had a chance, especially 'cause of the way it all started, but now…" Micki hesitated. "You are going to stay married to Riley, aren't you?"

Was she? An hour ago Amanda would have said unequivocally no, she was not. Now…now she wasn't so certain. And it had to do with so much more than what was best for the kids in the here and now. Or even the distant future. It had to do with what was in her heart.

Chapter 14

Tiny snowflakes, almost too little to see, were filling the air as Riley parked his SUV in front of his house. The night sky had taken on the soft white glow of a winter storm. Down the street, many of the residences had gone dark except for the festive Christmas lights. Inside his home, the upstairs windows were dark, but the lights downstairs—including those on the Christmas tree visible through the sheer draperies—were still burning bright.

Did that mean Amanda was still up?

And if so, was she waiting for him, or waiting for him to arrive and take charge of the children so that she could pack her bags and leave?

Figuring it didn't matter what Amanda had planned, so long as she heard him out, he stepped out of his SUV and headed for the door. Heart thudding with anticipation of seeing her again, Riley unlocked the front door and walked inside.

Amanda was where he had left her.

Only this time her hair was swept up on the back of her head and she was wearing a pair of red flannel pajamas festooned with ribbon-wrapped candy canes and reindeer-drawn sleighs. Riley wasn't sure what was sexier, the soft warm fabric over softer, warmer skin, or the fact she was ready for bed and waiting for him. All he knew for certain was that she had never looked more beautiful—nor more determined—lounging on the sofa, a book in her hands. He took off his coat, and headed in to join her by the fire.

"We need to talk," she said simply, turning her eyes up to his. She tossed the velvety lap robe away from her knees, swung her legs gracefully off the center cushions of the sofa, and shifted her feet onto the floor. After a moment in which she stared long and hard at the fire, she turned back to him and forced herself to go on. "I think I was too hasty before," she continued introspectively as she motioned for him to sit down beside her.

"I think so, too," Riley said quietly. He dropped down next to her and turned, one leg angled toward her, so they were facing each other. Draping an arm along the back of the sofa, he made himself comfortable and waited for her to go on, his gut twisted into a knot of apprehension. He wanted so much for them—a happy marriage, raising the three children together…everlasting love. But she had to want those things, too.

Amanda swallowed. Turquoise-blue eyes shrewdly direct, she reached over and took his hand in hers. "We shouldn't end things this way."

"Also agreed," Riley told her solemnly.

She squeezed his fingers affectionately. "Christmas is a time for giving."

Riley turned in the direction of her gaze and for the first time noticed two gift-wrapped boxes on the coffee table, one small and square, the other rectangular and about the size of a shirt. He felt his hopes rise another notch.

"And although I wasn't initially at all certain about the gifts I selected for you," she said in a low, tremulous voice, "now I think they are exactly right."

Riley knew his were the correct gifts, too. The challenge would be in convincing her of that.

As she looked over at him, Riley thought, but couldn't be sure, there was a telltale sheen of emotion in her eyes. There was no doubt there was plenty of remorse. She paused, shook her head, "I thought I needed romance to be happy, Riley."

Knowing he'd never had so much at stake in his entire life, afraid she was going to tell him straight out that she didn't love him and never would, Riley cut her off with a recitation of his own regrets. He wanted her to know he was to blame for what had gone wrong between them, too. "And I thought I needed an immediate solution to our dilemma of where we go from here." His voice caught. It was a moment before he could go on in a voice anywhere near cool, "I don't."

She regarded him, perplexed.

"I denied you a proper courtship," Riley explained, achingly aware he had moved way too fast for Amanda's comfort, in an effort to make her his. "I thrust you into the mother and wife role you weren't prepared to take on and then made the case that just because we could live together harmoniously, loved the kids and had great sex that we could live happily ever after. You told me it wasn't enough, and you were right, Amanda. It's not. But at the same time, just because you don't love me...yet," he told her hoarsely, "is no reason to call it quits."

Amanda blinked. And this time there was no doubt, Riley noticed. Her eyes were full of tears. "Wait," she said thickly. "What did you say?"

"Just because you don't love me..." he repeated gruffly.

"But I do!" Amanda protested.

Riley inhaled deeply. He let his breath out slowly as the first glimmer of hope rose in his chest. "Say that again?" he asked.

Amanda shifted over onto his lap, wreathed her arms about his neck. She smiled at him, all the joy he had ever wanted to see on her beautiful face, and looked directly into his eyes. "I. Love. You. Riley McCabe."

Joy filled Riley's heart. He could only stare at her in wonderment. Hot damn, this was one great Christmas! "I love you, too, Mrs. McCabe," he told her in a low, rusty-sounding voice.

"Well, why didn't you say so?" Amanda demanded, clinging to him as if she never wanted to let him go. Her eyes were overflowing, her voice was clogged with tears.

Riley held her closer still, loving the way she felt in his arms. Wondering how he had ever managed without her, glad he was never going to have to do so again, he told her softly, "I thought I had told you." He paused to search her face. "Every time I kissed you or held you or made love to you, I thought you knew." He tunneled his hands through the silk of her hair, loving the way she felt cuddled so close against him. "I thought words were cheap, that it was actions and intent that counted. But now I know words are every bit as necessary as deeds." He caught the shimmer of happiness in her eyes and couldn't help but grin. "So plan on hearing those three words from me every day for the rest of our lives."

Amanda kissed him sweetly. "I promise to say them, too. Because I do love you, Riley, so very much."

They kissed again, even more passionately. "Speaking of love," Riley said, when the languorous caress finally came to a halt. "I have two gifts to give you that speak to what is in my heart." He handed over two boxes.

Amanda noted that both looked as if they had contained jewelry. Could they be…? With shaking hands, Amanda opened the smaller one first. She caught her breath at the sight of the sparkling marquise diamond.

"Oh, Riley," she breathed, so moved she could barely speak.

He looked deep into her eyes. "This is the engagement ring you should have had if we'd done things properly," he told her in a gruff, tender voice.

He slipped it onto her finger.

Amanda admired the exquisite jewelry against her skin. It was perfect. He was perfect. "It's absolutely beautiful," she said softly.

Grinning, Riley drawled, "I'm glad you think so." He handed her the next gift. Her hands still trembling, she opened it, too.

Inside were two matching gold bands.

Before she could take the smaller one out and slip it on, he cautioned her, "I don't want us to wear these just yet."

She looked up, disappointed.

He told her in the firm masculine voice she had come to love, "I want to wait until we've said our vows again, in front of family and friends, so there won't be doubt in anyone's mind that we are really married this time. I've already spoken to Reverend Bleeker. He's ready to do it any time we are."

"The sooner the better," Amanda vowed, knowing Riley was right—they needed to wait to wear these rings until they said their vows. For real, this time. It would mean more.

She handed him the large box. "And how about opening this?"

Riley picked up the box. She had an idea what he was thinking—it was surprisingly light. To the point it felt almost empty. He unwrapped it, took off the lid. Inside was a single printed page. Across the top it read, Application For Texas Marriage License. Amanda's section of it had already been filled in. "I know we have thirty days, but I thought—hoped—we might want to make it indisputably legal."

Once again they were on the exact same page. "You thought right." Riley brought her closer for another searing kiss.

"And the last one." Amanda gave him the smaller gift.

Riley opened it and saw the watch inside.

"At first I thought it was a lame gift," Amanda explained, as she took out the expensive, elegant timepiece and helped him put it on his equally elegant and masculine wrist. "But then I began to really think about what it meant." She paused, looking deep into his eyes. "Me giving you the gift of time. From here on out."

The grin on his face was as wide as the Texas sky. "I can't think of anything I'd like more. Except this." He stood and led her to the stairs and their bed, where they came together once again, loving each other, body, heart and soul.

The kids woke at six o'clock Christmas morning and were as delighted as Amanda and Riley to find a blanket of pristine white snow covering the ground.

"Guess who came to our house last night?" Amanda said as they waited for Riley—who had gone down to put the coffee on and turn the lights on the tree—to come back and join them.

Chloe's eyes sparkled with excitement as she jumped up and down on the bed.

"Pretty?" Amber said, jumping, too.

"Santa Claus," Amanda confirmed, catching them both in her arms for a hug.

Chloe's eyes got even bigger.

"Everybody ready?" Riley appeared in the doorway, looking sexy and handsome as could be.

"We sure are," Amanda said. She handed Amber to Riley,

picked up the cooing Cory from the bassinet and took Chloe by the hand. "Let's go downstairs and see what's under the Christmas tree."

Chloe gasped in delight when she saw the presents. Letting go of Amanda's hand, she ran right over to them. Amber soon joined her.

Together, they unwrapped the gifts.

It was hard to say who was happier, Amanda thought, the kids or she and Riley.

"Looks like we scored a hit," she said as Chloe sat on her pink-and-white roadster-tricycle, and Amber toddled around with her push-and-pull wagon full of blocks.

Riley took Amanda's hand and kissed the back of it, everything he felt for her reflected in his tender gaze. "In every way," he promised.

"I love you," Amanda whispered, her heart filling with joy.

"I love you, too," Riley whispered back.

Hearing, Amber perked up. "Wuv!" she shouted, dropping her wagon handle and toddling over, showing off her new plush toy kitten.

"I think we've got a new word here," Amanda said happily.

"Wuv!" Amber repeated jubilantly again. Lacing her arms around Amanda's neck, she kissed her, then turned to Riley and did the same.

Chloe turned and stared at them both for a minute. Then she slid off her roadster-tricycle and came over to join them, too. Once again looking desperate to communicate, Chloe smiled at Amanda and Riley shyly.

"Did Santa bring you what you wanted?" Riley asked.

Chloe nodded. Imperceptibly, but it was a nod.

Amanda could barely contain her excitement. "What do you like best?" Amanda asked her.

Chloe smiled. Broadly. She took one of Amanda's hands and one of Riley's. And then she did what they had been waiting for—for what seemed an eternity—she spoke. "My new mommy and daddy," she said.

Once Chloe started talking again, it seemed she couldn't stop. The four-year-old chattered all morning, whispered through service at the church and continued talking at the family gathering at Sam and Kate McCabe's.

Micki—who had been unable to keep her secret any longer—had gone ahead and confessed to the McCabes the tragedy that had befallen her family. Sam and Kate had made her an honorary member of their family on the spot, a move seconded by one and all. Kate had offered unlimited grief counseling. And Sam and Kate made up with Laurel, now that they finally understood why her grades had taken the nosedive the previous semester.

It seemed to Amanda the holiday simply could not get any better.

Until, that was, they heard the clomp-clomp of horses and the ringing of bells at four that afternoon.

The kids all ran to the window. "It's Uncle Travis!"

"And he's got a sleigh!"

Travis McCabe came in, stomping the snow off his boots. Travis looked at Riley. "We're all set," he said.

"For what?" Amanda asked.

With a grin, Riley reached over and squeezed her hand. "The wedding we should have had," Riley said.

Twenty minutes later, they were all back at the church. Reverend Bleeker was waiting for them. And this time he looked very happy to be presiding over the ceremony that would join them together forever as man and wife.

Amanda placed the wedding ring on Riley's hand. "I promise to love you unconditionally…respect you…laugh and cry with you…"

He put the wedding ring on hers. "…comfort and encourage you…and stay with you for all eternity…"

Reverend Bleeker smiled as he completed the blessing and said, "I now pronounce you husband and wife. Riley—"

"I think I know what to do next," Riley cut in playfully as everyone laughed.

And he did.

* * * * *